THE APPRAISER

THE APPRAISER

R. FRANKLIN JAMES

THORNDIKE PRESS
A part of Gale, a Cengage Company

**LIBRARY OF CONGRESS CIP DATA ON FILE.
CATALOGUING IN PUBLICATION FOR THIS BOOK
IS AVAILABLE FROM THE LIBRARY OF CONGRESS**

ISBN-13: 978-1-4328-7921-1 (hardcover alk. paper)

Published in 2020 by arrangement with Camel Press, an imprint of Epicenter Press, Inc.

Printed in Mexico
Print Number: 01   Print Year: 2020

To earth angels and soul mates.

ACKNOWLEDGMENTS

This is the first book in the Remy Loh Bishop series, and many persons helped me to bring her into being by providing the support and encouragement I needed. First, I have to thank Phil Garrett of Camel Press and in particular, Jennifer McCord, my publisher and editor who keeps my feet to the fire, but makes sure I don't get burned. I count her as a friend.

I want to give a special thanks to Joy Viray, DNA Technical Leader for the Sacramento County District Attorney's Laboratory of Forensic Services. Her work as a criminalist analyzing case work, crime scenes, and examination of biological evidence made a tremendous contribution to giving a reality check to my story's background.

Special thanks to Linda Townsdin and Kathy Asay for beta reading *The Appraiser.* It's a better book because of them.

To Kathleen Asay, Cindy Sample, Pat

Foulk and Karen Phillips who share their knowledge, experience and friendship as the best critique group a writer can have.

To my family who put up with my absences from social gatherings and periodic mumblings to myself as I spun out the book in my head.

To Joyce Pope, Geri Nibbs, and Lindy Young who urge me to step away from the keyboard for short breaks. To Barbara Lawrence and Bern Mullen who make me smile and literally stretch every week. To Carol Oliveira, whose friendship I cherish, and generously produces a platform so that I may reach readers who have followed me for years.

CHAPTER ONE

She wasn't going to look at the clipping.

Remy Bishop shivered in the San Francisco morning air. Her breath released in small puffs of cloud, as she stamped her feet on the BART platform. A moment later, the blast of a horn and the accompanying computerized female voice, announced the arrival of the commuter train. She boarded, grabbed a seat and almost immediately reached inside her purse for the newspaper clipping. She wondered if a psychologist would diagnose the unfolding and reading of the same news clipping every morning as neurotic or compulsive. In all likelihood both, especially when they discovered the article was over a year old and proclaimed her as the forensic lab tech that tampered with evidence in the Sandra Lenox murder investigation. She read the words as if for the first time, and then with care re-folded the clipping, tucked it into her wallet, and stared out the train window.

She wouldn't stop until the truth about what happened, whatever it turned out to be, was laid bare.

Tomorrow she would have to bring her car. Mendleson was a small town that shied away from public transportation links to the rest of the Livermore valley and Bay Area. Less than an hour drive from Silicon Valley, it was a well-kept secret from non-locals who would have been surprised at its charm. With a population under ten-thousand, she'd been born there, and her parents, after several renovation projects, still lived in their first home.

Today, she was starting over with a new job and the promise of a clean slate.

Grayden Lane's car was already in the lot, even though she'd arrived to work thirty minutes early. In her last employment, she'd set her own schedule, now it was a hassle getting used to having someone track her whereabouts. She touched the hood of his white Mercedes — it was cool, he'd been there for some minutes.

The Bay Area spring fog clung like a sheer veil as she searched in her purse for the key to the rear door of LaneWilson, the East Bay Area's most respected and renowned dealer of antiques and vintage items. At least that's what Lane never hesitated to proclaim. Letting herself in, she dashed past his closed office door, turned on the coffee machine, and started the sound system. Remy looked out at the showroom floor; the truth was she needed the job. To be accurate, she needed any job from a prominent auction house if she were going to advance in her new career. Unlike real estate appraisers, independent appraisers were not licensed. The industry's growing number of fakes and reproductions, both digital and physical, complicated confirming the validity of goods in the antique world. Having descriptions and pictures logged in an individual appraiser's cherished binders, helped to identity imposters. Having her own auction binders were the single most important part of her credentials.

No sooner had she returned to her desk; Lane's office door opened.

Grayden Lane was reminiscent of a stereotypical middle-aged aristocrat, with graying blond hair, black wire rimmed glasses, a stout build and an unctuous smile. His meticulous appearance reminded her of a teacher in her appraisal program — a legend in his own mind. Antique rugs, furniture and artwork filled Lane's office, all selected with a deliberateness to announce refined

11

taste. He was in the right business.

He paused in the hallway wrapping a wool scarf around his neck. "I don't have a lot of time this morning," he said. "I'm appraising a home in Santa Cruz. I came into Mendleson because I knew you wouldn't know how to deal with the office alarm system. Remind me to teach you, in fact, put it at the top of your list." He stuffed papers and a small camera into his briefcase. "I'll be back later this afternoon, and we'll discuss your job duties in detail. We have a sale coming up, and we can go over what needs to get done when I return. There are no appointments for today, so you can use the time to get acquainted with the showroom facility and client files. It's pretty quiet on Wednesdays."

"I've got it under control, Mr. Lane."

He frowned. "Call me Grayden. I have no intention of calling you Ms. Bishop."

Remy listened with close attention over the next five minutes as he went on to point out the layout of the building, phone operations and the copy machine buttons. "If you get in over your head, here's a contact number for Evelyn." He handed her a slip of paper. "She's our receptionist and office manager. Right now, she's on maternity leave. But if you get stuck and can't reach me, you can call her — at least for the next couple of weeks."

"Got it," she said. "Evelyn for emergencies."

"She can be a little testy. If you don't want her to hang up on you, her name is pronounced 'Eve-lyn' with a long 'e'." He glanced at his watch. "It was poor planning on our part that we waited until the last minute to hire you. Evelyn could have been here to give you footing."

"Grayden, I'll be fine."

At last, satisfied she could be left alone, he waved goodbye and dashed out the back exit.

After locking the door behind him, she took an in-depth tour of the showroom. This was her first full day, and the first time she was able to explore the premises without notice. LaneWilson was a modest-sized store occupying two floors of a re-purposed nineteenth-century assay office. She went up the back staircase and turned on the lights. A large single room was packed with stacked chairs and long folding tables. Several display stands lined one wall positioned across the room from a massive walnut storage cabinet, containing desk phones, pads, pens and laptops. Next to the cabinet were three large area rugs stacked on one another. With a final look, she

13

turned off the lights.

Downstairs, she walked over to an over-sized vintage sideboard situated at the rear of the store behind a shoji screen. A computer, monitor, keyboard, and printer comprised the office machines area.

Grayden had been fast to tell her that the CDs playing were of his daughter's chamber music trio, and not any commercial artist. Whatever the source, the music was perfect for the plush furnishings simulating a comfortable living room. LaneWilson had an admirable collection of china and glassware. Still, Remy knew antiques enough to know that except for one small Ming vase on the top of a high shelf, the art pieces were all imitations, good imitations, but still imitations.

Searching for antiques and vintage pieces was her private pastime. She'd never thought she would be making it a career.

The landline phone on her desk rang and she picked it up before the second ring.

"LaneWilson."

"Joan?"

Who was Joan?

"Er . . . no, my name is Remy Bishop, I'm the new Assistant Appraiser. Can I can help you?"

There was a pause and then the phone

14

went dead.

Puzzled, Remy put the phone back in its cradle just as a little harp-like trill signaled the opening of the front door. A woman wearing a navy cashmere cardigan with a fox fur collar and trailing Guerlain perfume entered, followed by a wavy long-haired, blond two-year old.

Remy smiled, walking over to the door and introduced herself.

The woman lifted off her sunglasses and held out her hand to shake Remy's. "Is Grayden here?"

"No, but he's expected back this afternoon." Remy frowned at the toddler who had pulled away from her mother and was jumping on the Queen Anne loveseat. "May I help you?" she said to the woman as she handed the child a magazine.

Oblivious to her offspring's antics, mom tossed her hair, sat down in the tufted maroon leather chair in front of Remy's desk and began rummaging through her purse. It was evident, she was able to ignore the behavior of her child, who was now removing the glass beads from a crystal vase, one at a time.

"Do you have some paper? I'll write him a note."

Remy handed her a note pad with the

15

LaneWilson logo. "May I have your name?"

"Tess Perry," she said, not looking up from her writing.

"Er . . . Mrs. Perry, excuse me, but your daughter might hurt herself playing with that glass vase." Remy got up and with one hand lifted the vase out of the child's raised hands and with her other hand, returned the glass beads.

Perry slammed down her pen. "That is my *son,* Fenton." She gathered her purse, stood and held out her note. "Where's Joan?"

Remy took the note and shook her head. "I'm sorry, this is my first day. I don't know Joan." She scribbled her own name on a blank business card. "Here's my card."

"And yet they still left you in charge." Tess Perry looked at her with distrust, slipping the card inside her handbag. "I see." She pulled her son's hand from yanking at the sequins covering a sofa pillow. "Just let Grayden know I came by to see the Molini."

"Of course."

Remy walked the pair midway to the door and waved them a smiling good riddance.

She sat down to her desk and picked up the client file listing, searching for the Perry name. Too bad she didn't know Joan's last name.

The phone rang.

"Lane Wilson, how may I assist you?" Remy repeated the introduction Grayden had given her.

"Remy, this is your mother."

She looked up to the ceiling. "Mom, I know your voice. What's the matter?"

"I wasn't going to call you, but your father insisted. I told him this was your first day and the last thing you needed was to have your boss think your parents were checking on you." She paused. "By the way, where is your boss? Is he standing over you? If so, just cough and say: thank you, we're open from nine to five, and then hang up."

Remy rubbed her forehead with her fingers. "Mom, Grayden's not here so I can talk, but I'm not going to because I'm an adult, as you said, and I don't need my parents checking up on me at work."

"I know, I know," her mother rushed. "But tell me, so I can tell your father, you know how he worries. How is it going so far?"

Remy glanced at the faux crystal clock on her desk. Her father was likely asleep in the den or getting ready to show a house. "Well, so far . . . after a total of one and a half hours on the job, I'm doing fine."

Her mother didn't catch the sarcasm. Or, Remy thought, she didn't want to. It was a fact that to resist her mother was useless, and prolonged certain defeat.

Her phone vibrated — a text.

"Mom, I've got to go."

"Call me later," her mother urged.

They hung up with Remy promising a full account of her day after she got home. Remy pulled up the text:

"Sorry to take so long. I can't get access to your closed files. But found something interesting. Call me."

She wrinkled her brow. She hadn't heard from Andy in days — make that a month. They had worked together at the forensic lab until he had accepted a promotion to information technology in another section. When she was fired, or allowed to resign, he was one of two people who defended her. He believed her incapable of damaging the evidence. Privately, he'd offered to go behind the scene and ferret out who was the true culprit. What had he found? He tended to understatement, so if he said he found something *interesting,* it could be a game changer. She tried calling, but his phone went to voice mail. She texted him back:

"Sounds good. Will call before I leave for home."

She got the hot water for tea and sat down with LaneWilson's client list. The front door trilled.

Remember, Wednesdays are quiet.

At first glance, the woman appeared to be in her fifties or sixties. She walked tall and carried a large canvas tote bag on her shoulder. Dressed in black leggings, and a colorful tunic with swirls of maroon and soft yellow, she looked like a Bohemian artist.

Remy came around the desk and held out her hand. "Good morning, may I help you?"

"I hope so. Is Grayden Lane here?" She lifted her gaze as if to see past Remy.

"No, I'm sorry. He left for a meeting."

"Good, I was just making sure. I don't want to see him. I can talk to you."

Remy held back her look of surprise and pointed to a side chair in front of her desk. "Ah, all right. Have a seat."

"My name is Audra Dunlap. I moved to Mendleson to handle my son's estate." Her eyes misted over. "Martin is . . . was my only child. He died three months ago. There's . . . . Now there's just me."

A tear slipped down her cheek, and Remy handed her a tissue. At the same time,

Audra ran her hand over her head and pulled off the wool slouchy hat that covered her hair. Fog-gray curls sprung free, and Remy realized Audra's age was closer to sixty or seventy.

"Can I get you coffee or tea?" Remy offered.

"No, I can't spare the time. I need your help." She reached into her tote and brought out a somewhat wrinkled brochure. "This is yours, isn't it?"

Remy glanced down at the slick booklet. "Uh, yes, it's one of ours, but I must tell you this is my first day, and I'm not familiar with our store's —"

"Just hear me out." Audra leaned over and opened to the middle of the catalog. She pointed with an unadorned finger. "See this? It belonged to my son. I know this because his grandmother gave it to him to hold on to. It was handed down from his late father."

Remy peered at a photo of a Fernier clock listed for thirty-five hundred dollars.

"Mrs. Dunlap —"

"Call me Audra."

"Audra, it is a beautiful clock, but it's not rare. How do you know it's the one that belonged to your son? The names of the owners are not shown in a catalog, except in rare circumstances. Are you saying your son . . . ?"

Audra stood and walked over to the glass cases along the wall that held a variety of artifacts and clocks. She peered into each one and then returned to her chair.

"I know this brochure came out last month. How can that be? Martin had already been buried, how could he have put it up for sale? Even so, I know him; he never would have given up that clock." She went on pointing to the brochure. "It shows the front and back. You see that tiny maple leaf in the rear corner? That's our insignia. It's been in my husband's family for years. His grandmother knew he loved that clock, that's why she left it to him. He never would sell it, no, never."

"Well, maybe when Mr. Lane returns, he —"

"No, no, no." The woman shook her head. "You don't understand. I came to see Lane about three weeks ago; I showed him the catalog and explained my story. He claimed he couldn't reveal the seller's name, but that it was a reputable party. He said the same thing you did, that the clock was not uncommon. He wouldn't even consider the mark." She paused. "Then I got upset, and he asked me to leave."

21

She looked crestfallen.

Remy reached and put her hands around Audra's thin shoulders. "I grant you, the mark is unusual. Did you see who bought the clock at sale?" She picked up the booklet. "It was last month."

"No one bought it because it never went on sale."

Remy frowned. "There must be something wrong; LaneWilson is an esteemed auction house. They would never lure buyers in for items that weren't available." Remy wrinkled her brow. "Are you sure? Is that why you're here, to find out what happened?"

"I know what happened." Audra looked over her shoulder. "Grayden Lane knew I was suspicious about how he had gotten hold of Martin's clock. So, he never brought it out. He'll sell it through another house, or . . . or . . . ." Her voice faded, and she squeezed Remy's arm. "There's more, I can't find out what happened to my son's other things."

Remy's internal radar started to ping. The elderly woman appeared sane.

"What do you mean?"

"When I started out looking for the clock, I went to the thrift shop first, the one here on Main Street." Audra looked over her shoulder in the direction. "They didn't have it, and the owner said I should make a list, and she would be on the lookout if something should come in. I was on my way out that's when I saw a stack of LaneWilson upcoming sale brochures on the counter. It caught my eye, and that's when I saw Martin's clock."

That answered one of Remy's questions about how Audra got her hands on a brochure to begin with.

"You said other items are missing," Remy prodded.

"Yes, several more. For the past years, I've been traveling. When my husband died, Martin's father, I found I couldn't stay in one place, I had to keep moving. It kept me from having a nervous breakdown. I guess it also kept me from thinking how I was going to have to face my future alone." Her expression turned bleak. "Martin was just twenty-five. He said he would take care of our family heirlooms and keepsakes until I settled again. I've been trying to make a list, but I can't remember everything. I think he bought quite a few on his own. Any valuable artifacts came from my husband's side of the family. We packed things in crates and Martin took them home. But his house is big, and I can find just one or two crates in the garage."

"You want to keep the clock?"

"I'm not going to lie. At first, I was going to sell it," Dunlap said, holding her head down. "I need the money. My travels set me back, and I've had to dip into my savings. But now, no, I'm going to keep it. I'm determined to get back on my feet." She reached across the desk. "I know you don't know me, but if you could help me find out what happened to that clock? Your showroom had it at one time. Who has it now? I tell you, my son's clock was stolen."

"Audra, that's hard to believe. Mr. Lane wouldn't risk the store's reputation for thirty-five hundred dollars."

The woman lifted her face and stared at her.

"Maybe you're right, but remember there are other items missing, other items I have questions about. Martin sent me pictures of his house, and he had beautiful things. He was a collector of fine artifacts. I didn't see them myself, but from his photos I have no doubt." Her eyes narrowed, and she said with emphasis, "I would consider selling them through you."

"I appreciate that, but. . . ." Remy glanced at the catalog. "I'm sorry, but there's nothing I can do. I'm new here and —"

"And you don't want to lose your job."

Audra rose with stiffness out of her chair. "The clock was one of the few things that he cherished. I have a detailed picture of it, and of a beautiful vase he owned. It's missing, too."

Remy's hesitated. "It's not that I don't want to help." It was true, she didn't want to get involved in what seemed to be a matter of family missed communication. "Maybe you should contact the police."

"I did," she said. "They told me I couldn't prove a crime had been committed since my son could have sold the items on his own."

A tear trickled from her eye.

Remy didn't want Audra to know she agreed with the police. "Listen, let me figure out how I can best help you — if I can help you," she said. "I can go through LaneWilson's sale logs, and maybe something might shake loose. You said you had a picture of the clock? Can you bring it to me? It would be good to have something other than the catalog."

"The clock is pictured in a large framed photo," Audra Dunlap said. "Perhaps you could come by and take a look for yourself? There are still a few pieces of value in his house. You could tell me if they were worth appraising. It would also help you to see what has me upset."

"All right," Remy agreed. "But it will have to be tomorrow after work. I'm having dinner with my parents this evening." After work, she'd be on her own time, and therefore avoiding any objections Grayden might have about her assisting Dunlap.

"That will be fine." Audra Dunlap scribbled the address on a piece of paper.

Remy recognized the location. The home was in the Fremont hills, known for its mini-mansion neighborhoods.

"When I come out tomorrow, I may have some information," she said. "Between now and then, it will give me a chance to find out what happened to the clock on this end." She held up her hand when Dunlap reached out to give her a hug. "Remember, I'm not saying the clock in this brochure is what you think it is," she said. Seeing the woman's deflated response, Remy reached for her hand. "I will check into it. That's all I can do."

The woman came up to Remy's chest, even when she straightened her shoulders to stand tall. Audra patted her arm and turned for the door. When she got there, she paused.

"Thank you, I could tell you were a nice person." She shoved the knit cap on her head. "I'm sorry if I came off so shrill. But you should know you work for a crook. I hope I'm wrong for your sake, but you need to be prepared."

She left in a gust of chilled air.

CHAPTER TWO

Where to start her search for the Dunlap clock?

Remy thoughtfully chewed her sandwich while she stared at the clock in the catalog. She'd barely finished when the door trilled again.

Good thing nothing ever happens on Wednesdays.

She rounded the desk to greet a tall, brown haired, young-ish looking man in a Saville Row suit. Mendleson was a small community, and she knew almost everyone on sight. This gentleman was not from Mendleson.

"Good morning, welcome to LaneWilson. Can I help you?"

He looked her up and down, but she didn't draw back.

"Yes," he said. "I'd like to talk to someone about appraising an antique my aunt is leaving me." He took the chair in front of the desk as Remy took her seat behind it. "I've heard about your showroom. If things go well, I would want LaneWilson to sell it as well."

A commission.

Remy kept her adrenaline in check and gestured understanding. "My name is Remy Bishop and I'm the assistant appraiser." She wrote her name on the bottom of a LaneWilson generic business card and handed it to him. Grayden had assured her that her own cards would be ready by the end of the week. Based on today, she would need them sooner than they both thought. "Yes, we are expert at appraisals, and our ability to get top dollar for your heirloom is evidenced by our reputation as one of the best in the Bay Area. And, your name sir?"

"Kieffer, Edmund Kieffer. Hmm, yes, as I said, I'm familiar with your reputation. That's why I chose your showroom." He took a small brown envelope out of his inside pocket, lifted out a photo and handed it to her. "My aunt used this picture for the insurance policy she got years ago. This is the piece I would like to sell."

Remy squinted and tilted the picture back and forth.

She raised her eyebrows and handed it back. "This looks like a George II painted mirror, from the mid-1700s. If it's authentic — and in good condition, it could be worth anywhere from seventy-five thousand to more than one-hundred thousand."

Kieffer pounded his fist into his other hand. "I knew it."

"Mr. Kieffer, you showed me a faded polaroid picture. The estimate I provided is just speculative, assuming it's a real George II, the condition deter—"

"How soon can you come out? The house is in East Mendleson." He shoved the picture into its envelope and back into his pocket.

The phone rang, but she allowed it to go to voicemail.

Remy frowned. "It's unfortunate, but this is my first day, and I'm the only one in the store. Mr. Lane won't be in until late this afternoon. He will want to give the appraisal his personal attention. I can have him contact you for an appointment as soon as he returns."

It was Kieffer's turn to scowl. He shook his head. "No, I want you. My aunt is suspicious of men. She's a spinster. Besides, you recognized the piece at once, and you said you were the assistant appraiser, aren't you qualified?"

"Yes, but —"

"Good, be at this address at two o'clock." He went back into his coat pocket and pulled out a card. "I don't have any more of my own business cards. I'll write on the back of this one." He scribbled an address. "Don't worry. I'll explain everything to your boss. If Lane Wilson handles this transaction to our expectations, there could be several other items of much greater value that would come your way."

Remy glanced at the address. "This is the address for the old Crandall house."

"Yes, we bought it. Is there a problem?"

"No, not at all. I didn't know anyone had moved in. I know where it is."

"Fine then, I'll see you this afternoon."

He was gone in the same matter-of-fact fashion he entered.

Remy leaned back in her chair with a slow creeping grin on her face.

This could be her first deal . . . during her first week.

Then the reality of her situation struck her. Remy's mind raced. Could she leave the store unattended? For the next half-hour, she tried several times to reach Grayden who was not picking up his phone. She left a voicemail and texted him, but still no response. She remembered seeing a file drawer of forms; it should contain the contract Kieffer would need to complete before LaneWilson undertook any formal assessment. She would have a signed agreement, subject to management approval, of course, ready for Grayden Lane's return. He would realize he'd underestimated her abilities and would recognize that she was ready for a commission arrangement.

She noticed the small flashing red light on the phone indicating a message.

It was Grayden.

"Remy, I'm caught in traffic on the Nimitz freeway, so I'm going to stop for lunch. I won't be into the store until just before closing. I hope everything is going well. I'm going out of cell phone range in about five minutes. Not sure where you are. I'll call you when I'm back on the road."

Now what? She'd planned to convince Grayden to let her go, but she would have to decide without his go-ahead. With a deep breath and much trepidation, she picked up the phone and punched in Evelyn's home number. She alternated between hoping the aloof assistant would pick up and, by the fourth ring, glad she did not. Remy could imagine a frosty response.

Evelyn's voice answered on the sixth ring. Remy rushed to introduce herself.

"Evelyn," Remy said making sure to pronounce the long 'e'. "I hate to bother you, but I'm in the store by myself and even though it's a Wednesday, it's been a little crazy and —"

"What do you want? I'm on my way out." Remy was a little taken back with her abruptness, but she forged ahead.

"A potential new client wants me to come to his aunt's home and appraise a George II mirror, but I would have to close the store for at least an hour and a half, Grayden is stuck in traffic and can't answer my calls, and —"

"*Really,* Remy? Look, stick the sign on the door indicating the time you'll be back. Believe me, Grayden would understand. He'd kill for a new client." Her voice seemed to soften. "However, you need to think about this. Do you know what you're doing? Because, if you don't sign this client, Grayden will not hesitate to fire you for leaving the store."

Remy wavered and then pulled her shoulders back. "Yes, I can do this."

"Fine. Good luck and goodbye." Evelyn clicked off.

CHAPTER THREE

Mendleson prided itself on its historical homes and great Victorian mansions that clustered on the side of a hill overlooking the vineyards of Livermore.

Remy paused at the driveway entrance to stare at the Crandall mansion from inside her car. There was no doubt it was a mansion, because the word "house" wouldn't even begin to describe the large stone building at the end of a paved, curved driveway that stretched for almost a quarter of a mile. Eucalyptus trees lined the roadway and she could smell their unique and pungent scented leaves even through the car's closed windows.

When she was a child, her parents would drive their children to East Mendleson at Christmas time to see the decorations. At night, most of the mansions situated in the ten-block area opened their garland laden iron gates to the public. For a small fee, the proceeds of which went to Mendleson's community park, tickets could be purchased to view the opulent festooned interiors. It was one of her happiest memories.

The Crandall estate had never opened its doors for viewing.

But now it was spring, and while the signs of the holidays were gone from the neighboring homes, the grandeur remained, except for the Crandall mansion which in daylight appeared tired and bleak.

The home was Edwardian with a tall and wide middle building centered between two modest wings. Profuse clusters of ivy edged its way up the sides of stone pillars, softening the corners, but just enough to ensure the invasive plant would not do structural harm. The windows were large, modern and double-paned. Her father loved real estate and he'd passed the gene onto his children. Growing up, they had spent Sunday afternoons taking family drives to open houses. All her siblings could walk through a home and point out its faults and features, and double-paned windows were the first thing they were taught to look for.

Remy parked her car under the *porte cochere* in front of the door. She did a double check to make sure her folder held the LaneWilson sales contract as well as an item assessment checklist she discovered in one of the file drawers.

The pebbled path to the entry was understated, decorated with four urns, overflowing with limp geraniums and lanky coleuses on either side of five expansive stone steps. A small collection of litter drifted across the front, probably brought down by the rain and wind from the previous night. A crumpled bright yellow advertising flyer clung like a trespasser to one of the bushes and she reached down to free it.

Compulsive habits die hard.

Noticing the ornate doorbell next to a glass side panel, she almost pushed it before catching sight of a note taped right above it: *Enter, and wait in the library to your left. My aunt is resting. I will look for your car and be right down. Kieffer.*

Remy opened a tall front door with ornate carvings, and she stepped into a white marble foyer encircled with several closed doors. A huge crystal chandelier hung with drama from the ceiling, its bulbs appearing as sparkling jewels of glass. The entry was lit by the sunlight that poured through the long narrow windows on either side of the door. The walls were painted a calming blue, and an ivory colored chair-rail encircled the spacious foyer. A huge faux palm faced the door and off to its side was a staircase that rose to a circular overlook. The double door on the left was wide open and she stepped in.

She smothered a gasp. It was by far one of the most beautiful rooms she'd ever seen. Most home libraries were dark and close-feeling. Even cluttered, this room was expansive and airy. It resembled a solarium, with its huge ferns, twenty-foot tall French windows and row after row, shelf after shelf of books. There were two large window nooks with pillowed seats that looked out over what appeared to be an English garden. Antique vases and curios of various sizes were scattered with artfulness throughout the room. But it was the long mahogany refectory table with elaborate carved reeded legs that took center stage. Remy ran her fingers over the beauty of the wood grain.

"It's my most favorite piece in the house," Edmund Kieffer said from the doorway.

"It's by Gillows and Company and quite valuable." She bent to look underneath and pointed. "Yes, you see. Here's their numbered mark." She straightened. "But you know that."

He nodded. "Yes, it's been in the family for several generations, and we had it appraised." He walked over and shook her hand. "Thank you for coming. I suppose you must get back to the store?"

"Yes, I should." Remy had to remind herself she wasn't touring the beautiful home, but working.

She caught his eye looking with curiosity at the ad in her hand.

"Oh, this was stuck in one of your plant containers." She placed it in his outreached hand. "Where is the mirror?"

Kieffer looked irritated for a moment, and then he squeezed the paper into a ball and tossed it into a tall empty vase. "I'll speak to the gardener about picking up behind himself." He turned to the doorway but stopped when he saw Remy's focus on the antique vase now turned trash receptacle. "I see. I may have compromised your professional sensibilities. Don't concern yourself; I'll get the help to empty it. You should come this way; the mirror is in the living room."

He led her back out into the entry and through another set of double doors, straight across from the library.

The living room paled in comparison to the library; not that it wasn't an impressive area, with its massive fireplace and expensive artwork hung to an advantage. Remy tried to put her finger on what caught her attention, and then she realized the living room had far fewer furniture pieces than the library and none would be considered collectible. However, the room looked coordinated to perfection, almost like a living space arrangement in a department store.

She spotted the mirror standing in the corner across from a baby grand and walked to it. With care, she stepped behind and peered at the mirror's back. The markings and other evidence of age seemed to be present. After a few minutes, she stepped back around and faced Kieffer.

"Mr. Kieffer, I think LaneWilson can help you, but before we can go any further, you'll have to have your aunt sign an agreement with our company."

"Yes, of course," he said. "But you do think it's worth something?"

Remy hesitated. Her mentor and friend, Victor Camden, had warned her of clients who would pick her brain, quote her as an expert and go on to deny her a commission. The mirror was in excellent condition. She pulled out her phone and took two pictures — front and back, and then she held out the envelope with the paperwork she'd prepared.

"Mr. Kieffer, I can tell you're a businessman. I'm sure you'll understand why I need your aunt's signature before I take the additional steps needed to verify the authenticity of the mirror." She held out the envelope. He snatched it from her hands.

"I told you my aunt is resting." He opened his mouth to say more, but seemed to change his mind. "But it's not a problem; she has a doctor's appointment tomorrow. So, I will bring the signed paperwork to you day after tomorrow." Kieffer pitched the envelope onto the coffee table and glanced at his watch. He looked her in the eyes. "You know I have many friends who are either locating art buyers or selling their own antiques. I may have other business for you."

"That would be very nice," she said. "But why don't we make sure you're pleased with how I handle this business — first."

"Point taken." He bowed. "Then I will meet you on Friday."

Remy sensed the tension that seemed to rise from his shoulders. She picked up her purse and folder. "Mr. Kieffer, it's no problem for me to drive out here again and save you a trip to the office. That way I can take some time to assess the mirror and complete the appraisal."

He appeared to be weighing her offer. He looked at his watch. "All right, that should work out. Let's set a time for nine a.m."

Remy's grin lasted all the way back to the store and into the LaneWilson parking lot. But it faded to a wrinkled brow when she pulled into the space next to Grayden's car. She hadn't expected his return so soon, which meant he knew she'd left the store.

She entered the hallway and stood outside his office. He was talking with animation on the phone and glanced up when he sensed her presence. Her smile disappeared, when he glared and swiveled in his chair, turning his back. Her heart pumped with a fast staccato. She noticed the closed sign was still on the front door, which meant either he did not want to be disturbed, or his call had come through before he noticed. She walked over and took down the sign.

Before she reached her desk, Grayden emerged from his office, his face set in an unhappy expression. He motioned for her to follow him back to his office. He sat behind his desk.

"Remy, before I say anything, do you want to tell me what's going on?"

Remy moistened her lips. "Grayden, it was not a quiet Wednesday." She took him through the day's visitors.

He leaned back in his chair. "I'm sorry for

your difficult introduction to LaneWilson; my appointment went much faster than planned," he said. "However, it sounds like you handled things in a decent manner. Audra Dunlap is a nuisance and I don't want her business anyway."

She started to protest but resisted the urge. She wanted time to look into the woman's claims and she didn't want Grayden to stop her.

He picked up a pad of paper. "I can take over things from here." He scribbled a note. "I'll give a call to Tess Perry. Thanks for keeping the breakage to a minimum. Her son's damage has cost us plenty of dollars; however, we don't hesitate to bill it back to her."

"It came close, but I was able to save the Rosenthal vase," Remy said. "Here's a note she left for you and the message that she came to see the Molini."

He frowned as he read the note, but said nothing and shoved it in his top drawer.

"Now, tell me why you abandoned the store. I was quite shocked to find you weren't here."

Remy took a deep breath. "I tried to reach you several times, but I couldn't get through. We also had another customer this morning, a new client," she said with an emphasis. "A Mr. Edmund Kieffer. He wanted to retain LaneWilson to evaluate an item his aunt plans to leave him from her estate. He showed me a photo of a George II mirror that looked authentic." She hesitated at Grayden's wrinkled brow and rushed, "He insisted I come out this afternoon and look at the mirror. And rather than risk losing a new client, I agreed. I even called Evelyn and she concurred. She told me to put the sign on the door. I just came from there."

Grayden perked up when she mentioned *new client,* and then shook his head.

"He insisted *you* do an appraisal, how absurd."

Remy blinked, curious maybe, but absurd? She wasn't *that* inexperienced.

"Grayden, I thought the benefit of gaining a new client would offset leaving the office for less than two hours on a Wednesday, when nothing happens." She said this half-hoping he'd catch the sarcasm.

For a brief moment, he looked contrite.

"Remy, I didn't mean it to sound as if I thought you were incompetent. It was smart of you to think of the contract," he added, with a note of sincerity. "I meant you've just started, and with our new clients I go, or we send someone with more experience with the LaneWilson way."

"Like Joan?"

She tossed out the name without thinking, but Grayden's face flushed red. He should not play poker.

"How did you hear about Joan?"

Remy raised her eyebrows. "Uh . . . I didn't. Tess Perry mentioned her and there was a call for her earlier. Who is she?"

Grayden's color was returning to his face and he moved to go back to his office. "A silent partner. Now I had better call Mr. Kieffer. I can't make a nine a.m. appointment until Friday. I'm tied up at a trade show. We'll have to reschedule." He spoke over his shoulder.

He returned a minute later.

"He's not answering, and I couldn't leave a message." Grayden paced in front of her desk, not bothering to hide his irritation.

His cell phone must have vibrated. He answered and began a conversation that sounded like fielding another customer. Signaling to her he was taking the call; he walked back to his office and closed the door.

Remy sat back in her chair in thought. She didn't see Kieffer relenting. Then, shutting Grayden's reaction out of her mind, she logged onto the computer and began searching industry sites for sales of mid-18th century mirrors.

The desk phone rang.

Edmund Kieffer's voice greeted her. "Miss Bishop, I'm late for a meeting. I'm calling to let you know the contract is signed. I'll see you at nine Friday morning."

"No, Mr. Lane can't make that time. Can we arrange for another — ?"

"I thought I was clear, it's to be just you."

"Will your aunt — ?"

He hung up.

Remy rubbed her forehead in consternation, but a slow grin eased onto her face. She rammed her fist into the air.

She was still smiling when Grayden emerged from his office and stopped in front of her desk. He was trying to compose himself. She adopted a look of concern and stiffened her back. She opened her mouth to speak.

He held up his hand.

"Remy, before you say anything, I was abrupt earlier. This was your LaneWilson transaction. And, I can't fault your quick thinking in how you handled Edmund Kieffer. It was an out of the ordinary busy Wednesday." He raised his hand again when he saw a smile easing onto her face. "But this could be a major client. We are professionals. We must maintain our credibility and our judgment, as our appraisals must be right the first time. When we go out to the home of a new client, we take an information sheet on the client as well as on the piece we are evaluating. As regards new clients, we *don't* speculate on the provenance until we have a contract."

She let her shoulders sag and said nothing. He must have noticed her shift to a solemn air and felt satisfied she'd gotten his message.

"Well, now let's not dwell on the negative." His voice cheered. "Tell me about the house. I'm not familiar with the Kieffer estate. And I know most of the homes in East Mendleson."

"I have the address here. It's the old Crandall home." She held out a slip of paper. "The house is his aunt's and . . . and I didn't get her name."

Grayden looked smug. His words had struck home. He glanced down at the address, and a slow frown creased his forehead.

"Hmm, you're right, this is the Crandall house," he said. "I've never been inside. Supposedly, Lionel Crandall inherited it from his cousin right after the Korean War. He and his family lived there for decades, almost in seclusion. In the end, there were financial difficulties, and they sold the house about six years ago. It's been empty for some time. I didn't know someone had moved in. What did it look like?"

Remy, spoke with care, "Well, it's charming from the outside, though a little run down. I had access to the library and the living room, both of which were impressive. The rooms seemed a bit stocked and over-furnished, but the pieces were real . . . I mean at first glance."

She provided a description that included naming the Gillows table and other precious items she'd seen. Grayden's expression brightened and took on an air of expectation. He seemed to have forgotten Remy's misstep.

"Good . . . good. When Kieffer calls arrange for us to go out there." He looked at his cell phone's calendar. "Yes, we can go out there, Monday. I'll clear my other appointments."

"I was trying to tell you." Remy took a deep breath. "Er . . . Mr. Kieffer called while you were in your office to confirm a meeting for nine a.m. Friday."

"What?"

She didn't miss the transition from anticipatory glee to mass irritation. "He said it was the only time he had. He clicked off before I could ask for another time. He was in a hurry and —"

"Get him on the phone — now."

Remy punched in the numbers. In a few moments, she returned the phone to its cradle and offered Grayden a sheepish look. "His voicemail is full."

Not hiding his annoyance, Grayden turned to his office.

"I must make some calls."

She waited until she saw his phone line light up on the display and made her own call.

"Okay, Andy your text got my attention, what's so interesting?" Remy asked.

"I did as you suggested. I went back and traced your entries in the database," he said. "Sandra Lennox's samples had a chain re-action from a PCR technique, with the original sequencing amplified at least double, and when you signed off —"

"I don't care if my signature was on that file. I didn't sign off."

"Right, I know." Andy continued, "I went into archives and got your physical notes, that's what took me so long, they hadn't been shelved yet and were still in boxes. Anyway, I saw you never made mention of certain matches. Yet, they were entered into the lab's database."

"No, that's impossible." Remy shook her head. "Now, *that* I would remember. First, I never used the polymerase chain reaction technique; it's too rife with variability. I always used short tandem repeats — the industry standard. And, second, I always used my notes to justify my final analysis. Andy, I'm telling you, those samples weren't there, I would never overlook something that critical . . . and . . . and basic."

"I know."

A silence fell between them.

Remy exhaled a deep breath. "Do you think I should give up? Are you giving up?"

He gave a short laugh. "Give up? I don't know the meaning of the words." He paused. "But you might have to close the door on this whole episode, and just move on. I don't think it's going to make a difference even if you can show a pattern that all your other case files were always handled according to your notes." He hesitated. "It was just a mistake."

"A mistake I didn't commit," her voice rose. "I'm not moving on, I can't. I need to think. There must be some way to prove my innocence."

He took a breath. "Look, you don't have to prove your innocence; you weren't arrested for evidence tampering. You weren't charged with anything. Besides things are starting to turn around for you. You've got this new job."

"Andy, I can't believe you just said that," She snapped, then paused to hear Grayden's voice still on the phone. She lowered her tone, "I was all but fired for incompetence."

"What do you want me to do next?"

"I don't know," she said. "You sound like Melanie. She wants me to stop searching for an answer."

His silence spoke his agreement.

She ran her fingers through her hair. "I'll get back to you. I know you're doing this on your own time. Waiting around is making me pretty disagreeable."

"I know."

They both laughed.

"I've been thinking," Remy said. "Suppose I could prove that the sample results I analyzed were tampered with, but not by me. I could tell my own work. The original samples would back up my analysis. But how would I get access?" She mused.

She could hear Andy rustling papers.

"Well that's not going to happen. They're not going to let you back here," he responded. "I've got to get back to my own work assignment. Let me think on what more we can do. My parents are moving into a skilled nursing facility, I've got to put in more overtime to help pay for it. It may be a week or so, but I'll get in touch with you."

"Andy, I'm sorry. I didn't know about your family," she said.

He exhaled a deep breath. "No, I apologize for being for being so curt. Look, it's getting late. I'll get back to you as soon as I can. I know this means a lot to you."

Not a lot — everything.

They said their goodbyes.

Remy picked up her purse and coat and gestured good night to Grayden as she poked her head in his door. He gave her a flash smile and waved her off.

CHAPTER FOUR

Sitting in her car gazing at the beautiful façade of her family home, Remy looked on with admiration. The house was painted in muted marine blue with cream with cinnamon red accents. She thought back to the Metropolitan Home magazine interview with her parents, when they declared that after twenty-five years in the same house, and with their children gone, they could make the space their own.

Belinda and Mitch Bishop lived in the one of the oldest neighborhoods in Mendleson. Their four children had been born and raised in the old Victorian. When they were assured their offspring weren't planning to return, they painted the exterior, redid the landscape and underwent a complete renovation of the inside.

Andy could be right, maybe things were turning around. Frowning, she stared out the car window. After she was forced to leave the county, she had worked for her real estate broker father while undergoing formal appraiser training in Victor Camden's auction house. She always had an affinity for appraising. Her father hired her part-time, not to sell, but to use her analytical skills doing backgrounds on properties and recon on sellers who were thinking of selling. For her, it was mindless, but had it kept her busy and allowed her to settle into a not-as-deep depression.

Even so, it was a well-deserved depression. Her fiancé of four years had broken their engagement, timing it right as she'd been forced to resign. Having bought into his plans for a well-financed future of their dreams, she was caught off guard when he told her he had found someone who wasn't as intense. Her pride had taken a major hit. The last she heard, he and his new household were making beads in Nepal. She shook her head as if to clear the memory, she wasn't a "what if" person.

What had been her pastime was now her life raft. Her family never questioned her innocence or her abilities. She didn't want her old job back, but she was determined to be vindicated.

Her eyes caught the movement of the shutters in the living room. She'd been found out.

"Remy," her mother called from the front door. "Why are you sitting in the car? Are you debating whether to come in, or what?"

She gestured with a quick wave and got out of the car.

Hanging up her coat in the small mud room entry, she slipped off her shoes before walking on the gleaming distressed oak floors. It was one of the few memories she had of her *wàipo* before she passed away, and one of the few traditions her Chinese grandmother insisted the family continue to follow. The smell of roast beef greeted her as she made her way to the kitchen. This was her favorite room in the new house. It was airy with tons of natural light. Her parents had chosen an open floor plan and even though the style of the home was contemporary-comfort, the kitchen with its cream, almost pale-yellow walls, sky blue cabinets and oversized slate-gray granite island appeared to be an entertainment space versus the work center it was.

Remy bent down to kiss her mother's upturned cheek, and then she peered into the oven.

"Mom, why such a big roast?" She stared, and then a scowl appeared on her face. "Oh, no, Mom, you didn't. Tell me you didn't invite someone for me to meet at dinner."

Belinda held up her hand struggling to keep a straight face. "Not me. Talk to your father."

"Where is he?"

Her mother looked at the clock on the stove. "He's showing a house. He said he'd be home by six."

Another twenty minutes.

Her mother paused over the sink. "How did your day go?"

"It was great," Remy said, plopping a cherry tomato in her mouth, reconciled to the inevitable. "It's nothing I didn't do before, and I've already scheduled my first appraisal."

"Good," she said. "Now, it's time to get back on the horse."

Remy narrowed her eyes and faced her mother. "I'm not nervous about my job. What horse are you talking about?"

"The relationship horse, you want to be able to share your happiness."

Remy sat on a bar stool at the island and shook her head. "Why, oh why, oh why can't I come home for a visit without being the center of a plot?"

Belinda leaned against the sink with a dish towel over her shoulder. "When are you going to accept your father and I can't help ourselves? We worry about you; you're our chick with a broken wing." She put her arm around her daughter's shoulder. "You know you're my favorite child, our youngest, and I can't bear to see you struggling. We raised you to be independent and to think on your feet, but with a mate by your side don't you think it makes things more interesting?"

"First, I didn't get a broken wing. My engagement ended." Remy shook head. "Second, you've told each of us we're your favorite child, and we all know it. Third, it's because you raised me to know I can make it on my own, that I get irritated with these . . . these obvious attempts to manipulate me."

Belinda Loh Bishop was a petite woman whose features reflected her mixed heritage, her Chinese mother and Irish father. Her wide brown eyes were framed by long, thick, black hair which she wore in a low chignon at the nape of her neck. A child of the seventies, Belinda, although protective of her children, had instilled in them an innate sense of rebellion and individuality. Her inter-racial marriage to Remy's father brought together a melding of cultures that would make the United Nations proud. Remy had three siblings, Bevin the oldest, Zoe, and Charles, who had all moved out of the area. Remy, the youngest, was the one who'd lagged behind.

Belinda put her hand on her daughter's shoulder. "It's not manipulation, it's nudging."

"Good grief, nudging." She kissed her mother on her forehead. "Mom, you and Dad have got to pretend to be patient and let me find my own interesting times — when I am ready."

"You see, I told your father that."

"Told me what?" Mitchell Bishop came into the kitchen.

Her father was getting a little paunchy. His kept his hair clipped short, but it had thinned and revealed the start of balding. Still, he was a handsome man, with tan colored skin and striking hazel green eyes, his gift to his daughter.

Belinda turned up her face for the brush of his kiss on her lips. "She knows, Mitch. I told her we wanted her to find a companion, not necessarily a life partner."

Mitch bent down to kiss his daughter on the forehead. "No, not necessarily," he said smiling. "It's just dinner, Remy, not a wedding."

He took off his jacket and put it on the back of a dining room chair. Motioning to his daughter, he got a bottle of white wine out of the refrigerator. She brought two glasses from the cabinet and watched as he poured. The three of them tapped their glasses and sipped.

"Hmm, this is good," Belinda said.

Her parents were wine purists and they loved nothing more than to discover northern California's small vineyards and the best wineries.

Remy sighed. "All right, I'm too tired to argue. Who is he, and what time is he coming?"

The doorbell rang.

Her father glanced at the clock. "That would be him." He went to answer the door.

Remy took a sip of wine and ran her fingers through her hair.

Her mother whispered, "You look okay." She reached over with two hands and pinched her daughter's cheeks. "A little more color."

Remy gazed toward the ceiling.

"Belinda, Remy, this is our dinner guest, Jay Ross." Her father escorted a man, thirty-ish wearing black rimmed glasses into the kitchen. "Jay, my family."

Jay's deep baritone voice responded. "It's good to meet you."

"Hello." Belinda held out her hand. "And welcome."

"Hi, I've heard so much about you." Remy shook his hand.

She had to admit; he was easy on the eyes. A good four inches taller than she, he looked fit and his dark brown eyes held hers.

"She's kidding." Mitch clapped Jay on the back. "That's a joke for us, Jay." He sent Remy a stern look and poured Jay a glass of wine. "Why don't you guys finish setting the table and I'll help my wife get the . . . the appetizers together."

Belinda shook her head. "We're not having appetizers, and the table is set." She motioned her husband with a pointed look. "Why don't you sit down in the den where I can hear the discussion, and I'll join you in a bit. Dinner will be ready in a little bit."

Remy gave Jay a sheepish grin. Her parents were trying hard to look like they weren't trying hard. Still, dinner was pleasant, if not with a little forced gaiety. She couldn't miss their guest's right knee bouncing up and down.

Mitch and Belinda sat on the overstuffed sofas that formed a half square facing the limestone fireplace. Her father picked up a remote and clicked. Flames appeared behind the glass screen.

"Now, that's nice," Jay said, sitting next to Remy on the sofa facing. "I'm a fire log man, myself, but a gas starter is even better."

Remy laughed. "Don't get Dad started on gadgets. He's addicted."

"Not addicted, more like fascinated," Mitch Bishop said. He cleared his throat. "Jay is going to hang his broker's license in our office next month."

Remy's eyebrows went up. "Oh, you're an agent. Then be prepared for my father to work your butt off."

"Remy," her father chided. "He'll be working on his own."

"Hey, I'm counting on it." Jay moistened his lips and straightened. "I live just outside Santa Cruz in Colton and I've been working solo out of my home office there. I'll be coming here two or three days a week, and the rest of the time I'll be working the Colton area."

"Colton, ugh," Belinda said, as she entered and sat next to her husband. "It's a terrible commute. They're always reporting accidents along Highway 17."

"Jay won't be driving during commute time, Bee," Mitch said. "I want to use his talents to focus on selling to our younger clients who are buying their second home."

Remy frowned. "Why not their first home? I thought first-time homebuyers were good business."

"They are," Jay said. "But the Mendleson office already has two agents specializing in first-time homebuyers. I want to target those who are ready to move up."

"Sounds like a plan," Remy said.

Belinda cleared her throat. "Well, I'm going to put dinner on the table, Mitch do you want to help me?" She stood.

"Ah, now she wants me to help her." He followed his wife into the kitchen. "Remy, tell Jay about your new job," he said over his shoulder as they both left.

Remy sighed and faced Jay. "Right now, I work as an assistant appraiser for an auction house in Mendleson."

"Right now? What did you do before?"

Remy wasn't ready to reveal her past career and the questions that would follow. "Oh, I was a public servant, nothing glamourous like what I'm doing now."

"Do you get a lot of people coming in wanting to appraise the furnishings in their fancy houses?" he asked. "I bet you're in demand in this region."

"As a matter of fact, I did one such house today," Remy said. "This is a new job, but I've been appraising for some time. I started out working under my Dad, then I took a . . . a break for a while. At LaneWilson, our business is comprised of conducting appraisals and facilitating the liquidation of estates. We conduct sales of high-end antiques and vintage items."

"What's the difference between antiques and vintage?"

"Vintage items are pieces less than one hundred years old." She sipped. "So, do you enjoy real estate?"

"Yeah, yeah, I do." He grinned. "I like finding the perfect house for a client."

"Dinner is ready, you two," Mitch called out. "Let's eat while it's hot."

The meal was pleasant. Her parents, if anything, were always entertaining and the consummate hosts. She loved the fact her mother could fix soul food like a true southerner. She enjoyed seeing the expressions on her African-American cousins' faces as they wolfed down Aunt Bee's "long" gravies and smothered chicken. And then there were her Chinese cousins' pointed looks as they consumed her father's specialty, Peking pork chops. Tonight, was an all-American menu.

Remy sneaked side glances at Jay who seemed reserved and quiet. He said little about himself even when prodded by an expert like her mother.

"Each of our children has a special gift,"

Belinda said out of the blue, avoiding her daughter's piercing stare. "Remy is a curious problem-solver. She would always take things apart so she could see how they worked. What about you Jay? What's your gift? What are you good at?"

He coughed as if stifling a choke.

"Me?" Jay replied. "My gift? I guess I'd have to give it some thought." He paused to think. "I'm good at reading people. It helps in my career to anticipate people's needs."

"Hmmm," Belinda said, uncommitted.

Mitch dabbed his mouth with his napkin. "Let's go sit in the den. Leave the dishes. Cleaning the kitchen is how Bee and I bond."

Belinda led the way. "Don't believe him. I don't think he knows where the dish soap is. I'll take care of the dishes."

Remy touched Jay's arm and leaned in laughing. "Don't believe either one of them. Why do you think they had kids? I'll be the one doing the dishes."

Jay laughed.

"Good, well, that's settled." Mitch grinned.

Remy had to admit the evening was a needed break from the stress of the week. She glanced at the clock; she was starting to feel a wave of tiredness. The conversation was going well without her, and she left to clear the table. She was stacking plates when Jay offered to assist her.

"It will help us to bond," he teased.

Remy chuckled. "All right."

It wasn't a surprise that her mother just remembered they had promised to take some food to Mrs. Clarkson across the street.

"She's been housebound all week with a bad back." Belinda lifted her jacket from the entry coatrack. "Thank you, darling, and you too, Jay, for tackling the dishes. We can use the time to visit. I don't have to stay as long if your father comes with me."

As she spoke, she was putting together a plate of assorted dinner items and covered it with foil.

Remy could see her father trying to decide if visiting with the neighbor was better than staying and helping clean. Her mother made the decision for him.

"Mitch?"

Sighing, he grabbed his coat, and they closed the door behind them.

"They are so obvious." Remy shook her head. She started rinsing off plates and putting them in the dishwasher.

"Yeah, but they mean well."

He handed her dirty plates.

"Are your parents as . . . as overwhelming as mine?" she asked.

"No way," Jay said. And then rushed to add, "Wait, I didn't mean it to sound like —"

Remy laughed. "Hey, no worries, I'm used to them."

After her parents' repeated "goodbyes," "drive safes" and "call me when you get home," they left at the same time, and Jay walked her to her car.

"I enjoyed myself," he grinned. "Can I give you a call?"

"If you still want to call after all that, sure," Remy laughed, and gave him her business card after writing her cell number on the back.

Her mother must have had a stakeout watching Remy's front door, because she called as Remy entered her apartment. She picked up the phone and sank into a kitchen chair.

"Your father wanted to make sure you got home okay," Belinda said. "What did you think of Jay?"

"He seemed nice, Mom."

She knew better than to mention he might be calling.

"Yeah, he didn't impress me either. But

65

what can I do? You know how your father is."

Remy wondered why all her life, her mother would not admit her own concern and funneled her feelings through her father.

"Tell Dad I'm fine and I'm going to be fine."

They said their goodnights.

Remy poured a glass of wine and punched in a phone number.

"Melanie, I had to share. Today was a riot," Remy took the next minutes to bring her friend up to date.

Their friendship had started on the job where Melanie's lab table had been a few feet from her own. She and Remy had clicked from the beginning; they discovered they shared the same quirky humor and view of life. Melanie was there for Remy's breakup, and Remy was there when Melanie needed a shoulder to cry on. They were a study in contrast; Remy's almond shaped eyes, and honey brown hair contrasted with Melanie's blond patrician looks. It was Remy's adventuresome spirit that protected the gorgeous, but sometimes abrasive, Melanie from a world she wasn't good at confronting. Remy had negotiated Melanie's condo rent and car purchase, but it was

Melanie who gave her moral support to re-build her confidence after her fall from grace.

"Wow, you don't live a boring life." Her friend paused, then said, "This Kieffer guy sounds interesting. Don't let him mess up your job."

"What's that supposed to mean? How can he mess up my job?" She swallowed the last of the wine in her glass.

Melanie's voice turned flat, "He reminds me of a guy I used to know — good up to a point."

"Why would you say something like that? I was feeling pretty good." she said. Remy was slipping into weariness. "Look, I just wanted to check-in. I'll be perkier tomorrow."

Remy was surprised at her calm when her thoughts went to the day's happenings. Either she was exhausted, or the day's events were so taxing she was in shock. It was probably a little of both. She fell asleep as soon as her head touched the pillow.

CHAPTER FIVE

Fortunately, the next day the showroom was quiet, and customers were few. Unfortunately, it meant keeping busy would be a challenge, leaving Remy to mull over the conversation with Andy. Remy had liked her job as a forensic technician for the county. She liked her co-workers, her boss, the cases, and even her non-descript cubicle. After almost two years, she'd thought she would work there forever. Looking back, she still wasn't convinced the mistake was hers. Each tech had a badge with a barcode that was scanned with every transfer, ensuring a secure chain of custody. The blood samples had been so tainted, even a rookie would have seen a problem. It ate at her core, and she was determined to clear her name.

Sandra Lennox was twenty-six years old when she was brutally stabbed four times and buried in a three-foot grave under bramble bushes near a regional preserve in an unincorporated area of Patterson County. Her body was discovered by two hikers who stopped to pick up what they thought was litter, but turned out to be her pants leg. The coroner estimated the body had been there about a week, and if the area hadn't had a once in a hundred-year rain storm causing the soil to shift, it would have been there still.

Lennox had been a successful software designer and an only child, which made it more painful for her mother, who was blind and spoke English as a second language.

While the police had identified possible suspects, none was ever charged because the evidence discovered at the scene had been tainted during the chain of custody by the authorities.

Tainted by her.

Until the Lennox case, Remy had a perfect performance record and was set for a pro-motion to supervisor.

Until then.

Even she couldn't explain how someone had gotten into her locked table. Hers was the assigned key, and it was still in her pos-session. When the paperwork had been reviewed by the prosecution's legal team, they caught the discrepancy before a suspect could be identified and an arrest made. The case stalled and never came to court. The DA couldn't find any reason for conspiracy and she wasn't charged. Her boss had no choice but to allow her to resign, and making the nightmare even worse, an unidentified murderer walked free.

The days and months that followed had been her personal hell. She hadn't been allowed to view the original records, but it was clear that the lab's secured database system showed only her access and entries, including a weapon with a broken tip.

The system showed she'd never recorded the damaged knife.

She would lay low in Mendleson until she could get her bearings.

During her hiring interview, Lane had tried to entice her with, "You'll be overseeing the Mendleson store, so a minimum commute for you. And you'll be working almost all on your own. Evan Wilson is always on travel spotting new acquisitions and almost never comes in. There's free coffee and lunch, both of which are on us." No enticement was necessary.

Over the next few hours, she answered phone calls, followed up on a potential client referral, and organized a sales tracking spreadsheet to function as a follow-up tickler. Her sole customer that morning was a young man who looked for antique jewelry. He wanted to give his girlfriend an engagement ring. Remy told him about their upcoming jewelry auction, and he said he'd be back. She was going to give him a brochure until she realized she still needed to check on the auction brochures for the upcoming sale. However, this time she was determined to stay in the store until Grayden arrived.

She was glad she did. He noticed she was there when he arrived before lunch.

"Well, Remy, it feels good to see the store open and you behind the floor desk." He had come in from the rear entrance with coat in hand, and was untwisting the wool scarf from his neck. "Everything okay?"

"Quiet as a Wednesday," she teased.

She heard him unloading his things in his office, then silence. He came out holding pages. "Your master tracking list, this is thorough and well done. Good job."

Remy tried not to beam. "Thank you. The brochures will be ready on Tuesday. I'll pick them up and make sure the ad is set to run in the paper and on our website." She made a note.

"Good idea," Grayden said. "Tell them to invoice us. Make sure you double check all the information is correct — *before* you pay for them." He turned and went back into his office.

She sat still until she heard the lock click on his office door. Bending, she pulled out a small cardboard box containing LaneWilson sales transactions for the last six months. For the next hour Remy poured through the folders until she placed the last one on top of the stacked files at her side. If Martin Dunlap had put the clock up for sale, it would be documented by an agreement with LaneWilson. She was able to account for every item listed in the last six catalogs covering four months – except for the clock. There was no agreement with Dunlap, and there was no agreement at all for the clock in the catalog.

Remy returned the files to the cabinet and sat still in thought for several moments. She had already researched LaneWilson computer records with no success. Questioning Grayden a second time was unlikely to reap any results — not positive ones anyway.

Still, she waited until he emerged from his office to go home.

"Well, this is what I meant by a quiet day." He picked up the mail from the corner of her desk. After sifting through it, he said. "I'll be leaving in a short while; do you have any questions for me?"

"I do have one." Remy cleared her throat. "Er, I was making sure I understood Evelyn's instructions about the store's agreements matching items in the catalog. I used our last sale as an example and tried to match each item with an agreement."

"Very good."

"Yes, well, I was able to for every item except one." She didn't look up to see Grayden's expression.

"Which item?"

"The Fernier clock, I couldn't find the owner's agreement." This time she glanced up to see his face pale.

"No," he said. "There wouldn't be." He sniffed. "The owner pulled it at the last minute. We tore up the agreement. I told Evelyn to remove Dunlap from our client files. We will not do business with her." He pulled out his phone and tapped its screen. "I've got to attend a dinner. Make sure you lock the doors and set the alarm."

Remy reached for her pad. "What was the owner's name?"

"Why do you need to know that?" he asked, irritated.

"How am I to know which person you don't want to do business with?"

"I told you I'm already late, I've got to get

going." He turned to go back to his office, and then he exhaled a long breath. "Huntington, the woman's name was Huntington. I don't remember her first name." He looked down at his phone. "Now, I've got to leave. I hope I can count on you to be here tomorrow after your visit to the Crandall house. I'll be in the San Francisco office all day, returning in the evening."

"Yes, of course."

He muttered a "harrumph."

Martin Dunlap's house was built in a contemporary Mediterranean style with an expansive view of three bay bridges. Unlike the Crandall house, the Dunlaps lived in a well-manicured, if somewhat cookie-cutter home. Audra Dunlap must have been waiting by the window; she opened the door before Remy rang the bell.

"You came," Dunlap gushed with happiness.

"Of course," Remy said, handing over her coat.

"Come this way. I spread some photos out on the dining room table. There were in my son's office. I mean —" Audra stopped herself. "Can I get you something to drink?"

"Tea?"

"Perfect." She hurried into the kitchen. "I

was finishing up a cup."

Remy stepped down into a sunken living room with a massive white marble tiled fireplace that rose to the twenty-foot ceiling. The connecting dining room was a little smaller with modern glass French doors on one side leading out onto a covered patio.

Audra returned with two steaming mugs and coasters, handing one of each to Remy. Grasping one of two large flat boxes, she pulled out several photographs, and motioned for her visitor to come closer. She reached inside a folder.

"Look at this. See, this is the picture I told you about."

Remy bent down and then looked up again to peer at the fireplace. The 8x11 photo showed a young man smiling into the camera. He leaned against the long, simple styled walnut mantle topped with what appeared to be a Fernier clock, a period Italian vase, and two porcelain figures of peasants with veined hands scooping down into their baskets on either side of a Baccarat crystal bowl. Now however, the actual mantle in front of her was cleared of all objects.

"It was taken in this room."

"Yes, yes, you can see that."

Audra laid out the remaining photos on

the dining table, grouping those of each item, with photos of their authenticity marks or manufacture stamps, and in some cases letters of provenance. The photos appeared to be produced by a professional commission; the details were distinctive and clearly visible.

"Odd everything is lined up in a row," Remy said.

She leaned over the table, taking a sip from her cup. "Martin either took these photos or had them taken," she said. "I found these boxes on the bottom shelf of his bookshelf. My guess is he would have taken them for insurance purposes."

"Yes, that makes sense," Remy said. "But are these other items family heirlooms, too? You just mentioned the clock."

Audra frowned. "The clock is the heirloom that I know belonged to our family, the rest he must have purchased on his own," she said. "Do you think they might be valuable?"

"Maybe," she said, noting they were recognizable art items, that is, if they were real. "It could be he started a collection on his own."

"It's possible," Dunlap said. "But even so, none of those pieces are here. I've checked all over the house." She moved toward the doorway leading to the entry. "There is something else I want you to see. There are more photos of other rooms." She dug into the next box and pulled out additional photos. "These are pictures from the master bedroom. Things are missing there, too. Would you like to see?" She pointed toward a flight of steps. "Please, let me show you."

Remy followed her up the staircase. She stood aside as Audra pointed to a photo in her hand and then to the space that had once held items.

"I don't like to come in here," Audra said, turning to look around the room. "It's not just empty of artifacts, it's empty of spirit."

"I have to agree," Remy said. "At first glance, it does appear as if there are some missing pieces." She noticed the outlines in the light film of dust, then she peered at the photo that depicted a Tiffany lamp on a contemporary side table and a nearby art deco smoking stand.

She turned to scan the room. Both were gone.

"I don't know where they are." Dunlap sighed. "But I'm glad you believe me, now. You can see my alarm. You do believe me, don't you?"

Remy nodded. "It looks like you're right to question what's missing."

"Thank you for giving me some small peace of mind."

"I can see why you might be concerned," Remy said, looking at the pictures as she walked around the room. "Can I take a few of the pictures with me? I'll make copies and get them back to you"

"No, Remy, no need, take these photos with you," Audra insisted. "I know you'll take care of them. In other boxes there are sets of duplicates. Just take what you want and return the rest to me later."

Remy took another look around the room and ran her fingers over the table where the Tiffany lamp had once stood. No scratches, and a clear spot where the base had been.

Dunlap led the way downstairs to the dining room.

"Audra, did you check with your son's insurance? You need to make sure he didn't report them stolen, or maybe he sold items and removed them from the policy. He may have taken all these photos for his insurance files," Remy said, gathering her purse to leave.

"Yes, yes, that's a good idea. As executor I need to do that anyway. But . . . but if things are stolen, they'll tell me to get that police report."

"Let's not get ahead of ourselves," Remy

said. "Let me poke around and see if any of Martin's items are on the market." She paused. "One thing we haven't talked about is, assuming the items were stolen, how would someone get access to the house to clear it out? Do you have any ideas?"

Dunlap's face flushed red. "What are you insinuating?" she spat.

Remy was taken back by Dunlap's response. She hadn't meant anything, but knew the police would ask the same question.

"Audra, if you say Martin would never have sold or given away the family clock heirloom, then someone had to have taken it. But how?"

"I guess I never thought about that part. I mean when I saw the clock in the LaneWilson brochure I . . . I never thought about how they got it."

"I see," Remy said, opening the front door. "I've got to leave, but with these photos you've given me a lot to check up on. I'll get back to you in a few days. You may want to go ahead and get that police report; you'll need it for the insurance if nothing else."

"No, I don't want police involvement, just yet," Dunlap said. "A friend of mine told me I might have a better chance of retrieving things if I can negotiate with the thief, without the shadow of a crime over their heads."

"That assumes the thief contacts you." Remy shook her head. "I don't think that's wise."

"Perhaps not, but I'd rather try it my way first." She bit down on her bottom lip. "I'm sorry. I know I'm not making it easy for you to help me. I . . . I think it's because I feel guilty about not staying in touch with my son. I don't want to be judged, but I don't want to be taken advantage of, either. Can you understand?"

"Of course. I wish us both luck."

Back at her condo, Remy sat on the balcony with a cup of tea, and stared at the photos of Martin Dunlap's artifacts and antiques. Tiffany lamps were associated with the Art Nouveau movement in the late 1800's. Their extravagant decoration was rare and sought after by collectors. For that same reason, forgeries continued to flood the market, making it difficult to verify the authentic. Dunlap's lamp appeared to be of unique design, but she needed to inspect it.

The base should be bronze and hollow with a heavy ring of lead inside, and the shade should rattle just a bit when lightly tapped. True originals were produced by Tiffany Studios under the watchful eye of Louis Comfort Tiffany. If a true original, Dunlap's lamp could be worth, depending on its condition and size, over one million dollars.

CHAPTER SIX

Friday morning, Remy took a deep breath when she tucked the clipping back into her wallet. Andy was her last hope; he still had access to the Lennox case files. Unless he came up with something out of place, he was right; she may have to live with the outcome. The old article was starting to wear, but not her focus on clearing her name. The headlines foretold her career downfall and her inability to find out who had set her up. She had failed at that, and of more importance, Sandra Lennox had been failed.

Grayden had arrived early, leaving an email for her to message him an update as soon as she returned from the Kieffer appraisal. He also indicated he'd be in the store all of the following week, and they would have a long talk.

". . . you've got the check list. If you get in over your head, tell him that you want a

second opinion."

Grayden had already put the sign on the door that the showroom would open at eleven o'clock. Remy double checked the contents of her briefcase. It was time for her to go.

The drive to East Mendleson was a cold, foggy one. It was a break that the roadway to Mendleson was off the beaten track and most of the commuter traffic into the Bay Area had died down. As she pulled in front of the house, it seemed like the fog was at its thickest and had settled like a blanket absorbing all sound. The muffled crunch of gravel under her footsteps marked her approach.

She was greeted with another scribbled note on the front door: *Aunt is asleep, go to the living room.*

Once again, she pushed on the door, and it gave way without a squeak. With a glance to the left, the doors to the dining room were shut. She turned to the right and entered the living room. Unlike the afternoon before, the light was dim and to Remy it seemed like the room was less cluttered. Or to be exact, it had less furniture and the paintings were gone. The two sets of candlesticks on the mantle were gone as well as the silver tea set that sat on the Louis XVI side table, both were absent. She looked down at the impression the table had made in the area rug.

Remy paused; there was a sound of hurrying footsteps fading down the hallway. She sidestepped a long sofa and headed for the door. From the corner of her eye, she noticed a rumpled suit of clothing on the floor extending out from the sofa's edge. She tiptoed to see closer.

Inside the suit was a body.

Her scream stuck in her throat, even as she bent to get a better look. Edmund Kieffer's lifeless eyes stared at nothing. A stream of blood oozed from the bullet wound over his left eye. From the pallor of his skin, rigor had started. She backed up and pulled her phone out of her purse and reached the 9-1-1 operator.

"There's a body," she rushed, explained the circumstances and gave the address.

"We'll get someone there as quick as we can," the operator said. "Do you want me to stay on the line with you?"

"No, I'll wait in my car."

She was on her way to the front door when she remembered the footsteps and Kieffer's aunt. She went down the hallway.

"Hello, hello, is anyone here?" she called out. "Please, help!"

No answer.

She ran in the direction of what she thought would be the kitchen. She was right. The huge room had large, white 1950s appliances and a huge butcher block table centered under a bare rack for pots.

Other than that, the room was empty.

It was clear from the layer of dust on the table it had not been used in some time. She opened the refrigerator and stifled a cry when there was nothing to be seen. She ran into the hallway and took the steps upstairs two at a time. The hallway was dark with closed doors leading off from it, and there was a vague musty smell.

"Hello is someone here?" she yelled. "Mrs. Kieffer?"

Still no answer. She started opening doors along the length of the house. The rooms were all bare. Returning downstairs, she pushed open the doors to the dining room. It had been emptied.

CHAPTER SEVEN

Remy sat in her car with a pounding heart and a racing brain. What happened to Edmund Kieffer? Who did those footsteps belong to? Where was his aunt? Why did the house have all those empty rooms? The police were there in less than fifteen minutes. These weren't Mendleson police. She knew all of them. These uniforms belonged to the county sheriff.

"Remy Bishop?" one of the team asked as he took out his badge and handed her a card. "I'm Detective Tuft. Can you tell me about how you came to be here and found the body?"

She got out of her car, seeing more uniformed officers hurry into the mansion. She went through the actions leading to her discovery.

"Mr. Kieffer, that's the body, asked me to come out this morning and appraise a mirror for his aunt. He wanted our auction house to handle the transaction."

Detective Tuft was old enough to be her father. He was dressed in slacks, white shirt, tie and a navy-blue V-neck sweater. He was also wearing a black bombardier jacket with "Patterson County Sheriff" stenciled on the back.

"Who let you in?"

"No one, he left a note for me on the front door saying to enter." Remy pulled her jacket tighter over her arms. The fog had not lessened, and the chill was biting. Or, maybe the shock of her find was finally settling in.

Tuft raised his eyebrows and wrote a comment on a small pad. "Ms. Bishop, please wait here with the deputy." He motioned for a female officer to come forward. "I haven't been inside the house and I'll have questions for you when I finish."

Remy remembered the sign on the showroom's door. "How much longer, Detective? I have a new job and I'm supposed to be in the store and —"

"This is a murder investigation, Ms. Bishop. I'm not sure we can accommodate your work schedule, but we'll let you get on with your day as soon as we can."

Remy dropped into the passenger seat of her car and glumly sat facing out.

"Remy, you wanna' tell me what's going on?"

The familiar voice drew Remy to look up into the eyes of Mendleson's police chief, Ned Warren.

"Hi, Chief," she said, giving him a weak smile. "I knew you'd be here next. There's a dead man in the house, an Edmund Kieffer."

He leaned his broad but firm frame against the rear door, looking at the hustle of enforcement personnel going over the grounds. "Kieffer? Don't know him. What was he doing in the Crandall house? More to the point, what are you doing here?"

Remy sighed and explained her job assignment, the note on the front door, and the discovery of Kieffer's body. Warren let her speak without commenting. When she finished, he looked up.

"Let me go in and talk to the sheriff's people. Stay here 'til I get back."

She motioned her head toward the deputy standing a few yards away. "I have no choice."

Warren walked with hurriedness to the house.

Remy leaned back in the passenger seat. Her thoughts raced over the events of the morning, though the sight of Kieffer's body kept coming to the forefront. There was something else, something she should pay attention to, but it was an elusive thought, and she couldn't get a clear picture of what was bothering her.

It wasn't long before she caught sight of Detective Tuft and the chief heading in her direction. She got out of the car and the three of them stood in a loose huddle.

Tuft spoke first, "Ms. Bishop, I know you gave me a snapshot of what happened, but could you go over the details of how you know Mr. Kieffer? Why you're here and what happened after you arrived?"

Her mouth had gone dry and she licked her lips. "It's not a long story. I met Edmund Kieffer for the first time Wednesday morning. He wanted me to do an appraisal of an antique mirror that belongs to his aunt. I came out in the afternoon and did a preliminary assessment. I gave him the authorization papers for his aunt's signature. Later, he called me in the store to say his aunt had signed, and we arranged for me to come out this morning."

"Who set the time?" Tuft prodded.

Ned held up his hand. "Why don't you let her finish, Detective?"

Remy felt uneasy, and her voice was started to shake. "He set the time. I got here a couple of minutes after nine. The note on the door said for me to come in and go to the living room which I did and . . . and I found . . . him."

The chief and Tuft exchanged looks.

She hurried to finish. "I immediately called 9-1-1. I thought I'd heard footsteps just before, so I ran to the kitchen, but it was empty. Then I ran upstairs trying to find someone to help, I didn't know if his aunt was okay. But those rooms were empty too."

"Did you find any indication that someone else had been in the house while you were here?" Tuft asked.

"No, I . . . I thought I heard footsteps. I don't know. I didn't expect the house to be empty. Like I said, there was his elderly aunt. I wasn't thinking about me. I thought his aunt . . . she might be in trouble, too. Maybe the footsteps belonged to her. But . . . but . . . ."

Tuft raised his eyebrows. "But there was no aunt." He made another note on his pad. "So, who let you in?"

She didn't know if it was the repeated question or the way he asked it, but Remy's sensed she was entering murky waters. Even Ned took a step to the side and looked over his shoulder back to the mansion.

"I told you," she answered. "No one let me in. The door wasn't locked. There was a note on the front that told me to go straight to the living room, and that's when I saw the body."

Ned turned to her. "What did the note say exactly, Remy?"

She closed her eyes in remembrance. "It read, 'Aunt is asleep, go to the living room.'"

"Where's the note now? Do you have it?" Tuft questioned.

Remy frowned. "No . . . no, I left it taped to the door."

Tuft looked skeptical. "Where's the note from your first visit? Do you have it?"

Remy shook her head.

Ned pursed his lips and looked over to Tuft who was putting away his notepad.

"Ms. Bishop, I'm going to have to ask you to come with me to the police station in Mendleson," Tuft said. "We have a lot more questions to ask you, and I think it will be more efficient if we talk there." He slipped his pen and pad into his jacket pocket. "We need to eliminate you as a person of interest in Edmund Kieffer's killing."

Remy thought her heart would pound out of her chest. "Chief?"

He shook his head. "We checked the door.

There was no note."

Mendleson did not require a full-service police department. With just the one holding cell in the station, it was staffed by Chief Ned Warren, two newly hired beat officers, and Roberta, the combination receptionist and booking clerk. The small town contracted with the county for its fire and law enforcement protection. Located on Lincoln Street, all the streets in Mendleson were named after former US presidents. Lincoln was the main street that contained the majority of commercial activity.

Remy gave thanks there was minimum mid-morning activity going on in town, for anyone to notice her police escorted visit to the station. She would be spared being the center of town gossip during lunch.

The officers left her in the glass-enclosed coffee room a few feet from Roberta's desk. Roberta's lighthearted and cheery hello was stifled when she saw the chief and one of the sheriff's men following her in.

"It's okay, Roberta," Remy said. "I witnessed a . . . a dead body this morning."

Roberta nonplused, turned to the chief for orders.

"I need to meet a few minutes with Detective Tuft from the sheriff's office." Ned

Warren was terse. "Give Remy a cup of something warm and let her sit in the break room with some privacy."

So, there she sat. After a moment, she took out her phone and punched in a number. She left a message, "Er . . . Mr. Lane . . . er . . . Grayden, I'm going to be late getting into the store. I . . . I'm at the police station because . . . because I found Mr. Kieffer dead when I went out there this morning." She paused realizing how her message would be received. "Anyway, I'll come to the store as soon as I can . . . I . . . well, that's it."

She clicked off.

She was returning the phone to her purse when Roberta opened the door.

"Remy, the chief and that detective want to see you in the interview room. That's the one at the end of the hall on the left."

She strode down the linoleum hallway. Tuft was seated at a metal table and the Chief stood watching out the window overlooking the enclosed loading area.

"Have a seat, Ms. Bishop," Tuft directed. "We are opening an investigation into the murder of Edmund Kieffer and right now, you're our primary source of information."

"Murder," she repeated. "I was sure of it. I saw the bullet hole. It had to have been a large caliber gun. The killer was a good shot. He or she stood pretty close because there was powder tattooing." She looked up into two pairs of startled eyes. "I mean on his forehead — gunpowder was embedded in his skin like a tattoo."

Warren sat down and said to a surprised Tuft, "Remy used to work in forensics."

Tuft responded with, "We're still looking into the details on that. We won't know particulars until we get an autopsy report."

"Of course," Remy murmured. Her thoughts returned to the murder scene. "What about his aunt? Where was she?"

"Remy," Ned Warren said. "We checked. No one lives in that house. It's been empty since the last Crandall moved out about six years ago. Maybe your father had the listing. Didn't you think it strange going into an empty house? No utilities, no people."

"There was no real estate sign." She shook her head. "It wasn't empty at all. The rooms were full of furniture. I mean at least the two rooms I went into. I didn't know the rest of the house was empty." Her words sounded like an echo. She frowned at Tuft. "There was plenty of sunlight; I didn't notice there wasn't electricity. I went into just the two rooms. The mirror I was there to appraise, was in the living room."

Tuft leaned in. "Then maybe you can tell us how your fingerprints were found throughout the house." He added, "They were in all the bedrooms upstairs as well as the kitchen downstairs."

"Oh, right, I forgot. I did go in other rooms," she sputtered. "But . . . but that was later, after I found Mr. Kieffer. I was looking for help. My prints will show up on the doorknobs."

The chief frowned. "How long were you in that house by yourself?"

"I . . . I . . . I don't know," she stuttered. "Maybe ten minutes, fifteen at the longest. It's a big house."

Tuft's cellphone must have vibrated. He took it out of his pocket, glanced down and then held it out for the chief to take a look. They both turned to Remy.

The chief pulled the chair out to sit at the end of the table. "Remy, we didn't know the prints were yours, except through your own admission just now. We haven't checked for your prints in the system," he said, his tone changing to one of official concern. "We got the ID on Kieffer. *He* was in the system, out on parole for grand theft. He operated as a fence buying and selling stolen goods."

"How long did you know Kieffer?" Tuft asked.

"About a day," she replied, trying to keep her voice from shaking. "Does that mean he didn't have an aunt?"

Tuft straightened in his chair. "That's exactly what it means. He didn't have an aunt and he didn't own that house."

She felt her stomach knot and her voice choked. "I'm sorry, but I don't know anything more."

Tuft and the chief exchanged another set of looks.

The chief held open the door. "Detective, can I speak to you in my office for a moment?"

The moment turned into ten minutes and Remy could hear raised voices. At last the chief returned, but without Tuft.

"Okay, young lady, you can go home." His expression was grim. "But you can't leave the area. There are a lot of unknowns, and until Tuft and his outfit get some answers, your movements are going to be restricted."

She nodded understanding. "Because I can't prove anything." She paused and then straightened. "But what about the mirror? How would I have known about the mirror?"

"There's no mirror like you've described, Remy. The mirror's gone."

Gone.

With a hollow feeling in her stomach, Remy made it back to the store in time to face Grayden's scowl. He was on the phone and shook his head at her appearance in his office doorway and pointed for her to take a seat. She sat tense on the edge of her chair, her mind racing with the morning's events.

The mirror was gone, Kieffer was dead, and she was the deer in the headlights.

Of all the things that had occurred on this horrible day, the fact the mirror was missing struck her as the most unbelievable. She went over and over every minute in her mind, but she couldn't remember if the mirror was there when she found Kieffer's body. After she saw the body, everything else was a blur.

Her overwrought recall was broken when she realized Grayden had put his phone down and was addressing her.

"I'm glad you were able to drop by your job."

"I'm sorry, Grayden. This day has been the worst. There is so much going on. I can't even begin to tell —"

He held up his hand. "Not necessary to explain, I've been fending calls all day. Someone saw you go into the police station, and a client came in and told me they were taking a body from the Crandall house." He

97

folded his hands on the desk. "I know you've been dealing with the police, but can you take me through what happened?"

For the third time, Remy recounted the day's events.

When she finished, Grayden was silent and just looked at her as if assessing a painting. She was silent, too, because his next words would set her future.

"Remy, I am very disappointed. I mean you don't appear to be able to stay in the store for any length of time. However, I do not believe you are guilty of murder. Go home. We'll start over first thing Monday morning, I don't have any appointments. I want to wrap up your training, I'll be here all day and we can talk."

He continued, not looking at her. "That said, as much as I appreciate your ability to hit the ground running, we must be sensitive to our image. Many of our clients choose us because we are trustworthy. They want to be reassured we are of the highest character, ethics and do not attract those of disrepute."

She opened her mouth to protest, but Grayden raised his hand and continued to speak.

"If there is another incident, I'm afraid

LaneWilson will be compelled to let you go."

CHAPTER EIGHT

Remy stared at the blinking message light on her home phone announcing four voicemails. She kicked off her shoes and went to the cabinet for her favorite Malbec. She only drank it on special occasions, and this time, while it might not be special, warranted special treatment. Sitting in the kitchen, she sipped while going through her mail.

The phone rang. She glanced at the caller's ID but didn't move, listening instead for the message.

"Remy Loh Bishop, this is your mother. Please call as soon as you can. We're worried."

Remy sighed. When her mother called her by her middle name, it was just a matter of time before she showed up at the door. Still, she needed a moment more to process the day and going outside, leaned against the rail on her balcony to watch the sun set.

After a minute more, she went back to the phone and played the remaining messages.

"Remy, this is your mother. I just spoke with Mrs. Kirby. Her son is the one who works across from the police station at the ARCO. He saw you going into the station with the chief. He said something was wrong at the Crandall house and you were there. Call home."

Delete, next.

"Remy, this is your mother. Where are you? Call home."

Delete.

"Remy, I know things seem crazy. Call when you get a chance." Melanie's voice sounded her concern.

She paused, then pushed delete.

"Honey, your mother is driving me nuts. She's standing over me, now. If you have any mercy in your heart, you'll call her." Her father paused. "We love you."

Remy sighed. She adored her father. It was his calm and caring that had carried her through a bad relationship and a worse job loss. Growing up the youngest, she always knew her father's love and never felt in competition with her siblings for his attention. None of them did. But she knew he worried about her and just wanted her to get on with her life.

She picked up the phone and punched in the numbers.

"Hi, Mom," Remy said.

"Oh, my God, Remy, are you all right? Where are you?" Her mother's voice choked with worry. She called out. "Mitch, pick up the phone in the bedroom."

"Mom, I'm fine," Remy said. "I'm at my apartment."

After her father greeted her, she repeated what had happened, but left out the parts which implied she might be considered a suspect.

"Do the police think you did it?" her father asked.

Remy heard her mother's gasp.

"They let me go so I think I'm okay. I . . . I just can't leave the area."

She could hear her own voice crack.

Her mother spoke, "Remy, why don't you come home until this is settled?"

She shook her head. "No, Mom, like I said, I'm fine. I'm going to work tomorrow and . . . Grayden Lane appears to understand. So, I'll be fine."

Her Dad spoke, "Come on, Bee, let's leave the girl alone. She's got it under control." His voice lowered, "But maybe, kitten, you could come over for dinner next week? No match ups, I promise, but it would be good to see you."

"Sure, Dad," she conceded. "I'll be there."

Remy needed to think back.

She'd spent the rest of the weekend with the radio, television and her phone off. She wasn't a jogger, but she went for an hour walk that ended up three hours long. Sitting in her living room looking out the window, she watched the fog cover the sun and slowly drift into the horizon. With a deep intake of breath, she picked up one of the sofa decorator pillows and screamed as loud as she could into its fullness.

That felt better.

She hadn't done that since the break-up of her engagement. She hadn't needed to.

But . . .

The mirror had been in the room with the body.

Now, in her mind's eye, she saw the space where the mirror stood as she rose from Kieffer's body; her reflection catching the edge of the frame. She was sure, the mirror and the stand had been there.

It had been stolen while she'd been in the house, or in the car. How? How could she have missed seeing it taken out? Or, missed someone driving it away?

As Remy readied for bed, she knew she

would tell the chief about the mirror. He would think — she didn't know what he would think, but it wouldn't be good. She didn't even know what to think herself. She would see the chief straight after work.

Remy turned on her cell phone and messages dinged in a stream. She punched a number.

"I was hoping you'd get back to me," Melanie said, her voice strained. "I've been trying to get in touch with you. What's going on? What happened?"

She took a deep breath and summarized the events that had landed her on center stage. "I wanted to get back to you, but . . . well, things are pretty bad. I'm trying to deal with it in my own head."

There was silence on the other end.

"Sure, of course," Melanie said. "But you don't have to deal with it alone. Don't forget I'm your friend."

"I won't forget. Dinner tomorrow, okay?"

"Yeah, sure."

"You sound kind of strange. Are *you* okay?"

"Yeah, yeah," her friend said. "I'm . . . I'm tired, that's all."

They clicked off.

Returning to silence, Remy stared at her bedroom ceiling. A thought occurred to her.

It had been the nudge she felt as she looked through the art pieces in the Crandall library and the furniture pieces in the living room. Everything was so beautiful.

Everything.

But now she knew the assortment of fine goods was just that, an assortment. It supported the contention that Kieffer was using the Crandall house as a collection point for stolen goods. So many exquisite items, the true owners must be devastated.

It would help to identify the art pieces and objects to track them back to their source. The sheriff's office might even be grateful.

She reached for several binders and books from her nightstand and tossed them on top of her bedspread. These were her prime references that had served her through her appraisal certification classes and apprenticeship at the Camden Auction House. Victor Camden was her teacher, as well as an art historian and collector, and he'd made her his protégé. The "why" always left her with a question. He said she reminded him of his dead daughter. But whatever the reason, fate had been with her when she walked into his office after class and told him she intended to be an art expert for the largest auction houses in the world.

Now her primary intent was to stay out of jail.

Remy reached for a pad and pencil and jotted down a list of items she had seen in the Crandall house, placing them throughout the rooms starting with the corner right wall in the library. Vases, candlesticks, platters, bookends, Queen Anne chair, Victorian fainting couch . . . her list went on for two pages before she came to the end of her memory.

She opened up Miller's Antique Handbook. It was the industry guide book on antiques and pricing. First on her list was the large cloisonné vase centered on the library mantel.

This was going to be a long night.

CHAPTER NINE

There was nothing like waiting for the other shoe to drop.

It hadn't helped that dinner with Melanie was less than relaxed. Her friend seemed distracted and kept looking at the time. They had brought take-out to Melanie's stylish townhome. Now, finished eating, they nestled on opposite ends of her just paid-off sofa, their feet curled underneath them.

"A killer is out there because of me."

"Don't be so hard on yourself," Melanie said. "The case isn't closed."

Remy looked away. She wasn't ready to admit, even to her friend, she couldn't and wouldn't go on with her life until the Lennox case *was* closed and the guilty jailed. Melanie and Andy were the last of the original group to remain as her friends. Remy felt awkward about going around Melanie and asking Andy to help her, but she'd promised Melanie she wouldn't let the Lennox file get under her skin. And rather than hear Melanie's reproach, she opted to ask for her forgiveness once she got her job back, and she swore Andy to keep silent about her ongoing search.

"Wonder if they kill again, because my work was tainted?"

"Remy, let it go. It's been months now," Melanie said, sliding a glass of wine across the table. "You've just started a new job. You can't let the past mess that up for you."

"I won't, but there must be some way to prove I didn't blow a murder case. And now, it's possible I could be a suspect in another homicide. What is going on?" She reached for her glass. "I refuse to accept there isn't someone or something out there to substantiate I'm not incompetent. And I don't know how all that furniture disappeared from the Crandall house. Then there's the mirror. There's not a day that goes —"

"Enough. You're starting to repeat yourself," Melanie said, squeezing her friend's hand. "I hate to see you so stuck on events that can't be undone. You're making yourself crazy."

"Don't worry; I know I'm lucky to be working for LaneWilson. With most of the prominent auction houses located in San

Francisco. And, I'm really happy I don't have to go into the city every day. That alone will start to make up for the salary." She took a deep breath. "So, I guess what I'm trying to say is, I'm doing my best to move on, but I won't ever forget."

"And no one believes you killed that Kieffer guy," Melanie said. "But I will admit, your timing lately has not been good."

Remy nodded and caught Melanie's smile. She laughed.

"You are so right about that."

"Good." Melanie patted Remy's shoulder. "I promise you, after a while it will fade, and you will have moved on. As a friend, I'm advising you to let it go."

"You're right," Remy said. "I need to pull myself together, start a new chapter and make sure I keep this new job."

"Sounds great to me," her friend said. "You're fortunate this is all you have to worry about."

"Yeah, I know." She dabbed her lips with a napkin after draining her glass. "Thanks, for the therapy session. I'm going home. Do you have to work tonight? How's your budget?"

Melanie was a whiz at statistics, but she was terrible with her personal finances. For as long as Remy knew, except for a few months, her friend had worked two jobs. For the past year, she'd been working part-time in the technology section at the Blue Feather Casino outside of Gilroy.

"I'm doing fine, thank you." She rose to take their glasses to the sink. "Things have started to look up. My school loans are paid off," she said from the kitchen. "I've got a half shift to do tonight, so it's not so bad. And, I have a date for a midnight supper." Her friend pushed reading glasses up on the bridge of her nose and patted Remy's arm. "This one might be around awhile."

"Hmm, I'm not that self-absorbed. Have you told me about him? Why haven't you brought him around?"

Melanie dropped her smile. "Now, you know I don't introduce you because they tend to end up not meaning anything. Just forget I mentioned it. If things continue to work out, you'll be the first to know. I forgot how nosy you could be."

Remy frowned. "I'm not being nosy — curious maybe, but not nosy."

Melanie's love life amazed Remy. It was one area where her friend didn't need anyone's help, and it showed in the regular cadre of men who sought her attention. She was single and said she liked it that way.

The phone rang and Melanie picked it up

in the kitchen. It was clear the call was private, and she motioned she was going to take it outside on the patio.

Remy waved her on. Straightening her shoulders, she went into the bathroom, combed her hair, washed her face and stared into the mirror. She sometimes felt her failure at the lab showed in her face. She'd loved the hunt forensic detecting provided, and she'd been good at it, too. Now, life had thrown her another curve and the murder of Edmund Kieffer threatened to disrupt an already disrupted existence.

What she hadn't told Melanie, or Andy, was that she'd started a Lennox file on her own. A few things didn't make sense. Everything had happened so fast, those lab samples had her tags, but not her biohazard labels. That damaged knife sample could not have been there. She remembered because —

"Hey, you okay?" Melanie tapped on the bathroom door. "What are you doing in there?"

"Just thinking," she called out, checking her makeup one last time in the mirror. She opened the door to a curious Melanie; they both headed back to the living room.

"Now, promise me, you'll stop dwelling on the lab." Melanie stood in the living room and picked up a full paper bag from the coffee table. "Here's your care package: tissue, tea, wine, you've got a new job to focus on. Let it go."

On Monday, Remy made sure she arrived at the showroom first. She'd promised herself to make the effort to achieve some modicum of normalcy in her career life. She had tea ready and a small box of fresh baked croissants in the break room ready for Grayden when he arrived a little after eight.

He looked at her attempts to placate him and accepted her offerings. "Good morning and thank you." He motioned with his head toward his office. "Give me fifteen minutes to settle in, and then let's talk about your training."

Remy took a deep exhale, she was still on payroll. She used the next minutes to dust items around the store with a duster she'd found in the storage closet, add water to the large floral centerpiece that sat on a sideboard against the wall, and repositioned out-of-place furniture. Taking a quick look around with pad and pen in hand, she went to Grayden's office.

He rocked unhurried back and forth in his executive chair, the only modern piece of furniture in the store.

"First, I don't want any suspicion or bad publicity about this Kieffer murder falling back onto LaneWilson." He stopped rocking. "So, I think it is best that other than the police, you don't speak about what happened in that house to anyone. We will proceed as if it has nothing to do with us. Agreed?"

Remy moved to the edge of her chair. "Agreed. All I want to be is a contributing employee. I'd like nothing better than to put the whole . . . whole . . . incident out of my mind." She waved her hands in dismissal. "I came here to learn and to contribute to the store's success."

"Yes, well, that *sounds* good." He took a sip of coffee. "Now, do you remember the antiques and vintage items you saw in the Crandall house?

So much for never speaking of the house again.

Amused at the question, she raised her eyebrows. "Yes, I made a list last night. I wanted to —"

"Great, let's see it."

She stood. "But I haven't catalogued anything. I listed the items by category and estimated age. I didn't finish the —"

"No matter, I'd like to see the list. This could be a commission for our store. With your involvement, we could get in on the ground floor by appraising the items for the court."

"Grayden, I think these are stolen goods. They'll seek out the owners —"

"Perhaps, but at first they'll need the value in order to make their case."

Remy had her doubts, but tilted her head in acknowledgment. "I didn't think of that. But I can see how you could be right." She left to retrieve her list and returned with a copy for Grayden.

"That's why I'm the owner." He glanced at the sheets. He raised his eyebrows. "Impressive, I'll review this in detail after our talk." He put the paper to the side. "Now, we have the jewelry sale coming up in two weeks. We typically don't do them, but it's a favor for a friend who's the executor and he's liquidating an estate."

He handed her a thin file. "It will be a good chance for you to get your feet wet. There are a modest number of items for sale. Look over the list, do some research and then we'll talk about it this afternoon."

"What about advertising?"

He looked at her in surprise. "Why, Remy, I'm impressed with your question. That's one of the most important tasks of a sale — letting people know we're having one. But in this instance, Evelyn made all the arrangements with the newspapers, social media and industry news outlets to get the word out. She put everything in a file with the sale date on it. You can —"

The front door trilled.

Remy jumped up and peeked down the hallway. She felt her heart thump as she turned back to Grayden. "It's the chief and Detective Tuft from the sheriff's office."

He moved to join her, and they both walked out onto the showroom floor.

"Morning, Remy," Chief said. "Grayden, this is Detective Tuft. He's with our sheriff's office out of Patterson County. He's been assigned to the Kieffer case. I'm sure Remy has caught you up."

Grayden shook hands. Remy kept to the rear of the group. She wanted to get the tone of the visit before she engaged. The visitors turned down his offer of coffee, and Grayden pointed for them to sit on a loveseat facing the center of the store. He and Remy took chairs opposite.

He said, "I know what Remy's told me and what I read in the paper. I don't know any Edmund Kieffer. I tried to reach him by phone once, but I wasn't able to connect."

Tuft took out his notepad, scribbled a note

and looked up. "When was the last time you were in the Crandall House?"

Grayden was caught off guard. "I can't say if I ever was. If so, I don't remember. Why?"

"So, we shouldn't find your fingerprints anywhere?" Tuft persisted. He ignored the rise he saw coming from the reddening of Grayden's face and the shake of the head. He shot out another question, "How's business?"

Grayden couldn't hold back his temper. "Wha—"

"It's all right, Grayden." The chief put out his hand as if to calm the rising waters. "We're just doing our job. But Detective Tuft I think we need to get on with our objective." His voice sounded concerned and firm. "Remy, we need you to come back with us to the Crandall house and walk through all your steps. There're a lot of questions we can't answer."

"I was going to come by the station anyway after work," she stammered. "But I just started working here. . . . My job is —"

"That won't be a problem, will it, Mr. Lane? I'm sure you want to cooperate." Tuft peered at him.

"No, no problem, not at all." Grayden ran

his hands over his hair. "Remy, go with them. I'll be working late. We can finish our conversation when you return."

She grimaced. She didn't want to go. She didn't ever want to go back to that house again.

They pulled up in front of the Crandall mansion behind a couple of county sheriff cars. Remy got out of the front passenger seat and looked up at the house she had just days before thought of as a dream.

Now a dream turned nightmare.

"All right, Ms. Bishop," Tuft said as he directed her to the front pathway. "Tell us the first thing you did when you visited here."

Remy took a deep breath. "I walked up to the front door, ready to push the doorbell when I saw the note telling me Mr. Kieffer's aunt was resting, but for me to enter and go to the left into the library. I was to wait for him to join me."

They exchanged looks.

"I know," she sighed. "Another note that's not there."

The chief shook his head.

Remy pushed open the front door and they followed her to the left. The drapes were pulled back to let daylight pour in from all the windows into the almost empty room. There were a couple of furniture pieces covered with sheets and books still lined the shelves.

"On my first visit, this room was full of furniture," Remy said. "There were art objects everywhere alongside the shelves of books. It looked nothing like this."

Tuft looked skeptical and the chief walked around the room. Neither said anything and Remy stayed by the door.

Tuft glanced out the window. "They must have worked fast. Did he threaten you?"

"Threaten me?" Remy cocked her head. "With what? Why?"

"Perhaps, he thought you would help him out in his . . . endeavors."

"No way, I'm telling you, this room was full — completely full of furniture." She turned around. "Nothing was covered." She lifted the sheet over a reproduction 19th century English fainting couch. "This room is where I met Edmund Kieffer for the first time. He gave me the history of . . . of . . ."

Remy stood in the middle of the room where the massive refectory table once stood. This couldn't be happening. It must have taken half dozen men to empty a room that size. The fragile table alone could have taken that many. The shine of the bare floors seemed to mock her.

She turned around, trying to register what it all meant.

Her eyes sought the items in the room. "Wait, Chief, there's something odd. Detective Tuft, look around. There's no dust on anything. And if . . . ," she said as she went over to open one of the drapes. "If you look on the area rug in front of the fireplace, you can see the impression of table legs."

Both men circled the room and ran their fingers across the shelves, sills and tops of sheets. Tuft squinted at the book shelves.

"Remy, Edmund Kieffer had been dead some hours before you found his body," the chief said.

"I'm not surprised," Remy responded. "I could tell that rigor mortis had begun. And that makes sense. The furniture must have been removed the day before." She stood next to the chief. "Were there tracks in the rear of the house?"

"She's right, Tuft," The chief said. "We need make sure that forensics picked up any heavy tire impressions. This room was cleared out, and not long ago."

Tuft nodded slowly. "Maybe, but I can think of a couple of other explanations." He looked at Remy. "What did you do next, Ms. Bishop?"

She rubbed her forehead. "I looked around at the beautiful pieces and then in about . . . oh, less than five minutes, Mr. Kieffer came in and he saw me admiring a valuable antique table. He said he already knew its worth, but he wanted me to appraise a mirror in the living room, and we crossed the hall."

The chief frowned. "Remy, why didn't he tell you to meet him in the living room first?"

It was her turn to frown. "That's a good question. I don't know."

They left the library for the living room. This time the almost emptied room was as she left it, after discovering Kieffer's body. The drapes were drawn back, and the hardwood floors echoed their footsteps. The old-world Persian area rugs were gone.

Except for the one with a large blood stain.

She paused in the middle of the room and continued. "Anyway, the living room wasn't as decorated as the library, and he seemed to be in a bit of a hurry. Kieffer showed me the mirror; it was sitting on a stand over in that corner." She pointed. "I went over to it and —"

"Where was it, exactly?" Tuft interrupted.

"That's what I wanted to tell you." She turned to the chief. "The mirror was still

120

here when I found Kieffer's body."

He and the chief exchanged frowns.

Remy walked over to the far corner next to the mantel.

"It was right here." She tapped her right foot for emphasis. "Day before yesterday, it was on a stand. I turned it around to see the back, and then I examined the front. From my initial evaluation, it appeared to be genuine. It was a George II white painted mirror, circa 1740, with the original beveled rectangular plate. The frame was carved with scrolls and foliage, and the pediment was crested with a putto surmounted by a vase of flowers."

"What's a putto?" the chief asked.

"Sorry, term of art," said Remy. "A putto is a cupid image from the Renaissance period."

Tuft started to pace. "So, this thing is pretty fancy. Is it heavy?"

She shook head. "It's elaborate but relatively lightweight."

He stopped pacing and squinted at her. "So, you could carry it out?"

Remy felt herself flush and no coherent words emitted from her lips. The chief rubbed his face and was about to speak when Tuft held up his hand.

"I'm not saying you stole the mirror, Ms.

Bishop. I'm saying someone your size could have removed the mirror."

She felt like she was falling down the rabbit hole without Alice to hold on to. "I couldn't have emptied two large rooms of furniture and art works, Detective. I couldn't have —"

He held up his hand again. "No, *you* alone couldn't do it," he said. "Now take us through one more time, how you found Kieffer's body."

Remy couldn't help but hear the insinuation in his voice that she could have had help. Her temper was replacing her feeling of helplessness.

"Same thing, the note on the door this time said to go straight to the living room. I went in and almost immediately saw Kieffer's body behind the sofa. I bent down, he . . . he wasn't moving. I could tell . . . and I knew better than to touch anything. Then I called the police." She stopped.

"Remy," the chief interrupted, "you said the mirror was there when you found the body?"

"Yes."

"Then what did you do?" Tuft prodded.

"I ran to the kitchen to get help, but it was empty and then —"

"How did you know where the kitchen

was? You said you'd only been to the living room and library."

Remy squeezed her fists. "I'm familiar with real estate, Detective. I know houses, and it's pretty easy to find the kitchen. You don't need a map."

"Remy . . ." Chief Warren cautioned.

She conceded with a small nod and took a deep breath. "I ran from room to room calling out, trying to find his aunt or . . . or anyone. I went upstairs, but all the rooms were empty, and there was no one there." She moistened her lips. "And I went to sit in my car, that's the whole story."

"Can you remember the items that were here from your first trip?" Tuft flipped a page on his pad.

"Yes," she said. "I already made a list." She reached into her purse for a folded paper and handed it to him.

He scanned it. "This is good." He slipped it between pages of his pad. "Now, you didn't hear anything? Or see anyone else all the time you were in the house?"

"Well, I thought I might have heard someone running, but I can't be sure. But, no, I didn't see anyone else, and then I went outside to wait. Someone could have . . . someone *did* come into the house once I was gone. The mirror was here."

The chief frowned. "That was pretty risky, someone taking that mirror while you waited in the car. What about the rest of the furniture? Where did it go?"

She shrugged and shook her head. "I have no idea, but three days ago, the library was full of items."

They walked out to the car. The forensic team hovered over the foot paths and others were prodding the shrubs along the rear of the house.

"I'll get a ride back with one of the techs." Tuft put his notebook back in his pocket and opened the car door for her. "I want to thank you for your cooperation, Ms. Bishop."

She looked at him with skepticism and gave him a brief nod.

"Please, don't leave the area without letting us know," he said, over his shoulder as he walked away.

The ride back to the police station with Chief Warren was a silent one. He said goodbye in the parking lot.

"Remy, I know this is rough on you. But right now, you're the only direct lead we've got." The chief pulled at his ear. "Are you sure you hadn't met this Kieffer guy before Wednesday?"

"I'm positive," she said. "He wasn't from Mendleson, and I didn't recognize him at all. Why?"

" 'Cause he had your name circled on a piece of newspaper tucked inside his jacket pocket."

Remy froze. There was only one time she'd been the subject of a newspaper article.

She closed her eyes. "Was this article about my involvement in the Lennox case?"

The chief nodded, not taking his eyes off hers.

She stared back at him as her heart beat stronger.

"I . . . I didn't . . . he never said."

"I just got a text from the coroner. He found the article on Kieffer," the chief said. "I'm going to have to tell Tuft."

"Of course," she'd murmured, resigned.

"I'll have one of the deputies drive you back to LaneWilson."

"No, I'd rather walk."

Chapter Ten

By the time she returned to the showroom it was close to the end of the day and she could hear Grayden on the phone in his office with what sounded like a customer. The walls were thin enough she didn't have to stretch much to overhear his raised voice. But for now, she wasn't interested. Exhausted, she slumped into her chair at the reception desk. The chief's revelation that Kieffer had sought her out struck down her hope this nightmare would be over soon.

Minutes later, Grayden's voice faded and the door opened.

"Remy, I'm glad to see you're back," he said, standing with one hand in his pants pocket and the other holding a cup of coffee, he sat in her guest chair. "You okay?"

"Yes, I'm fine. Grayden, I want you to know that —"

"Remy, in our business you have to be able to assess pieces in a limited amount of time." He reached into his suit jacket pocket and took out a pair of glasses. He put them on and peered at her. "I assess people, and I don't think you murdered Edmund Kieffer."

"I assure you I didn't." She took a breath. "But now there's the missing mirror, and . . . and all the stolen art."

He straightened in the chair. "What? You mean that list you gave me? All the items were stolen?"

Remy gathered herself. "Kieffer was a crook; he dealt in buying and selling stolen goods." She moistened her lips. "When I found the body, the rooms were almost completely empty. I don't know what happened to the contents from my first visit."

He removed his glasses and pursed his lips. "Whoever stole the furnishings will want their items back. Did you give the list that you gave me, to the detective?"

"Yes."

He leaned over and retrieved a binder from behind her desk. "Well, there's nothing we can do about that now, and we have a sale to get ready for." He opened the book between them. "This is your sales operation bible. It includes the background on the items to be sold as well as on the seller. If it's an estate, we also do a little family ownership research. The public is interested in the provenance of an item as well as the stories behind the sellers and the pieces. This will be the first focus of your LaneWilson training."

Remy reached for a pad of paper to take notes. "At Camden's, I was responsible for compiling the sales binder for the auctioneers." She opened the bottom desk drawer. "In fact, I brought a sample of what I'd put together there."

Grayden motioned for her to continue.

"It's similar to yours." She pulled out a two-inch white binder. "See, it's a ledger. Here's the seller's background, item provenance, sales history, if any, photos, and an appraisal worksheet of comparable high and low sales numbers of similar items."

He raised his eyebrows as he flipped through the pages. "I'm impressed. You're not the newbie to the business I thought you were." He handed back the binder. "We might be talking about a commission plan sooner than I thought."

Remy felt herself beaming. Then she wondered if he was just trying to be kind.

He continued. "Why don't you go ahead and prepare a to-do list for our upcoming sale and run it by me. It will give me an idea of your process and experience level."

"I'll have it to you by Friday." Then she hesitated. "Grayden, why did you hire me if you didn't know I could handle the basics of being an assistant appraiser?"

He stood. "To be honest, it didn't matter. We were desperate to replace Jo . . . Evelyn, and since you appeared to be intelligent and eager to work, I knew I could train you."

Remy pretended not to notice his slipping reference to the mysterious Joan.

At home, Remy poured a glass of wine and put her legs up onto the sofa. It took no time for her thoughts to run back to the events of the day. If she hadn't seen the proof, she would have said it was improbable to have emptied the Crandall mansion of all art, furniture, books, and area rugs in less than two days. And, for that same reason, she knew Detective Tuft wasn't sure she was telling the truth about the previous condition of the rooms.

She could tell the chief wanted to help her out, but it wasn't his investigation. Tuft had made that clear. He'd also made clear that until he had someone else in his sights, she was person of interest number one.

It had been one hell of a week.

But there was one memory that kept just out of her reach. Maybe if she could get back inside that house.

Enough speculating, if she wanted to keep the job she had, it was time to do some work. Snatching up a writing pad and pen, she started to itemize the tasks she would need to oversee the auction sale in two weeks.

Her phone buzzed.

"Remy, are you busy?" Melanie begged. "I know it's late, but can I come over?"

"Yeah, sure."

Melanie sounded nervous, which wasn't unusual, but what was unusual was her being free on a week night. With two jobs she often complained about her lack of rest.

Minutes later, Remy opened the door to her friend who entered in a rush.

"Share some of your wine. I need a drink." She flopped onto the sofa and ran her fingers through her hair. Her eyes were red-rimmed, and her hand shook.

Remy poured her friend a half glass of wine. "What's wrong?"

Melanie took a sip. "Yeech." She pushed the glass aside. "I changed my mind. Can I have some water?"

Remy brought a bottle out from the refrigerator and handed it to her friend.

"You've been crying. Will you tell me what is going on?"

"I got some bad news, but that's not why I'm here." Melanie took out a tissue and swiped at her nose. Then downed a swallow of water and leaned back on the sofa. "Remember, I told you I stopped seeing Greg? He reports for the *Mendleson Herald.* He's been assigned to follow up on the Kieffer murder."

"Ah, that was his article in the paper yesterday." Remy wrinkled her brow. "What about him?"

"He knows you and I are friends, and he wanted to know if I'd be willing to give him your background story."

Remy frowned. "What story? I don't have a story."

"I knew you would say that, and that's what I told him, but he talked to Roberta, who told him you'd been brought in to have your fingerprints taken." Melanie put her water bottle down. "Remy, did you get arrested?"

"No, of course not, they wanted to . . . to eliminate me as a suspect."

"I don't understand. Why were you even there?" Melanie asked. "According to Greg, by way of Roberta, you're a suspect; I wanted to let you know. Did you . . . did you see the body?"

"The body was my potential client, Edmund Kieffer." Remy took a sip of wine and squeezed Melanie's hand. "Thanks for the heads up, but this is little ol' Mendleson. You're not from here. Here, everyone already knows everything. And, there's nothing to tell. I was there to appraise an antique and . . . and I found Kieffer's body. Other than once two days before, I had never met the man and it turns out he was on a criminal watch list. He was a thief and a fence for stolen goods."

"What!"

Remy shrugged. "It's not uncommon in my business. We buy and sell high ticket items; we hope from the rightful owners."

"Sure, but not you?"

"Of course not," Remy snapped. "I was in the wrong place at the wrong time. One of the reasons I'm not in a cell is because I have no motive. They're going to start looking into all his associates and relationships to see who might know him and want him dead."

"Yes, that makes sense." Melanie bit her bottom lip and fidgeted with her purse strap. "Remy, there's something else. I'm going to need a favor." She took a swallow of water.

"What's wrong? I can tell something's bothering you."

"I need your help."

Remy said nothing and waited for her to continue.

"Er, do you remember my brother, Nick?"

Remy shook her head.

"I thought I told you," she said. "Well, he got into some trouble owing this guy. He was a loan shark. But anyway, Nick couldn't pay what he owed, and the interest, too. Well, anyway, Nick came to me for a loan to cover what he couldn't. You'd have to know Nick, but he has never asked me or anyone else for help. I knew he was in over his head this time." She coughed to clear her throat.

"Drink some more water."

"No." She shook her head. "I'm okay, and I want to get this over with. I need five hundred dollars. Can you help me?"

Remy blinked. She was torn. She was down to her last savings and five hundred dollars would put a nice dent in it. Somehow, she didn't think Nick would be responsible enough to pay her back on time. Melanie must have been reading her thoughts.

"Don't worry," Melanie said. "I'll be the one to pay you back before the month is out, make that in the next couple of weeks. I'm expecting a sizable check from the casino for working extra hours. It's just that

I'm short until then."

"Melanie, I don't —"

"Never mind, I didn't think you'd come through," she stood and slung her purse over her shoulder. "I didn't want to ask you, I knew —"

"Wait," Remy said and stood next to her. "I was going to say I don't know if I even have that much in my account, but if I do, it's yours."

Melanie leaned in and dropped a light kiss on the cheek. "Oh, I knew you wouldn't let me down." She headed for the door. "I'll fix lunch for us tomorrow, and you can bring the check then. If you're short, maybe your parents can chip in."

"What?" Remy frowned. "My parents? I —"

"Just kidding." Melanie waved her hand. "I meant, if you didn't have enough. But let's not even go there." She looked at the watch on her wrist. "I've got to get going. My shift starts at ten o'clock. See you to-morrow."

She rushed to embrace a silent Remy and hurried down the foot path.

Remy closed the door and leaned against it.

She reminded herself she'd known Mela-nie ever since she went to work at the lab, their friendship blossomed immediately. While Remy didn't care to lend money, she also wanted to be there for her friend.

The week from hell didn't appear to be over.

CHAPTER ELEVEN

The next day, LaneWilson had just two customers. In the late afternoon Remy picked up her purse and headed to the back of the store. Grayden was on a long-distance call. She gestured at his door that she was going to pick up the brochures. He waved her on, but not before he motioned to his watch — hurry back.

Able's Printing was in a small business park in the middle of old town Mendleson. Howard Able was the sole proprietor, and as far back as Remy could remember, its only employee. Concessions to his advancing years were the hours of operation being reduced. Over the years, he'd gone from being open twelve to twelve, seven days a week; to nine to six, seven days a week; to noon to five, seven days a week; to four hours a day, seven days a week. The trick was, customers didn't know which four, but at least you knew he'd be open sometime every day. Locals learned to call ahead.

"Good afternoon, Howard," she grinned. "I'm working for LaneWilson now, and I came to pick up our brochures."

He squinted at her over his bifocals. "Remy Bishop?" He rose from his graphics table to meet her at the counter. "You're doing auctions for LaneWilson? I thought you were helping your Dad."

She laughed. "I haven't helped out in the real estate office in a while. I used to work for the county, but . . . but the commute was making me crazy and I decided to stay local." The white lie rolled easily off her tongue.

"Well, it's good to see you. Tell your Dad hello for me. He's a good customer. Everyone else has gone over to doing their own printing on those dang computers. But he still comes to me, and I appreciate it."

"I'll tell him." Remy knew her father ordered his business cards and simple flyers through Able's; the bulk of her father's business printing needs were done through an online service. He'd told her he didn't mind paying a bit more to Able to show support for his business.

"Now, why are you here?" Able narrowed his eyes.

"The LaneWilson brochures," she repeated. "I'm here to pick them up."

"Oh, yeah, I'm sorry. I did hear you the first time." He ambled off to the rear of the service area and brought forward a large box. "What do you think of these?"

She lifted the top off and reached for a brochure. They were quite nice. She had to give it to Howard, you might not know when he was open, but the quality of his work was still superb and worth the wait.

"Howard, these are wonderful. I like the layout and the font. Did you do the design?"

"You don't think that uppity woman who works with you did it, do you? She's about as creative as a wooden ruler. Yes, I designed it." He beamed. "You think it looks pretty good?"

"I do."

He fingered one before putting the lid back on the box. "I need to tell you something. I told Joan that two different kinds of font made no sense. But she insisted so I said I would do it her way, but I didn't."

Remy almost dropped her purse.

"You've met Joan?"

He squinted at her. "Sure, haven't you? You said you worked for LaneWilson, didn't ya'?"

"She's been out of the office since I

started," Remy said. "What's she like?"

"Oh, I don't know. But one thing strikes you right off, she's all smiles on the outside, but the smile doesn't go to her eyes." He stroked his beardless chin. "You can tell she's not from Mendleson."

"Hmm, well, I can't wait to meet her."

"Well, maybe not, but she's a slick one." He pointed to the order form attached to the mock-up. "See, two different fonts."

Remy froze.

She realized what had been bothering her — two different fonts. She picked up the box in her arms and started for the door. "I've got to run, Howard. Just send me the invoice," she rushed. "I have some ideas for some other work. Thank you for doing such a great job."

"You're welcome. I'm glad you like it. Tell your boss that I give a good price for repeat customers." As she dashed out the door, he looked disappointed at her leaving so soon.

Remy placed the box in her trunk and half-ran the two blocks to the police station.

Remy walked up to the counter. "Hello, Roberta, is the chief in?"

"Yeah, he's on the phone with the sheriff's office about the Kieffer murder, seems like there's some new discovery about the victim." She peered at Remy. "Did *you* know him?"

Remy shook her head. "No, he told me his name was Kieffer, and that he was looking after his aunt's interests." She looked past the gossipy Roberta to see into the chief's office. It appeared as if he was finishing up his call.

He came out looking grim and was running his hand through his thinning hair when he saw her.

"Remy, you're just the person I need to talk to. Come on back to my office." He motioned with his head. "By the way, why *are* you here?"

She looked over at Roberta, who was practically prone in her chair as she leaned over to hear Remy's answer. But Remy waited until the chief closed his office door behind them.

"Chief, I've been trying to recollect something at the Crandall House. It was making me crazy, and then I remembered. It was the notes." She moved to the edge of her chair. "Those notes were written in two different handwriting styles. They weren't written by the same person."

"What?" It was his turn to straighten in his chair.

"Yes, even the wording style was different,

140

but yesterday was so . . . so crazy, I didn't recognize what was wrong. I came right here when it hit me."

The chief said nothing and stared past Remy's head. Then he looked at her, pushing a paper and a pen across his desk.

"Write them out for me, Remy. Can you remember the exact wording?"

"Sure, but without the notes, I don't see how this will help."

She scribbled the words, and pushed the sheet back to him.

"I don't either, but this case is turning out to be one big knot, and I don't want to assume anything is trivial." He lowered his voice. "You know, we found out from his fingerprints, that Kieffer was wanted by the feds. That's why I wanted to see you. Are you sure you don't remember anything else about him or about your visit?"

"My visit? No, I met with him on that one day. He was . . . dead the next time I saw him."

"And that's our other problem. We can't find anyone else who saw him except for you."

She winced. "I don't understand. How can that be?"

"Do you remember if he mentioned going anywhere, or coming from some place?"

Remy shook her head. "I don't think so . . . . I don't recall him saying anything like that." She went over Kieffer's words in her mind. "What about the Feds? What did he do to get their attention?"

The chief stood and then sat back down on the window ledge. "Kieffer was last known to be in Baltimore. There he was the east coast connection for a major import/export cartel out of Singapore. The Feds had him under a close watch, but he disappeared about a year ago."

She frowned. "And he shows up in little 'ol Mendleson . . . why?"

"If you were to ask Detective Tuft that question, he would say you should be able to answer."

"Me!"

"You're the only one who met this Kieffer guy — alive, and you're the only one that saw the Crandall house full of furniture — furniture that's gone." The chief looked down at his feet and said in a low voice, "Tuft is speculating if the furniture was there at all."

"There at all!" Remy shook her head. "Of course, it was there. I don't know how the house was emptied." Pausing, she self-talked herself to calm down. "Chief, I'm the one who's trying to help. I called the police, and

I'm the one who's coming to you with information to help. You believe me, don't you?"

He sighed. "That's why you're not sitting in County jail." He folded his hands between his knees. "But Tuft thinks you might be smart enough to hide behind appearing to be useful. He thinks Kieffer was hanging you out to dry and in a rage you . . . well . . . ."

"Great." She put her head in her hands, and then looked him in the eyes. "Well, I'm not going to let something else hang over me. I'm innocent of any wrongdoing."

The chief squinted. "What else is hanging over you?"

"Nothing, I . . . I meant that there's a murder and grand theft with the furniture gone. I don't want to be connected with it. It could mean my job." She recovered her composure.

The chief peered at her. "What are you going to do? Don't be getting involved, Remy. I'll pass what you said on to Tuft." He shook his finger. "This is going to be nasty. Too many law enforcement players, and that's never a good sign."

She sighed. "I've told all I know. I wish it would all go away."

The chief patted her shoulder. "That's one

thing it ain't going to do."

Melanie's condo was located in a gated community. A bored-looking, solid built security guard took Remy's name and punched in Melanie's phone number. She knew the other guards; this one was new.

He took out a sheet of paper containing the layout of the complex.

"I know where her unit is." Remy replaced her identification in her wallet.

"Yes, ma'am, but we have new rules." He pointed to a color key on the page. "Your friend lives in the green section. I'm giving you a numbered green pass for your windshield. It helps us identify people who might be lost or —"

"Shouldn't be there at all?" she offered.

"Yes, ma'am."

"This is just a residential complex, right?" Remy teased. "I mean no one is building bombs or anything."

The guard did not respond, but took a step back into his booth and waved her through.

"Why so much security?" Remy asked, after plopping a dip covered chip in her mouth and chasing it with a swallow of iced tea.

"Beats me. They probably told us," Melanie said, shrugging. "But I don't go to homeowner meetings and I toss the newsletters."

They were sitting on bar stools in the small kitchen. The table was covered with papers and a beeping laptop. Melanie appeared preoccupied and got up over and over to read the laptop screen.

"I can tell you want to get back to . . . to whatever you were doing before." Remy opened her purse. "I wanted to drop off the money."

Melanie spoke in a rush, "Remy, I can't thank you enough." She looked at the check and put it in her blouse pocket. "I . . . well . . . you were my last resort. I didn't want to ask you. My family's problems aren't yours." Her eyes returned to the computer screen.

Remy hoped she would mention when she could expect repayment, but it appeared Melanie was only there in body, her mind was elsewhere.

"Well, I better be getting back to work." She stepped off the stool. "The thing about a new job is it takes a while to get that first paycheck. My account will be almost empty until then."

"Hmm? What? Oh, yeah, don't worry." Melanie took her eyes off the screen. "I'll get the money back to you within a couple of weeks." She walked Remy to the door. "I've got to get this check to my brother. We'll talk later."

Remy turned to respond, but the door was already closing.

CHAPTER TWELVE

Over the next couple of days, Remy spent the bulk of her time mailing and distributing auction catalogs. She thought she would have a few days to further familiarize herself with the sale items, but she hadn't counted on the locals. It was clear, Mendlesonians were anticipating the upcoming sale event as a social gathering opportunity. Each Thursday and Friday afternoon, the week before a sale, LaneWilson served complimentary beverages and pastries, and in the evening wine and seafood appetizers.

Grayden was pleased. "These Thursdays and Fridays in conjunction with the release of the catalog are a lot of work, but the word gets out this way. On average, a quarter of our sales come from people who live right here in this region. The rest are customers from around the Bay Area."

"If you say so," Remy muttered. She had to keep one eye on replenishing the refreshments, and the other on potential damage to the storeroom furnishings.

For most of the morning she cleaned and re-arranged the glass cases that held the jewelry pieces for the sale.

"Let's have a rehearsal." Grayden pointed to a brilliant diamond necklace. "Tell me about this piece."

Remy was ready. "This is a Harry Winston vintage necklace. Founded in 1932, Harry Winston showcased exquisite quality and showmanship. Each piece has its own unique story and provenance. This is a sister piece to a longer necklace owned by a prominent New York heiress. Notice the two graduated rows of flawless circular pear and marquise diamonds? They are set in platinum and total 25 carats. Of course, it comes with reports from the Gemological Institute."

Grayden clapped. "Very good, very good." He walked over to another case. "And this?" He pointed to a ring.

"Ah, this is a breathtaking modern estate ring, circa 1940s. Notice the spectacular round brilliant cognac diamond bezel set in the center, with the rich rose gold setting encircling the center gem. There is a scalloped halo of round brilliant diamond accents. It was a Christmas gift to the owner from her husband when he returned from World War II, as a symbol of their good luck. Its setting is in 18 carat gold and totals almost 2.3 carats." She grinned.

"Enough, enough, I'm convinced," he said, amused. "I think you know enough to represent us. Next week I want you to make calls to our top collectors and buyers who didn't attend the preview to make sure they know about the sale."

"I'm on it."

Mid-afternoon Grayden emerged from his office where he'd been behind closed doors all day.

The preview reception was underway.

It didn't take long for the numbers of visitors to reach a crescendo of wall to wall clusters, and then lessen over the next two hours, until Grayden closed the door behind the last couple.

"Well, I think we have the public's attention." She turned off the music and stifled a yawn.

She realized it hadn't gone unnoticed. Grayden looked sympathetic.

"I'm not going to bring up how important this sale is to our bottom line," he said. "But next week will be hectic. We use the next couple of days to finish preparing for the sale."

"Not a problem," she concurred. "This weekend I'll continue doing my prep work and household chores. How about you?"

"My wife and I are driving up the coast to our house in Bodega Bay." He glanced at his watch. "Look, go ahead and take off. You worked late the last couple of nights. I've still got some work to do, and I'll close the store."

Remy protested. "But I wasn't here for a half-day earlier this week."

"I'm not worried about it. You'll work many more hours next week at the sale." He headed for his office and said over his shoulder, "Go home."

She did.

The reality of the past days had started to sink in, and she was more than a little tired. She had just flopped down on her bed when her cellphone rang. She was surprised to hear Jay Ross's voice.

"I was calling to see if you'd like to catch an open-air concert in Golden Gate Park tomorrow?" he said. "I know it's late notice. I tend to preview houses on weekends, but I just heard from a friend who needs me to cover for him and he'll do my rounds for me."

Remy grimaced. "Ordinarily, Jay, I would like to go, but I had a rough week and I

150

need to sleep late and recharge my batteries."

"Maybe what you need is to take your mind off of the Crandall house and all that's going on, and have some fun."

"Fun?" Remy rolled her eyes. "I can't remember the last time. . . . You know what, I haven't done anything spur of the moment, as in forever. I'd like to go."

"Great."

CHAPTER THIRTEEN

After a good night's sleep, in the morning, Remy put away the clipping, and with determination tackled the pile of laundry that had built up over the week. Alone in the apartment complex laundry room, she sat at the small table next to the warmth of a dryer and perused LaneWilson's sales reports. She was already impressed with their auction activity when she applied for the job, but it was a surprise to see the majority of their income came from private appraisals and brokering transfers of art assets. She did a quick calculation in her head, almost seventy percent. No wonder they wanted her as an appraiser.

Her phone buzzed with a text message.

A complication re: paying back your loan. Something came up. I know I promised a deadline. Don't be mad. I'll call you in a couple of days.

M

A twist in the pit of her stomach caused Remy to emit a low groan. She'd bet her friend would keep her word, and now she'd lost — big time. At least, her lease payment and utilities were paid, she could get lunch at work and dinner would be a bonanza of green salads until she got her first full check. She would have to scrape to make her student loan payment.

Remy slammed the file closed and sat staring out into the room. It wasn't fair. It had been just a few days. Melanie had to have known she couldn't make the payment at the time she asked for the loan. She took a deep breath and realized the dryer had stopped. Her clothes were done, and for that matter so was she. Her fiancé had used her, Melanie had used her and Kieffer had used her. She was tired of being used.

There was a different guard at the gate.

"I'm here to see Melanie Chase." Remy looked straight ahead as the guard punched in the numbers.

"This is the gate. I have a Miss Bishop to see you." He nodded, "Thank you." He

turned back to Remy. "Are you familiar with
—"

"Yes, just give me the green pass," she said
with more harshness than she meant. The
guard was doing his job. She put the pass
on her passenger seat and drove through
the web of streets.

Parking her car in the guest spot, she
couldn't stop the self-talk going on in her
head. Melanie never intended on paying
back her money. That's why she wasn't taking her calls. She knew Remy was lean on
cash, and Remy could not forget the dig
Melanie made about her parents.

She strode up the short path to the door.
A group of three women dressed in jogging
outfits chatted cheerfully as they went past.
One waved a good morning, but Remy
turned away and rang the bell.

No answer. She knocked on the door.

No answer.

*Ah, come on. It's not like she didn't know I
was coming.*

She walked around to the parking garage
entrance. Melanie's parking space could be
seen through the gate. Remy had to look
twice to make sure her eyes weren't playing
with her.

Melanie's car was in her space.

■ ■ ■ ■

Back at home and still fuming, Remy called
and texted Melanie again and again, but
there was no response. After leaving three
increasingly terse voicemail messages, she
realized waiting to hear back was making
her crazy, and she wasn't getting anything
else done. It was bad enough Melanie had
let her in the gate, then changed her mind
and didn't open the door to avoid telling
her to her face. On top of that, her childish
response by not answering her phone was
eroding their bond. She thought they were
friends, Melanie's behavior implied other-
wise.

She glanced at the time. She would be late
for her date with Jay.

He answered on the first ring.

"Jay, speaking of last minute, I'm going to
need a raincheck. We both seem to be
squeezing each other in," she said. "This
time, I'm in the middle of a dispute with a
friend and it has put me in a bad frame of
mind."

"Well, I'm disappointed, but I'd rather not
get together if you don't feel you can have a
good time. You're forgiven, if you agree to
see me when we both can make real plans.

No more squeezing in."

"Agreed."

They clicked off. Remy's smile returned for a moment until she remembered why she'd had to make the call. The frown returned.

Needing to let her anger slow to a simmer, she gathered the files she'd brought home from the office to do catch-up. Making room on the kitchen table, she'd started reviewing office records and set aside a slim folder tucked in the back of her desk in the bottom drawer. Evelyn had titled it: Evan Wilson, but there wasn't much. From the few forms and correspondence contained, she gathered he was an equal partner with Grayden from the very beginning. They'd bought the auction house from its previous owner. Grayden seemed to have the administrative skills, and Evan the eye for value. She was putting away the folder when her attention went to a file lying flat at the bottom of the box. Tugging with care, she pulled it up through the folders that hid it.

The tab read: Joan Lane Durbin.

Remy didn't try to contain her curiosity. She cleared a small space on the top of her desk. She lifted out the pages: there was a small stack of several letters and a document labeled, Agreement of Understanding.

She sorted the letters in date order and began to read.

They dated back to the start of the auction house. Joan was Grayden's sister. She was a silent partner in the start-up of LaneWilson. If Grayden was the management leg of the stool, and Evan the buyer, then Joan was the charmer and networker. She made the connections; she was the closer. The letters were more like memos from Grayden to Joan requesting her to make connections, and Remy couldn't help but read between the lines his growing dependence but concern regarding his sister's outreach tactics.

Spanning three years, in the beginning the memos and notes appeared to be in response to Joan's success in securing estate sales. Then over time, the correspondence dealt with the need for the sales contracts to reflect the integrity and values of the auction house. The last letter was dated the previous year. It acknowledged Joan's willingness to no longer represent herself as a dealer for LaneWilson, in exchange for remaining a partner and signing a new owner's agreement. Remy picked up the three-page single-spaced document. It was straightforward and didn't give any clue to the background details.

Remy leaned back in her chair and thought. The file explained the reactions she got when she said Joan's name. She still had questions: had Joan's activities gotten the store in trouble? What were her tactics? Her gut told her she couldn't approach Grayden for answers, and she didn't want to wait until Evelyn returned.

She would have to be patient.

Household errands and chores kept her busy the rest of the day. By Sunday morning she could no longer dodge her mother's phone calls seeking her "thoughts" about Jay.

"I know you just met him, but what did you think?" she asked.

Remy sighed. "He's nice, and he asked me out. But I . . . I couldn't make it."

"Oh, good grief. So, when are you going to see him again?" Her mother persisted, "Besides, what are you doing bringing work home? You need to get a life."

"Now, that's true. I do need a life and as soon as I . . . I make things right — it will be soon. But work is good for me, it keeps me focused," Remy said, knowing her mother was concerned. "Mom, I will let you know when Jay and I go out."

"Remy Loh, I worry about you."

"Don't. I'm fine. I promise."

The rest of the morning, she prepared her meals for the next few days. She went to the grocery to buy up salad greens and feta cheese. Thanks to her friend, it was going to be a wallet-tightening week.

Chores done; she'd picked up a book she was close to finishing when her doorbell rang. The thought crossed her mind that it would be nice to have a guard gate at her complex like Melanie, to give her a heads up on visitors. She peeked through the eye piece and frowned.

Two uniformed sheriff officers stood at her doorstep. They must have sensed her presence on the other side.

"Ms. Bishop, please. We'd like to ask you a few questions."

Just like on television.

She took a deep breath and opened the door. The officers were both middle-aged, one with a slight paunch, the other looked fit with graying hair. Her eyes went to their guns.

"What is it? What's the matter? I told Detective Tuft I didn't know any more than what I already told him about Edmund Kieffer the last two times I was interrogated by him."

"May we come in?" the gray-haired one

asked, looking past her.

"Yes, I suppose."

She stepped aside and the two men entered. Their girth took up the space of the small foyer, and she led them to her living room. The three still stood.

"I'm Lieutenant Crest and this is Officer Gaines," the gray-haired Crest said. "Do you know a Melanie Chase?"

"Melanie?" Remy frowned. "Yes, we're friends. Why?"

"When was the last time you saw her?" Gaines asked.

"Yesterday . . . Saturday." She raised her hand. "No, wait, I didn't actually see her, she wasn't home. I guess Wednesday was the last time I saw her. Why? What's wrong with Melanie?"

"We don't want to inconvenience you, but we're going to have to ask you to come with us to the sheriff's office to answer questions," Gaines said.

"It *is* an inconvenience, and I want to know what's happened to Melanie."

"She's dead," Crest responded. "Her body was found in her condo, and we think you're the last person seen entering her home."

CHAPTER FOURTEEN

"You need a lawyer," Mitch Bishop, her father, said. "I'll call Doug Ricks, he's our attorney and he can recommend someone who deals with criminal law. But I can tell you this — don't talk to anyone from the sheriff's office. Don't answer any more questions until a lawyer arrives."

"Dad, I'm not afraid to talk to them," Remy insisted. "This time I don't know anything. And I'm going to get my own attorney. Victor Camden has a great firm on retainer, and they know the business. I'll call him to recommend someone."

"I doubt he'll have a criminal attorney."

"Why don't I ask and find out." She paused. "I would prefer to handle this myself."

She was sitting in a small cubicle at the sheriff's office using a landline phone. Crest and Gaines had been accommodating and almost sympathetic. They let her make a call in private, or, whatever privacy a cubicle in an open work space in a police department could provide.

"Look, your call caught me in Seattle. I'll return home tomorrow," her father said, tired. "Tell them to bill me. And, I would wait until I got back to tell your mother. We won't do anything until we hear from you, and if —"

"Thanks, Dad, but I've got to go. They're coming back."

"Remy, remember don't say anything. And —"

She clicked off the phone.

Gaines spoke first. "Finished your call? Why don't you come with us to a decent office where we can talk?"

On its face, it was a question, but he was already leading her out of the room and down a short hallway.

"Now you already told us you were the last to see Melanie Chase." Crest took out a notepad. "Where did you go after you left her?"

"What? That's not what I said." Remy shook her head. "I didn't 'leave' her, I never saw her."

"That's not what the video shows," Crest pushed back.

Remy squeezed her hands. "I —"

162

The door opened and a woman dressed in uniform handed a note to Crest. He read and passed it over to Gaines.

Now what?

She didn't have to wait long to find out.

"Ms. Bishop, we located the guard on duty at Melanie Chase's complex when you went to see her. He tells us Melanie Chase answered and authorized you to come in. He says he remembers you because you were her only visitor that day, and you seemed upset."

Remy put her head in her hand and closed her eyes. When she opened them, Crest and Gaines were staring at her. She cleared her throat.

"Am I under arrest?"

"No. If she's your friend, we're hoping you feel obliged to do your civic duty and be a good citizen by assisting us in finding whoever killed her."

"I'm not answering any more questions until I see my attorney."

Remy glanced down at her watch. Thank goodness it was Sunday, at least she could report to work on Monday. She looked at the clock on the wall. Where was her attorney? Victor Camden had made his calls and assured her a lawyer was on his way.

"Look, Remy, you need a lawyer who will keep the cops off you," he said. "Don't worry, I'll get someone over there."

As she glanced at the clock for the umpteenth time, the door opened and a deputy stepped in.

"Ms. Bishop, your attorney is here." He stepped aside.

Remy rose and looked down on a nerdy looking man wearing a navy pullover sweater with a striped shirt and a tweed sports jacket. His glasses slid half-way down his nose, and his rumpled jet-black hair with manicured gray sideburns gave him the appearance of a kid trying to look grownup.

"Paul Scott." He held out his hand. "Victor Camden contacted our firm." Remy shook it, and he turned to the guard. "If you would leave us now, officer." He had a stern voice with an authority that contradicted his looks. He waited to hear the door click closed.

"Mr. Scott —"

"No." He shook his head. "Call me Paul. In court, I'm Mr. Scott. Let's sit down and you tell me what you think you know about why you're here." He took out a notebook and pen.

They sat across the table from one another. Remy used the next minutes to

164

recount Melanie's loan request, then her message about not meeting her repayment.

"I was disappointed, more than anything else," Remy said. "She was right, I know my parents would have given me money to hold me over, but I didn't want to ask them. And I thought it was a little presumptive to suggest." She frowned. "I guess also, I was angry that she wasn't too busy to come over to my house to ask for the money, but too busy to tell me to my face she couldn't pay it back."

"You were angry?"

"Yes, I was angry. I'm tired of being used. I'm tired of —"

"So, you went over to her house to . . ."

"To tell her off," Remy replied, slamming her back into the chair.

"That's all?"

Remy's brow wrinkled, then understanding crossed her face. "It was just five hundred dollars. I wouldn't have hurt her for any amount of money." She sighed. "She was my friend. Can you tell me how she was killed?"

Paul reached into his briefcase and glanced at a sheet of paper. "Blow to the back of the head."

"Have they found the murder weapon?"

He shook his head. "Not yet." He picked

up another file. "What can you tell me about Edmund Kieffer?"

Remy looked startled.

"Kieffer? What has he got to do with Melanie?"

"A friend in the sheriff's office mentioned you were involved in that case as well." He peered at her. "He was murdered a few days before Melanie Chase." He shrugged, and pushed his glasses up onto his nose. "Maybe it's a coincidence, but. . . . So, tell me about Edmund Kieffer."

Remy took him through the previous week and her discovery of Kieffer's body.

"You need to check with Detective Tuft," she said. "Looking back, I suppose I should have picked up some warning signs. A family living in the Crandall house would have been big news. I would have known if anyone had moved in." She rubbed her forehead. "But more important, this town hasn't seen a killing since the 1930s. Now there are two murdered bodies in the morgue within the span of weeks, and I know both the victims. That doesn't sound like a coincidence to me. The sheriff is right to be concerned." She took out her own pad and made a note.

Paul gazed out the window.

"Do you know if Kieffer knew Melanie?"

"What?" She struggled with the thought. "No, I mean I don't know. I have no idea."

He searched her face, and then took off his glasses. He wasn't a handsome man, but he had an air of competency that left Remy with a modicum of reassurance he knew what he was doing. Nor, was Paul a tall man, but he sat tall in the chair and met her eye to eye.

"Okay, I'm going to talk with the sheriff and see about getting you out of here. There's a chance he might want to hold you until Monday, but my bet is he can't get an arraignment calendared that fast. Most important, he doesn't have all the proof he needs to formally arrest you. He's been very generous with giving us time to talk, so I don't want to antagonize him."

"Do you believe me?"

"Doesn't matter," he said. "I've got to get a judge to believe you. Let's meet tomorrow morning in my San Jose office, and we'll see where things are."

He stood and handed her his business card, and then returned the notebook and paper to his briefcase.

She rested her hand on his arm. "It's important to me, to know you think I'm telling the truth. If I can't convince you, I'm not going to convert the sheriff."

He exhaled. "Look, it's been my experience that liars, especially killers, try to weave stories without holes in them. But the truth is rarely that tight. Your story has enough holes for a fleet of trucks to pass through."

Remy moistened her lips and smiled. "Thank you." Then she frowned. "I think."

He held the door opened for her.

"It's what I do."

CHAPTER FIFTEEN

Remy got up Monday morning, made time to read the clipping, and then dashed to the showroom. She left a note for Grayden summarizing her need to respond to the sheriff regarding Melanie Chase's murder. It had been the number one story on the local morning news. They didn't give her name, but mentioned a Mendleson resident had been questioned; she breathed a sigh of relief when they identified her place of employment as an unnamed local business. She hoped Grayden wouldn't be too upset about her absence, but there was nothing she could do.

Her meeting with Paul Scott wasn't until ten a.m. He'd been able to convince Detective Gaines that while she may have had the opportunity — means and motive were lacking in their case against her. The likelihood of her being a flight risk was also negligible. So, once more she was a person of interest and asked not to leave town.

So be it.

Her intuition nagged at her. She would bet a million dollars Melanie's murder was somehow linked to Edmund Kieffer's. She kept coming back to the fact of two murders within two weeks without a connection — it was doubtful.

Remy checked the time, while she was certain the forensic team had done their job, she still would have liked access to Melanie's condo. She was also certain staying as far away from the condo was what any attorney would tell her was a no-brainer, that is, if she didn't want to remain in the suspect column.

Paul was tapping away on his laptop when the receptionist knocked on his door to announce Remy's arrival. He worked for a small firm, and its modest circumstances were evident in the sturdy carpet and utilitarian chairs.

"Good morning, come in," he said, gesturing to a nearby chair. "Let me finish up this motion. I need five minutes."

"No problem." She took one of the two seats in front of his desk.

She glanced at the wall to her right. It was covered in the typical diplomas and certificates from prestigious schools and organizations. She squinted at an icon overlapping a gold seal. It seemed familiar but out of place. She was set to rise to get a closer look.

"Done," Paul said with clear satisfaction and pushed his laptop to the side. "Now, tell me what you know about Edmund Kieffer and why he selected you to represent the estate sale."

Remy sighed and took a breath. She recounted the details of her encounter with Kieffer and then fell silent. She looked Paul in the eyes. "In retrospect, he did insist on having me, versus Grayden, do the appraisal. But I got the distinct feeling he'd never been to Mendleson before, nor did he give any indication he knew me personally." She wrinkled her forehead. "Another thing, he was anxious to obtain an appraisal sooner rather than later."

"Interesting. I saw in your file that you have a background in forensics," he said, leaning forward. He made an entry on a separate page on his pad. "What else did you pick up?"

Her expression was thoughtful. "Nothing the police don't already know. My question is: why did he choose LaneWilson? He had my name on him, how did he know me?"

"I wondered the same thing," Paul said.

"He was referred to you, but by whom?"

"His business card," Remy said. "It's more like a calling card, except under his name it had an address in Palo Alto, California. It was on cheap paper stock and . . . wait!" She straightened in her seat. "I forgot. On the back of the card he wrote the address of the house. It's in my desk in the showroom. I'm not sure if the sheriff's deputies told you, but the notes were written by different persons. And, there's something else, he said he'd already had some pieces appraised. There was a rare Gillows refectory table; he said he knew its worth. I bet I could find out which dealer —"

"Whoa." Paul raised his hand. "Let's be smart about this. First of all, I want to see that business card. If it has his handwriting, it needs to go to Tuft in case those notes ever show up."

"You're right," Remy agreed. "I'll make a copy and get it to you."

"Now, about these dealers," he said. "What information would they have?"

"Are you kidding? Depending on what I find out, there are dealers and there are dealers." She tapped one of her fingers on his desk pad. "If I could find the dealer he worked with, the one who did those other appraisals, then there would be at least another viable suspect for the sherriff to look at. Besides, I need to call around anyway for another customer matter."

"And the connection with Melanie Chase?"

"It's hard to believe Kieffer knew Melanie," Remy murmured, then her shoulders sagged. "She was a good friend. I'll miss her. But, you're right, two murders in little ol' Mendleson, there must be a connection. I can't think of how they could have crossed paths. Melanie worked as a forensic tech and at night as an account clerk. She had expensive tastes, but wasn't an antiques buff at all, just the opposite. She liked contemporary style."

"But you said she needed money."

"Yes, but that was for her . . . brother." She stopped speaking and sat in thought.

"What? What are you thinking?"

"That he might be worth checking into."

Paul agreed. "Let me look into the brother, since you've never met him anyway."

She released a loud breath. "I know. I'll go to the funeral."

"No, you won't," Paul said. "Given the circumstances your presence may not be welcome. And I need you to keep a low profile." Paul put his papers into a stack on his desk. "Let's touch base tomorrow. I have a hearing in the morning but I'm free after that. I can do some background work on Melanie Chase's brother, and we can see where we are."

Remy looked at her watch. "If I hurry, I can get to work by noon. I need to keep my hours. Is there any chance we could meet at lunch tomorrow?"

"Sure. I'll meet you at the cafe down the street from your job."

"I'd better be getting back, or I won't have a job."

Grayden was on his cell phone when Remy entered the showroom. She'd made it before the clock chimed noon. A quick look at the top of her desk produced a couple of follow-up messages, catalogs, invoices, and return envelopes containing checks. With one ear listening for the end of Grayden's conversation, she was able to return calls and open most of the envelopes, which indeed carried checks.

"Well, good to see you, Remy," he said. "Before you go into some convoluted story about being late, your attorney's secretary called and explained you wanted her to make sure I knew you were on your way. There's no need to say more."

"Grayden I —"

"And, yes, I read the paper. Please," he said shaking his head. "Let's just get some work done. Are we ready for the sale?"

"Yes, we are."

Remy had taken the catalog home and converted it to a spreadsheet of items by current owner last name and the appraised dollar value. She took the sheet out of her tote bag and handed it to Grayden.

He peered at it with a long stare and then looked at Remy. "All right, we haven't done it this way before. In the past, we made a mock-up of the catalog and wrote the information next to the item. But this seems a bit more comprehensive." He handed the paper back to Remy. "We'll give it a try."

"Thank you," she said, reaching for a writing pad. "Today I want to work on the event itself, lining up the caterer, florist and . . . and I thought some music might be nice."

Grayden frowned. "It's not a party. Evelyn has already handled those details. Did you check her file?"

"Yes, I did." Remy could feel a rising blush. "I used her guidelines as just that. I wanted to push things a little further and do something different." She moistened her lips. "I know it's not a get together, but don't people buy more when they're comfortable and the atmosphere is congenial?"

"Grayden wouldn't know anything about that."

Remy and Grayden turned at the same time toward the voice coming from the rear of the store. She was a tall woman, blue eyes, with thick sandy brown hair clipped into a modern pixie cut. She wore a navy blazer atop gray slacks and a lime green sweater top. She looked beautiful and sophisticated.

"Joan," Grayden muttered under his breath.

CHAPTER SIXTEEN

Remy's eyes opened wide.

"Ah, my name is Remy Bishop." She put out her hand for the woman to shake. "I . . . I've seen your name in our files, but it's good to put a face to them."

"Hello," Joan said, shaking Remy's hand with obvious amusement. "I understand we've become your waystation as you go about murdering people."

"Joan!" Grayden blurted.

"Just teasing, dear brother." She set her purse on Remy's desk and sat down in an adjacent overstuffed chair. Leaning across she spoke to Remy, "I came in to look things over. We conduct a jewelry sale once a year. Each showroom tries not to compete on the calendar with the same items. Our next sale will be furniture and McCarthy's will auction jewelry."

But Remy was not ready to be distracted. "First, I am not a murderer. And second, I am already familiar with how to schedule auction sales. I did an apprenticeship with Victor Camden's showroom in San Francisco." Her voice sounded clipped, but she didn't care. "Today I plan on posting to the store's email list to make sure our customers are aware of our special."

"What special?" Grayden and Joan asked together.

Remy looked past them. "Our free shipping offer." She turned to Grayden. "I was going to provide you with my marketing plan, but . . . I never got the chance."

"Well, I stand, if not corrected, definitely curious about the marketing plan and our new employee," Joan said. "Perhaps you could take both of us through this plan."

"Good idea," Grayden said. "I'm interested in seeing what you've been working on."

They moved to Grayden's office, and Remy took the next thirty minutes detailing her ideas and actions she'd already taken for promoting not just the jewelry sale but LaneWilson sales in general.

Grayden was nodding as Remy came to the end of her presentation.

"There are a couple of concepts that don't fit our operation," he started. "But, overall, I have to applaud your initiative as well as

178

your instincts — well done."

Joan glanced at her cellphone which had begun to vibrate. She didn't look up. "I agree. We can follow your promotion plan for the jewelry sale, but I want to see the stats when it's over." She put her phone in her purse and stood. "We'll need to know if you've made a difference."

"Of course," Remy replied, feeling a drop of sweat slip down her back.

Joan turned to her brother. "We need to talk."

"I'll be at my desk." Remy stood and left the room.

She located Kieffer's business card and made a front and back image on the copier. Paul would want the actual card, but she wanted to pursue her own avenue of research.

Over the next hour, Joan and Grayden were still behind closed doors, so she used the time to set up the email alerts to clients for the sale. At one point the voices were raised as in an argument, but Grayden's office was too far down the hall for Remy to hear anything other than mumbled voices. It was near closing time before his door opened, and she heard the click of Joan's heels go out the rear door. A few minutes later, Grayden came into the lobby.

"I'm going home," he said not looking at her. "Have a good evening."

"You, too, Grayden."

Remy had promised her parents she would come by on her way home. Her father wanted to see her, and hear first-hand about Melanie's murder as well as Paul Scott's strategy for ensuring she didn't get arrested for being her killer. But she had a stop to make first.

"I read about Melanie," Andy said. "Everyone in the lab is yacking about it. But no one thinks you did it."

They were meeting at a book store located next door to her old workplace, the county forensic lab. Andy Carter had been promoted to a senior technician. His overweight frame and sparse brown head of hair belied his deductive brilliance. He was the only person Remy knew who could solve Sudoku puzzles with just one number for a clue. And he was her friend.

"Well, I'm . . . I'm involved . . . well, not involved exactly but you could say I'm . . . I'm connected to the recent murders in Mendleson." She looked down at her feet. "I . . . I haven't gotten used to Melanie being gone; and being gone in such an awful way."

Her voice choked at the end.

Andy scowled. "Yeah, you two were good buddies." He seemed embarrassed at her show of emotion and coughed into his hand. "I did like you suggested and went through the database for everyone who handled the Lennox evidence, but you were the one assigned from your section. I think we've gone has far as we can."

"As far as we can, legally," she said, looking at the customers standing in the cashier line.

"Ah, . . ." he stopped.

"What's the matter?" she asked, and then realization came over her face. "I'm sorry, Andy, I'm being self-centered. You worked with Melanie, too."

"I'm okay. Everyone at the lab is taken aback," he said. "The police can't think you killed her."

"Thank you for questioning their wisdom," she said. "I'm trying to deal with one thing at a time."

"I get it." Andy cleared his throat. "Now, tell me what am I checking for now? I know I told you it was a little slow around here, but I didn't mean I wanted additional work."

"It sounds worse when I say it out loud." Remy took a breath. "I need to narrow down possibilities, and hope to expand the pool of primary suspects." She sighed, "I need to have official fingers point away from me. When they find out about Lennox, there's a good chance they'll think I might have . . . maybe have some reason for . . . I don't know."

Over the next few minutes, Remy recounted the events of her contact with Edmund Kieffer. Andy moved his chair closer, leaned back with crossed arms and a deepening frown.

"I know the team brought a lot of forensic evidence in. But my section wasn't assigned the case. Still, I may be able to get access to the read-only files," he said. "It's no big deal."

"And Melanie's file?"

He shook his head. "Since she's an employee, they're giving her evidence special handling."

"That makes sense." She gave him a peck on the cheek. "I'll appreciate anything you can find out. Call, or text, if you find anything suspicious."

By the time she arrived at her parents' home, her mother had a fire blazing in the fireplace and her father had returned from showing a house to out of town buyers. He grinned with pleasure at seeing his daughter, but she couldn't miss the concern in his eyes. Over a satisfying meal, their dinner conversation was light and enjoyable, and Remy noticed both stayed away from the elephant in the room.

"For some odd reason," her father said. "My business is picking up from recent referrals. Mendlesonians have decided you're innocent, and it has resulted in a lot of new sympathy clients for me."

Her mother pointed a finger at her. "They're good people. They know us, they know Remy doesn't have a mean bone in her body." She paused, dabbing her mouth with a napkin. "We wanted to tell you that your father and I are going to cancel our vacation, for now. We'll go after all this is over."

"Oh, no, Mom," Remy said. "You and Dad have been planning this river cruise forever. No, if you don't go, I'll never forgive myself."

Mitch moved closer to his wife and squeezed her shoulders.

"We need to show a united front, princess. Besides, we can cancel now without losing all of our deposit," he reasoned. "It's either that or we'll encourage your sister to come and stay until your name is cleared."

There was a twinkle in his eye. Remy didn't need to ask why the threat. She rolled her eyes.

Zoe.

"Dad, you guys don't play fair," she implored.

"I don't know what you're talking about," her mother said, busying herself with stacking the plates. "Your sister loves you. It's good she doesn't have children in her life. Selling her business provided her with money, but she needs focus, someone to care about."

Even her mother couldn't look Remy in the face.

Zoe Bishop McKinney cared about one thing, making sure any and everyone was as miserable as she was. Her negativity could turn any festive and happy occasion from joy into gloom. She was four years older than Remy and lived in Reno. Her siblings had sworn to cover each other in the event Zoe ever ventured over the state line. She relished re-making her family over, under her standards. One hint or suggestion from her parents that Remy needed support, and she'd be here on the next flight.

Remy shuddered.

"All right, I can't clear my name and deal with her too. Your threat has worked. Postpone your vacation until I'm cleared," she said, putting on her coat. "I'm leaving."

Not bothering to hide their grins, her parents accepted her grudging hugs of good-bye.

At home, Remy checked her landline for messages. There was one from Paul changing their lunch meeting to after work. That suited her, she didn't want to run the risk of being away from the showroom when Grayden was sure to call and check on her. Besides she needed the morning to locate dealers in refectory tables and clocks.

She picked up a book by her bedside, but she couldn't concentrate on its fictional storyline, reality was too demanding. The idea that had nagged her all day was stronger than ever.

She was going to Melanie's funeral.

CHAPTER SEVENTEEN

"No, you're not. We've already had this conversation." Paul shook his head with emphasis. "I don't want to upset her family at the funeral. You're already in the papers as the last one to see her alive. At least, let me talk to them first and see where they're coming from. Besides didn't you tell me you have a big estate sale coming up?"

Neither was eating the French bistro dinner in front of them.

"The sale is Saturday. And Melanie's funeral is next week. I can handle the sale *and* go to Melanie's funeral." Remy's lips formed a thin line. She should have asked for forgiveness instead of permission. Now, she couldn't ignore Paul's objections. "All right, I won't go, exactly," she said.

"Exactly," he repeated. "What does that mean?"

"It means, I'll tuck myself away, maybe park at a distance, take pictures at the funeral home to see who attends. No one will know I'm there."

Paul ran his hand over his head and groaned. "Do you not get you are a suspect in two murders?"

Remy realized she was becoming more intolerant of his drama. "Look, there's a benefit in having a video. You'll be close up, but I'll have the overview and catch what you missed. We can compare notes when we meet in your office." She leaned in. "You're the one that said there's a link between Melanie and Kieffer. My independent observations could point out a connection."

He lifted his head and exhaled. "All right, but you've got to stay out of sight," he said, resigned. "The time for her funeral has been set for ten a.m., meantime, stay out of trouble. That means, in your case, don't go anywhere or talk to anybody."

"Ha, ha." She mocked. "Very funny."

With this matter settled, they both were able to eat.

Dabbing her mouth, Remy looked around at the half-empty tables, her eyes avoiding Paul's. "Do you know when they expect the crime scene tape to come down from the Crandall house?"

He put his fork down. "Why?"

"If I could get in there, I could take my

time and look with fresh eyes. As my attorney, don't they let you have access?" Her voice picked up. "I'm a forensics tech. I know what to look for. The last time I was there I was with the sheriff and I couldn't focus. But —"

"Remy, it's not a good idea. Didn't you get fired for tampering with case evidence?"

It was Paul's turn to avoid her eyes now boring into his. "How did you —"

"I'm sorry, but I always background check my clients."

"It was a lie," she said, her voice cold. "I couldn't prove it, but someone else altered those records."

Evidence tampering.

Remy's thoughts went to information she wanted from Andy.

Paul cleared his throat and spoke in a low voice, "I wasn't going to mention this, you were already upset, but Gaines and Tuft already know about your . . . your job history. If you go to that house, they wouldn't trust anything you found."

Remy stared at him. His bluntness spoke the painful truth. All she could do was nod in agreement. It was too late anyway.

"But don't give up," he rushed. "I'm the one that's supposed to fight your fight. What are you looking for anyhow?"

Her eyes started to blur. "That's just it, I don't know."

They ate the remainder of the meal in silence.

Paul waited until they finished eating to speak, "I've made a little progress in peeling away the onion that is Melanie Chase."

"Go ahead," she said. "Tell me."

He ordered wine for her and a spritzer for him.

"First of all, Melanie didn't have a brother. Nor was her family out of state, nor were both her parents dead, and while she had exceptional computer skills used in her position with the county, she did not work part-time for a casino in accounting." He acknowledged Remy's expression of amazement. "She was an IT specialist at the casino, or so said her obituary."

"I guess I didn't know her at all," Remy murmured. "She lied to me. All this time I thought she was my friend."

CHAPTER EIGHTTEEN

This time Grayden didn't question Remy's plans for the show's logistics. She went over in detail, the room layout, refreshments, lighting, and of course, the placement of the auction items. She'd arranged to be there after closing overseeing the staging crew as they came in with rental chairs, tables, and moving the furnishings from the upstairs storage area to the first floor.

"Grayden, I'll take care of all the last-minute items," she said. "You've gone over everything with me at least three times. I won't leave until it's all done the way you want it, and I'll meet you here at seven in the morning to set up for the final preview."

He looked skeptical over the notebook he held. "If I didn't have this high-profile client valuation in Pacific Grove, I'd never leave you alone to setup for a show."

"It's going to be fine. Camden trained me on jewelry auctions." She glanced at her phone. "I'd like to get a bite to eat before you leave, though. Any problem with me slipping out for about an hour? I need to share a sandwich with my attorney. I told the crew to be here at six, I'll be back before five-thirty."

"Yes, yes, go ahead now. I'm not leaving until you return." He wiped his glistening forehead with a monogrammed handkerchief. "There's too much going on. I hope I survive this."

Remy wondered how much of the *"this"* was her doing.

Paul was waiting for her with sandwiches when she arrived.

He tapped his laptop and a screen diagram appeared. "This is your case file. I spoke with Melanie's mother, and everything checks out. As a child of a single mother, she went to the local community college, got average grades, transferred to state college, got her degree in criminology, and pretty much stayed out of trouble." He clicked on another screen. "She got an administrative job with the county, worked there for a year then went to work for your former employer as a lab technician. And that's where her life started to go downhill. She got into a financial bind. And, like I told you, she did have

191

a part-time job at a casino."

He looked sympathetic and got up to sit in the chair next to her. "I'm pretty sure you're not going to have to hold your breath, waiting to be arrested for Chase's murder." He frowned. "But her murder builds on a bigger problem that may make things even worse."

"What do you mean, worse?"

"I admit, the connection is unfortunate," he said. "But you're a common denominator between the Chase and Kieffer murders. If you discover anything as we go along, I need to know as soon as possible."

Remy had already come to that conclusion.

"That reminds me," she said. "Here's Kieffer's business card. You said you'd give it to Tuft."

"Right." He put the card in the pocket of the folder. "I'll get it to Warren and Tuft later today." He leaned forward. "I hope you realize that both victims were using you. They knew your troubled background, at least Melanie did. You have to assume whoever killed Kieffer and Chase, knows about you. You could be next."

It was time to get back. Remy finished their meeting with a promise to be vigilant and to keep him informed. Pushing Paul's last comment to the back of her mind, she dashed out and drove to the showroom to say goodbye to an anxious looking Grayden.

"Good, you're back."

"Go," she insisted. "I've got this. We'll talk tomorrow."

He grabbed his coat. "Stay on top of these guys; we're paying them by the hour. I'll see you at seven tomorrow morning."

And he was gone.

She couldn't hear, but could imagine what he muttered under his breath as he headed for the door. She hadn't realized she'd been holding her breath until she let it out, as she saw his car pull out of the lot.

The specialty movers came on time, ready to get the job done. She had worked with them before in San Francisco, and for the next three hours she forced aside thoughts of murder and betrayal, and focused on proving her worth by setting up the show-room for her first LaneWilson auction.

Remy was glad to have the bustle of the workers going up and down stairs with furniture and taking her orders for placement for the show. It took her mind off of her visit with Paul.

Two murders and she was the common link.

■ ■ ■ ■

The Saturday sale was here.

It didn't matter that this wasn't her first sale, Remy's stomach still quaked with expectation and her mind was in a continuous check-off list loop. Even though the weather channel forecasted a thick fog bank later on in the evening, the day was clear, and the showroom was transformed.

Grayden was unable to cast his usual skeptical expression, and a slow grin of acknowledgment greeted Remy as he entered the main room.

"Remy, this is a wonderful job you've done," he said, fingering the pamphlets topping the draped tables along the walls.

"Thank you, Grayden," she said. "I have to admit I worked hard on this one."

She didn't want to tell him she'd returned to Able Printing with a new idea. It resulted in a rush print job she'd picked up that morning, after verifying Howard Able would be there. The new pamphlets highlighted selected individual pieces in addition to the catalog description. Customers would be able to see the expanded detail on items, in particular the higher priced ones. The catalog would be the teaser.

Scattered among the promotional material were small plates of crumb-less finger foods and custom napkins bearing the LaneWilson logo. Bouquets of flowers, just delivered, were positioned amongst the cases of jewelry. Deep purple sweet Williams and lacy baby's breath hovered over a case exhibiting sapphire and diamond rings. Vibrant red roses, their fragrance subtle and soothing, stood watch over the brilliant ruby necklaces, bracelets and pins. Tall white lisianthus sheltered a lustrous array of opals and pearls. Remy had taken the precaution of putting the flowers on an inconspicuous table apart from the showcases. This display was meant for the preview. For the actual sale this evening they would be removed to the rear room and brought out as the category came up for auction.

Grayden assessed the room and cleared his throat. "Your work shows. Now, let's go over again how LaneWilson conducts its sales."

She didn't mind his coaching as they walked around the room and went through his auctioneer calls. They had gone over his preferences twice before, but Camden had done the same. Repetition and rehearsals were meant to calm nerves and reduce error. The customer must see a seamless process — nothing to distract or discourage bidding.

And then it was time. An hour before the time advertised for the preview, a young woman knocked on the door. Remy glanced up at Grayden whose glasses were perched on his forehead as he reviewed the items list.

"I can tell her to come back," Remy said. "I guess she can't read the sign on the door."

Grayden squinted. "No, no, I know her. I'll get it." He took off his glasses and preceded to the front talking over his shoulder, "She's a regular."

Remy heard a polished voice.

"Good morning, Grayden. I've got to drive down to the peninsula, and I'll miss your preview, so I stopped by."

Tall and slim, the woman with the voice entered with a rush of Jo Malone fragrance. Dressed in jean leggings, an untucked crisp white shirt and navy blazer, their first customer appeared casual and expensive at the same time.

"Linda, Evelyn is on maternity leave. I want you to meet our new assistant appraiser, Remy Bishop." Grayden led her to the rear of the store. He motioned with his head. "Remy, this is Linda Fadden. She's a procurement manager with Glacier Corporation in Silicon Valley.

"Linda is one of our favorite customers," Grayden added jovially.

Linda laughed. "He means I buy a lot, and he's right." She pushed her sunglasses onto the top of her auburn hair. "I like LaneWilson because it has the more unique, and not necessarily the most expensive items." She turned to face Grayden. "I love your jewelry sale the best. I was hoping I could get a sneak preview."

"Well, I would say you won't be disappointed," Remy said, and waved her hand over the showroom. "Will you be coming back this evening to bid? Or, do you have a spotter?"

Linda winked at Grayden. "I'm using a spotter, this time it will be Nelson Horn." She said to Remy, "LaneWilson has a small but determined following, and I've discovered if my competition sees me bid on an item, they will feel the need to bid as well."

Grayden crossed his arms across his chest. "Linda buys gifts for her bosses to give to special customers, employees or their spouses." He pointed to a case. "Take a look at these sapphire pins. Last time we didn't have as wide a selection, but we were able to get a first look at items from the Parson's estate, and I remembered you."

He led Linda by the arm over to an oversized glass case.

It was a good crowd. But more than that, the energy in the room was positive and festive. Remy could tell Grayden was delighted with the turnout. Remy was pleased her cocktail party theme had contributed to the steady murmur of customers who took notes and jotted down item numbers from the interest tags. Grayden caught her eye and indicated his approval with a congratulatory nod.

Remy met Nelson Horn at the start of the evening. He was a heavy-set man with dark eyes and hair, appearing to be in his mid-forties. He walked around the room gazing at all the cases but settled at the case holding the sapphire collection. Then, as if to make sure no one saw his preoccupation with its contents, he ambled over to the ruby case across the room. Remy walked up to him and introduced herself.

"Is this your first time visiting LaneWilson?" she asked.

"No," he said. "I've been here quite a few times. I represent clients who cannot attend, but require, uh, representation."

"Sounds like a great job."

He laughed. "It is. I'm a retired cop with

a love of art and antiques. Neither of which were given much time when I worked at San Jose PD."

"Well, I'm sure in your business, you learned you can't judge a book by its cover."

He smiled, but it was quick and superficial. "I think your boss is trying to get your attention."

Remy turned to see Grayden retrieve the gavel, indicating he was ready to start. She flicked the lights, clients settled in their seats, and talking subsided.

The sale was underway.

Remy looked over the heads of fifty or sixty people and took a breath of relief. Grayden came up to her several times during the event grinning like a Cheshire cat, and all but rubbing his hands in glee. LaneWilson had contracted with an auctioneer from Marin County to conduct the actual sale. And it was clear he knew what he was doing. His auction chant was excellent and, thanks to the ringer he brought with him, any and all raised hands were recognized.

Earlier in the week, she'd asked Grayden how he conducted his sales.

"We hire experts." He was examining a porcelain vase on his desk. "We handle the preview period and the registration. But for the actual auction, we contract out, and ask he bring an assistant to spot bidders. Lester Moore knows what he is doing."

Lester had just announced a pair of sapphire necklaces and matching earrings were being sold as a lot and were the last items of the evening.

"On the final necklaces, three times the money," he called out.

There was a surprised hush in the crowd, and Remy looked over at Grayden who had given the nod. Whoever won the bid would get all three necklaces multiplied by the bid price. It was a great commercial ploy as all three necklaces were similar, each setting more elaborate than the other, but the stones were not flawless. Still, everyone loves a sale. The necklaces went for double the price had they been sold separately. A win-win.

Grayden couldn't stop smiling.

CHAPTER NINETEEN

Remy woke rested and content. Saturday's sale had been a financial and promotional success. Grayden had given her this Monday off. He would oversee the workers coming in to clean and restore order.

Her thoughts went to Melanie, and her mood slipped. She was torn between grief and apprehension. She still couldn't believe someone she knew had been murdered, no matter the secrets and the unnecessary lies.

She padded to the kitchen, dug in her purse to read the clipping and then retrieved the copy of Kieffer's business card. He had scribbled his name across the top of the used card, with the Crandall address after blocking out a location in Palo Alto. She opened her laptop and tapped it in. According to Google, the address belonged to a wine bar, the Best of Wine Bar. She checked Yelp and took notice the bar had received four out of five stars. She would have to pay it a visit, but for now she put it aside.

Today she wanted to pick up the trail on the Dunlap clock. Remy had to admit Evelyn had lived up to her reputation. She'd brought home a copy of the store's contact list. It was organized, detailed and provided an impressive amount of customer background information. Grayden's obvious reluctance to provide the name of the clock's seller was bothersome, but not insurmountable.

There were two Huntingtons on the store's contact list, but only one woman. Her name was: Mrs. Lucy A. Huntington of Oakland, California. Remy recognized Mrs. Huntington's address as being in the Lake Merritt neighborhood. If she were going to make contact without arousing suspicion, she would need to be cautious, and she would need Grayden to be out of the office. She would have to arrange the meeting so the store would be closed a minimal time.

As it was, Mrs. Huntington provided the way. She seemed agreeable enough and open to a meeting if held on a weekend.

"I have a new grandchild," Lucy Huntington explained. "I watch her during the week while my son and daughter-in-law work. It's our time together."

"This Saturday would be perfect," Remy

rushed. "I can make myself available any time that works for you."

Huntington hesitated, and then said, "Well, I do my errands in the morning, but I can see you in the afternoon, say three o'clock. What is this all about, again?"

"The clock you brought to LaneWilson for sale two months ago," Remy said. "I understand you withdrew it. I just started work for LaneWilson. We'll be holding another furnishing sale soon, and I know you don't want to sell your clock, but I'm doing a little research on the maker, Louis Fernier, and seeing your clock would fill out the collection. I can't locate another like it."

Her story sounded weak to her own ears, but Remy had tried to cover all possible objections to her request.

"But I don't have the clock anymore, to be honest I never —"

"What happened to the clock?"

"Well, I was approached by another auction house because —"

"You sold it to another house?" Remy said. "I'm sorry, I keep interrupting you. Please tell me what happened."

Lucy Huntington paused and then spoke. "It's kind of curious. I didn't sell the clock to another auction house; I was supposed to *buy* the clock from an auction house."

"I'm confused," Remy said. "LaneWilson's papers indicate you were going to sell a Fernier clock at our March sale, but you later pulled it."

"This is the first I've heard of the LaneWilson's sale," Huntington said. "A representative from an auction house in the city knows I love antique clocks, and she approached me about a recent find she had, but then after I made arrangements to see it, she called to say it had been pulled."

"Who was the woman, and which auction house?"

"It's a cute name, Seems Like Olde Times."

Still relishing her day off, Remy smiled her satisfaction. If she hadn't found Lucy Huntington, she would have been forced to contact Evelyn, and outcome would not have turned out as well. She spread out Audra's photos. She stared at the one showing a Tiffany lamp.

She was energized. The week before, she had checked for the object d'art items going up for LaneWilson's next sale, again matching seller agreements with a log sheet. She was still missing three items: a vase, a pair of silver candlestick holders and a porcelain figure. There was one owner, a V. Camden. She picked up her purse. She needed to inspect the lamp. She could combine two inquiries into one visit.

She'd seen a Tiffany lamp in Victor Camden's studio.

On Tuesday, Remy had a list of tasks she wanted to accomplish.

After college, she had worked part-time for over a year in Victor Camden's San Francisco showroom and prior to completing her training as a forensic tech. He had a reputation for working with new appraisers who were trying to earn their in-service hours. His program was respected, and an apprentice learned all aspects of the business.

Camden's was full of artifacts. Furniture was not his forte. She was sure she'd seen the Tiffany lamp displayed in a locked glass étagère in his main showroom when she returned for a visit before her hire with LaneWilson. Tiffany lamps were not common. Even though she hadn't taken the time to remark, its beauty drew one's eyes immediately to it, and the sun's rays through the transom window had caught the brilliant colors of the floral design on its shade.

Victor seemed glad to see her.

"Remy," he said, giving her a brief hug. "How are things going with your new employer?"

"Things are going very well. I was preparing for our next sale, and I saw your name on some of the items," Remy said. "Why are you selling through us?"

His voice was warm. "*I'm* not selling, I'm representing the seller," he said. "Tell me, how are *you* doing? I read about the Mendleson murders in the *Chronicle*."

Remy groaned. "It didn't mention me by name, did it?"

"No, it was a small article on the bottom of the second page," he said. "This Crandall House had a lot of beautiful items?"

"Yes, I made a list of as many as I could. But, don't go thinking like Grayden, it looks like everything was stolen."

There was a silence.

"Well, the article didn't say or mention your name," Camden responded. "Are you okay?"

"Yes, I'm fine. I thought I would drop over for a visit." She didn't want to get into a discussion about her state of mind. "As I said, I'm getting ready for our summer show, and we don't have your client's pieces."

"I apologize," he said. "It slipped my

mind. I know you had your jewelry sale last Saturday, and we have our fine arts show coming up, and I'm exhausted. You see, I lost my assistant appraiser to a competitor, maybe you know her?" He chuckled. "Nevertheless, a courier just came and picked everything up. You should have the pieces by late this afternoon."

She laughed. "Okay, you're forgiven. We had posted a clock for sale a couple of months ago, and it was a no show. I wanted to make sure this wasn't another instance."

"Hmm, clocks, we already have quite a collection on consignment. The Dunlap clock wasn't worth the suggested price. We had to turn it down. So, I can't help you," he said.

Remy stiffened. "How did you know I was referring to the Dunlap clock?"

He paused before answering. "You said Dunlap."

"No, I didn't," she insisted. "*Who* tried to have you sell it?"

"Look, you know how this business is. I can't remember every transaction, especially one we didn't pursue." He cleared his throat. "I think it was a woman, but I can't be sure."

There was something he wasn't saying. He always cleared his throat when he was nervous.

But why?

"You can expect those items in a couple of hours. I hope to get top dollar."

"We would like nothing better," Remy said.

Over the next minutes, they bantered back and forth in the usual industry pleasantries and light gossip. Remy glanced at Camden's bright flyers displaying an upcoming sale. But a frown settled on her face when she closed the door behind her.

That afternoon, Remy pored over her binders. She hoped she could settle two issues with one inquiry: the conversation with Victor Camden had sent off "pay attention" bells in her head. In the auction world, it was common that every showroom has a specialty, a focus on one or two industry items that set it apart. Refectory tables were a niche specialty, not many dealers could handle the space requirements — not just for storage, but access to customers that had the space to place them. Kieffer's use of the Crandall house had made that clear.

On the other hand, clocks didn't have that concern. They were in most households in one fashion or another. Collectors and sellers were abundant.

She first contacted Seems Like Olde Times, but from the recording on their phone the showroom was closed for three days for a small renovation. Messages would be returned, but Remy didn't want to leave one. While she researched other clock dealers, she also made a much smaller list of dealer showrooms of antique and vintage tables. She spent the rest of the afternoon calling around to dealers asking about the Fernier clock, but without success.

One dealer had confirmed her doubts. "It's a fine clock, but pretty common, even in perfect condition. It's more likely one of the other family members latched on to it as a memento."

"Yes, well, there are no other family members, but thank you for checking."

She was back to square zero and Victor Camden. *How did he know about the Dunlap clock?*

She called Audra.

"I want to thank you for all you're doing," the older woman said. "I . . . I think there may be other items gone as well, but I didn't want you to think . . . that I was just a crazy old lady who couldn't let go. Maybe Martin did sell his collection."

Remy felt a pull at her conscience because that had been her thinking as well. But maybe Audra was still dealing with grief.

"Audra, I'm not so sure about that," she said. "When you came by the store the other morning, you said you had the name of one of Martin's friends. I should have gotten right back to you, but things have been a little crazy around here."

"I didn't think anything of it. I knew you were busy. Let me get my purse," she said, placing her phone down. "Yes, here's his name, Ian Winter." She rattled off the number. "I wouldn't have his contact information except Martin said . . . he told me; Ian would always know how to get in touch with him."

Remy could hear the woman's voice waver then strengthen.

"Audra, it would help me if you could locate Martin's insurer and find out if he filed a claim, and if he did, get the particulars."

Having something to do, to contribute, would give the older woman focus.

"I don't know why I keep stalling. I . . . I guess it's because what they tell me will . . . will be like closing a chapter with Martin." Her voice shook, then came back strong, "No matter, it's what needs to get done. I'll get on it as soon as we get off the phone."

"Good, I'll check with you tomorrow. I'll be in the showroom."

CHAPTER TWENTY

Remy hadn't slept well, and Ian Winter didn't return her call. It was a foggy morning and the biting cold caused her to hurry to the showroom. Shivering, she put her key in the lock at the same time her purse fell onto the ground. She bent down and felt a push of air across her cheek. She heard a snapping thud. Still in a crouch, she turned to look over her shoulder. There was a figure coming toward her through the haze. She stood and took a couple of steps in that direction.

"Audra, what are you doing here?"

The woman must have dressed in a hurry. Her knit cap was askew, and she wore a man's raincoat that was at least two sizes too large.

"I couldn't sleep. I had to see you as soon as possible. I didn't want to talk on the phone," she said in a rush. "I think I found out something. I spoke with the insurer.

They had not received a claim under Martin's homeowner's policy." Audra gripped Remy's arm. "So, someone must have stolen those pieces in the photos."

"Maybe."

Remy looked around, and then back at Audra. "Come on, let's get inside. I'll fix some tea, and if you want coffee there's a pot you can put on."

Remy put an arm around the woman's shoulders, which were shaking from the cold, and walked her back toward the door. She turned the key and froze.

Audra looked up to see what had caught her attention.

"Remy, what's the matter?"

"Nothing." She shook her head. "Hurry, it's chilly out here."

She half-pushed, half-ushered Audra into the hallway and shut the door behind them, but not before she let her fingers trace the small hole where a bullet had lodged in the door frame.

CHAPTER TWENTY-ONE

Rattled, Remy fumbled as she set up the boiling water for tea. She tried to calm her nerves from thinking about the shooter, and almost getting shot. She didn't want to alarm Audra, but without speaking she dashed out the back door and returned just as quickly, locking it behind her.

"You seem distracted. I should have called first," Audra offered. She pulled her purse straps across her chest. "I wanted to tell you about Martin's insurance." She paused. "No tea for me, I can tell now is not a good time."

"No, it isn't," Remy said, noticing her hand was shaking. She sat on it. "Audra, did you — did you hear anything strange before you met me at the rear door just now?"

Dunlap walked back toward Remy, looking puzzled and curious. "Like what?"

Remy was cautious, she didn't want to

lead the woman's response. "Something that caught your attention maybe?"

Dunlap wrinkled her brow. "No, no I don't remember anything in particular," she said. "But then my hearing isn't what it used to be, and I guess I'm too vain to get a hearing aid. You okay?"

"Yes, I'm fine." Remy exhaled a long breath. "I need to take care of something as soon as possible. How about I call you this afternoon? Things should have calmed down by then."

"Yes," Audra responded. "There's an errand I need to run, anyway."

Waving her hand goodbye over her head, she headed back down the hallway.

"No," Remy almost shouted, and then in a calmer tone. "Go out the front door. It's . . . it's easier." She got up and walked to the entry.

Audra nodded, and waited for her to unlock the door. "We'll talk later. Go have a cup of tea," she said, patting her on the shoulder and waved goodbye.

Remy returned the wave, closed the door still shaking, and called the sheriff.

"Ned's not here, Remy," Roberta said in a lackluster tone that bespoke her boredom. "They're all at training down in Sunnyvale, and won't be back until tomorrow." Her voice took on a little energy. "Is everything all right? Bill's on duty. You want to talk to him?"

Remy leaned against the back of her chair. Bill Hoagg was an adequate deputy, but if it wasn't in his manual, he couldn't deal. However, she had little choice.

"Yes, I'm going to need to speak to Deputy Hoagg."

"He's not here. He went for a late breakfast."

"Roberta, someone just took a shot at me." Remy heard her voice rise. "I don't have time to wait for Bill to finish his breakfast." She took a deep breath. "Can you get in touch with him and tell him to come to the LaneWilson showroom as soon as possible?"

Roberta was contrite. "Of course, I'll get him right over there," she said. "Are you all right?"

She straightened in her chair. "Yes, I'm fine. I think they've gone."

Hoagg arrived tucking his shirt in his pants over his stomach. He pulled a small notebook out of his shirt pocket.

"Ms. Bishop, you want to explain to me what went on here?"

Remy went over in detail the events of the morning. "I didn't see anyone but Audra

216

Dunlap. She wanted to talk to me."

He looked up. "Who's Audra Dunlap? You think she could've done it?"

"Audra? No, not at all." Remy explained Audra's presence in Mendleson. "She came from another direction than the shot."

Hoagg peered at her. "Now, how do you know what direction the shot came from?"

"Because when you look at the hole and the angle the bullet must have taken, it's clear the shooter was almost directly behind me," she said, trying to keep annoyance out of her voice. "Audra approached me from the street side almost at the same time. It was not her. I was trained as a forensic specialist."

"Hmm, forensic specialist," he repeated. "Well, let's go get this bullet."

They both hurried out the rear door.

It was gone.

"No, no," Remy said, putting her hand to her forehead. "Not again."

The neat little hole in the door jamb was not only empty, but it was clear the shooter had used a knife to dislodge the bullet making the hole much larger and therefore much more difficult to identify the bullet type. He, or she, had had enough time while she was getting rid of Audra and waiting for Hoagg.

217

Hoagg shook his head. "Well, without that bullet, it's hard to say this wasn't done with carpenter tools. You can't even tell when this was done. It could have been anytime."

"For once I can prove my word." She patted her jacket pocket. "I went right back out and took a picture with my phone."

"Let's take a look."

Both heads bent over her phone as she scrolled to her photos. She tapped it to expand.

He squinted. "Too bad we can't get the ballistics off that photo. We'd know something about the gun."

"No, we can't, but it does say someone wants me silenced, or at the very least scared off." Remy looked over the parking lot. "Deputy Hoagg, why would someone carve out a nickel-sized hole in a door jamb? Would it be because they didn't want a bullet to be identified?"

"Maybe." He shrugged. "You tell me. The chief said the sheriff is looking at you for those murders." He opened the door for them to return to the showroom. "It's too bad we don't have that bullet."

The knot in her stomach grew.

Remy didn't contact Grayden about the shooting until after Hoagg left. She could

218

hear the expletives under the store owner's breath.

"Are you all right?" he asked. "Did they get inside?"

She was reassured to hear him ask about her health first before checking on the showroom.

"Yes, I'm fine, and no, they didn't get in. But you may want to get the rear door patched," she said, surprised at her own light tone. "I've got to leave and give a statement to Chief Warren. I'll be back to the showroom as soon as I can."

"I'm putting in cameras," he said. "I never would have thought Mendleson could harbor such desperate people." Grayden cleared his throat. "Take the time you need. Put the 'be back' sign out."

Remy didn't want to disavow him of his erroneous thinking. Why would a burglar shoot if they were trying to get inside? The shot was clearly meant for her. Once Grayden realized that, there's a good chance he would reevaluate his judgment in keeping her on as an employee. She was too much trouble.

She called Paul next.

"I told you your life would be in danger."

"That you did," she said. "But I'm planning on living that life while I have it. I'm

219

on my way to give a formal statement to the sheriff."

"I'll meet you there."

Remy and Paul sat in silence next to one another in the sheriff's lobby. Paul glanced at the time on his phone.

"You keep looking for the time. Do you have someplace you have to be?" she asked, noting they'd been there a bare five minutes. "I can do this by myself."

He looked up to the ceiling. "No, I need to hear how they respond to your claim of innocence. If, they believe you at all."

"Innocent, of what? Why wouldn't they believe me? I have a picture of a bullet hole with a bullet in it," she said. "If I didn't have a picture, I'd be discredited. But I've got proof." She patted her purse.

"Don't be too confident," Paul said. "You can't get ballistics off a picture." He ran his hand over his head. "Ever notice you attract trouble like a magnet?"

She frowned. "No, it's just been since —"

Ned Warren came toward them with an outstretched hand for Paul. "Remy, I came back as soon as Deputy Hoagg contacted me. What's this about a shooter?"

"Chief, someone took a shot at me," she said. "They were waiting and, but for the cheap lock that LaneWilson has on its parking lot door, I'd be history. I came in to give my statement." She looked over her shoulder at Paul. "And, I want you to have me tested for GSR."

"Gunshot discharge residue — that's not a bad idea." Warren pointed to an open door off the lobby. "You go right in there, and I'll have Deputy Hoagg take some swabs. When you finish with Hoagg, I'll take your statement myself. Give me a minute. I'm assuming you're going to join her, Mr. Scott?"

"Is that a problem?" Paul said.

Warren shrugged with a curious look. "Sir, you have every right to sit in with your client. Go on in."

Remy looked stern. She was familiar with the swab procedure and assisted as much as she could to expedite the process. She looked down at the treated sheet that had been rubbed against her clothing. With a triumphant expression, she looked at Hoagg.

"No pink specks," she said. "No evidence of nitrate results. I didn't fake that shot."

Hoagg squinted at the results. "I'd say you were right about that."

Paul gestured a thumbs-up from the corner of the desk.

■ ■ ■ ■

The interview room was small and set up with a tape machine on one end of a long table, and Roberta on the other end poised to take dictation. The chief asked a few questions and minutes later, Remy concluded her story and leaned back in her chair.

"We'll have that ready for you to sign tomorrow. Meantime, let's see that picture, Remy." Ned Warren reached for her phone when she pushed it over. "Can you email this to me? I'm going to need you to sign an affidavit regarding its circumstances."

Remy nodded and sent the email.

Paul edged up in his chair. "Is there a problem with proving the bullet came from a hole in the door? I mean proving the timing happened the way Remy said it did."

Warren raised his eyebrows. "Good point." He looked down at the photo. "It would have been better if Deputy Hoagg had seen it lodged in the hole. However —"

"Come on, Chief," Remy protested, giving a 'whose side are you on' look to Paul. "The picture carries some weight. Besides, Audra Dunlap was with me."

"Did the Dunlap woman see the bullet in

the hole?" Warren asked.

"Well, no," Remy said. "I wanted to get us inside. I asked her if she had heard anything, but she hadn't. And then once we were in, I went right back out and took the picture. I didn't want to alarm her, but I doubt she would have noticed it and not said anything."

Paul stood. "I think we should leave," he said. "Chief Warren, I don't want you interviewing my client without my presence. I hope I can count on you?"

"Wait," Remy said, raising her hand in objection. "What are you talking about, Paul? I'm the victim. I didn't shoot a gun." She turned back to the chief. "He's right, though, I've got to get back to the showroom. Do you need me for anything else?"

The chief looked her in the eyes. "I think it would be a good idea if you stayed with your parents for a while, at least until we catch the shooter."

Remy persisted. "Then you do believe me."

"Yes, I do," he said with a grim face. "But, Remy, it's clear to me you are in the center of something that led to the killing of two people and an attempt on your own life. I don't have the staff resources to put you under protection. I'm going to have to call

223

in the sheriff's people."

"Have they discovered anything on the Kieffer and Chase murders?" Paul asked.

Warren shook his head. "Nothing they've shared with me." He turned back to Remy and then pointed out the window. "Somebody out there thinks you know something, or thinks you're getting close to knowing something."

Remy was quiet for a moment, then she took a deep breath.

"Well, Chief, I don't know what that something is." She hestitated then said, "I know you think I'm nuts for not being afraid, but I assure you, I *am* afraid. However, my reputation has already been turned upside down once. I can't go through that again. I'm not going to live a half-life with a cloud over my days, no matter how long I have."

"Somehow I knew you were going to say that," Warren said, resigned.

Paul gathered his briefcase and coat. "Okay, then that's settled," he said. "Remy, I've got to get to another appointment. We need to go. Chief, keep me informed if the sheriff comes up with anything on the murders."

Warren ignored him and went to stand next to Remy. "If anything looks amiss, you contact us right away," he said. "I'll call the sheriff's office and let Gaines know what's going on. He'll get a copy of your statement." He paused. "You be careful."

CHAPTER TWENTY-TWO

Remy had decided not to say anything to her family about the shooting. Their alarm would make her more apprehensive. And while she found herself looking over her shoulder whenever she used the back door to LaneWilson, she wasn't willing to give in to fear. She must be getting close — but to what?

Her phone vibrated.

"There was nothing unusual in the post evidence handling in those cases you wanted me to check out, nothing at all," Andy said.

Remy put her head in her hands. For once, she had the showroom to herself for the day. Grayden was at a trade show in San Francisco, and for once it was a quiet Wednesday.

"Remy, you still there?"

"Yes, I'm here. I was counting on something to show up," she said. "I don't know what, but I'd hoped . . ."

He snorted. "So, what do you care? You told me you weren't a suspect anymore. Let the sheriff figure it out. You're done."

"Well, yes, I may be cleared as a suspect, but someone took a shot at me yesterday."

"What!"

"Hey, calm down. Obviously, they missed, since I'm talking to you."

Remy recounted the highlights of her recent encounter.

When she finished, she didn't rush Andy's silence on the other end.

He emitted a low whistle. "Okay, so what are you going to do now?"

"Go about my business. I've got a lot on my plate. I'm not going to go into hiding," she said. "Besides I think he, or she, just wanted to scare me off."

"And did they?"

"Well, let's say they caught my attention, except I was hoping the special evidence treatment in those cases would give the sheriff's officers some alternatives . . . some leads."

"Something you could see, but they couldn't?"

"Okay, I hear you. I was being a bit presumptuous, but it's my life on a rollercoaster."

"Hey, there's one thing I was able to follow through on," Andy said. "I went through your old files and found four cases similar to Lennox, and, more important, I found your case notes. You can stop speculating, but they don't say much."

Remy's heart went to a rapid beat. "That's great news. But now, I'm not sure what they would mean to anyone other than me."

"That's true enough," he said. "But I can take photos of the files and get a package ready for you. I don't want to send it in an email."

She understood what he wasn't saying. He could be exposed as her contact for retrieving confidential case information. Andy was taking care of his parents; he couldn't afford to lose his job.

"Don't worry. I'll meet you when you're ready," she said. "What you've done is more than enough."

He promised to call before the end of the week to arrange for the transfer.

Remy clicked off the phone. Maybe her old cases could show precedent. And then she put the thought out of her head. She was grasping at straws.

She turned back to work.

Her to-do list included after sale follow-up of thank you notes to clients who had made a purchase or showed future interest. She was so engrossed in writing, she didn't hear the footsteps, but she did hear a slight cough. She almost jumped out of her skin.

"I'm sorry. I thought you heard me come through the rear door."

Remy looked up at Joan. "It's all right, Ms. Durbin. I guess I was deep in concentration." She would insist Grayden install a rear bell over the door along with the cameras.

Joan was dressed in a tailored navy pants suit with an open collar, pale yellow blouse. Her hair was brushed back, and her large sunglasses added to her aura of drama without looking out of place in a town that was almost always under a cloud of fog. She oozed competence and professionalism.

"Please, I told you to call me Joan. Where's Grayden?"

Remy had gathered her composure. "He's at a San Francisco trade show today. I don't expect him in until tomorrow. Do you want to leave him a message?"

Joan turned down her mouth. "I thought he knew I was coming by. Did he leave an envelope for me?"

"No, not with me. And his office is locked, I can't check the top of his desk."

"What? He doesn't trust you with a key?"

she teased. "Don't worry, I have one."

She strode down the hall. Remy hesitated then followed. She stood by the door as Joan went through the few papers on top of the desk. There was no envelope.

"Do you want to call his cellphone?" Remy offered. "He's at a show, but —"

"No, no." Lane raised her hand in protest. "This is very much like him, the passive aggressive prick."

Remy didn't respond and returned to her desk. After a few minutes, Joan still hadn't emerged from Grayden's office and Remy wondered what she was doing. But as that thought came, she heard the lock click on the office door. Lane exited with her cellphone in hand.

"Remy, I'm going to make a couple of calls from the back office," she spoke. "Can you get me a cup of coffee?"

"No," Remy said. "I can't. I drink tea, and making coffee was not on my resume."

Joan Durbin looked up and grinned. "Good for you. I deserve that. Evelyn gave me a hard time, too."

Her phone buzzed.

She glanced at her phone. "Look, I'm going to get a Starbucks. I sent a text to Grayden. If for some reason he calls the showroom, keep him on the line." Lane was already heading out the front door.

"Not a problem," Remy said, wondering how the meticulous Grayden could have forgotten about a meeting with one of his partners.

She was spared any further moral dilemma by the phone ringing.

"Ms. Bishop," a familiar voice said. "Detective Tuft. We're hoping you could come to the Mendleson Police Department as soon as possible. Ned Warren sent us your statement and we also have new information we'd like to discuss with you."

"Detective, I'm at work," Remy responded. "I won't be able to come by until this evening."

"We'll accommodate your schedule in this instance and see you at five-thirty."

"Can you tell me what the new information is about?"

He paused, and then spoke, "Melanie Chase had an abortion within days of her murder. There's a possibility whoever killed her might have had feelings about it. Since you knew both Chase and Kieffer, we would like to run a couple of theories past you."

She raised her eyebrows. She was mildly surprised but not shocked. Melanie was a big girl and far from naïve. It was too bad her friend hadn't felt she could share the confidence.

"Yes, of course, I'll be there."

Remy made a couple of calls to clients thanking them for attending the sale. She took the opportunity to inform them the next sale would highlight Asian porcelain. Joan returned while she was making calls and gestured, she was going to use Grayden's phone.

Minutes later, the door to Grayden's office opened.

"Remy, I had to pull Grayden out of his trade show. He's on his way back. He'd forgotten about our meeting." Joan sniffed. "But he also said we had a burglar and you almost caught him in the act."

Remy weighed the possibility of correcting the burglar misconception and decided she didn't have the energy. "The police are looking into it. Nothing was taken from the showroom."

Joan looked around and then back at her. "Still, it must have been a little scary. Did you see him?"

"No, it was foggy that morning," she said and then, wanting to change the subject, "By the way, we did well at the Saturday sale. I just finished the report. Would you like to see the numbers?"

"Yes, but I noticed the change in subject."

Joan accepted the spreadsheets Remy held out. After a quick glance, she decided she'd look at the results over lunch.

"Maybe by that time, my brother will have returned."

"I'll let him know you'll be back." Remy said.

Joan must have received a call. She tapped her phone and spoke hushed tones as she headed down the sidewalk. Remy closed the door and went back to her desk.

When Grayden came rushing in, Joan was right behind him. He gave a cursory nod to Remy as his sister was already speaking with urgency. They remained behind the closed door until Remy knocked and put her head into the room to say she was leaving for the day.

Without looking up from his computer screen, Grayden responded, "We'll talk tomorrow."

This time the sheriff's lobby was almost empty. Still, Remy was glad she'd waited until after work to meet, she'd been waiting almost twenty minutes. The receptionist looked up from time to time to verify she was still there.

"Detective Tuft apologizes for taking so long," the receptionist called out from the

Plexiglas separation. "He's in an interview and it's taking much longer than he expected."

"No problem," said Remy.

It was good to know there were crimes in the county taking place that didn't involve her. She checked her phone for emails, but there were none. It struck her that Melanie had been her close friend, her main source of emails. She realized she didn't feel too sad about it, especially after finding out how much Melanie had lied to her.

"Ms. Bishop," Tuft said, walking toward her with his hand held out. "I hope you got my apology. It's been a very busy day."

"That doesn't sound good," Remy said, following him to a small windowless office.

He didn't respond, but went out into the hallway and motioned for what turned out to be a woman with an audio/video camera. He offered Remy a chair and took a seat across from her. The woman with the electronic equipment settled in.

"All right, I hope you don't mind giving your statement again," he said, opening a folder in front of him. "Let's get started. Because of the overlap in case details, the department is combining the Kieffer and Chase murders. I'll be investigating both. Do you want to tell me what happened yesterday morning?"

Remy went through the details of her encounter with a bullet. Tuft asked several questions, but she could tell he was distracted. "That's it," she finished.

"Can I see this picture you took?" he asked already holding out his hand.

She tapped her phone to photos and slid it across the table. This was a charade. She knew the chief had already sent him a copy. "I tried printing it out for a larger picture, but it loses details."

He squinted. "Well, it does look like a bullet. Can you email this to us? We have special equipment that will get the best resolution."

"Of course." She pulled out her phone and sent him a copy of the picture.

Tuft picked up his phone and gestured he'd gotten receipt. He put his elbows on the table and rubbed his forehead. "What do you think all this means, Ms. Bishop?" he asked. "Why would anyone want to kill you, or even scare you?"

"I assume it's because someone is afraid, I know something or maybe saw something."

He raised his eyebrows. "I see." He glanced at the clock on the wall and spoke to the woman whose fingers were poised over the steno machine's keys. "That's it for

235

today, Sharon. See you tomorrow."

The woman departed from the room, and Tuft turned to Remy.

"Do you know the father of Melanie Chase's child?" he asked.

"No, I knew she was seeing someone," Remy replied. "But romance was one side of her life she didn't share."

"Strange for close friends not to become involved with each other's relationships," Tuft said with a wrinkled brow.

Remy shrugged. "That's the way it was. What are you thinking?"

"Two avenues of thought cross my mind. One, and I like this the least, is there never was a bullet. You meant to distract us. Your picture didn't capture the entire door. Dunlap never saw it and couldn't verify it was ever there. A defense attorney would say it could be from anywhere."

Remy started to protest.

"Just a minute. It has been a long day," Tuft said, raising his hand. "My second avenue of thought says someone does want you, at the very least — silenced, either through fear or elimination."

She leaned back in her chair. "Which 'avenue' are you inclined to follow?"

"Until we get definitive evidence to the contrary, the second. Now, we have to figure

236

out if this has to do with the Kieffer, or the Chase murder, or perhaps both — and who wants you out of the way."

Remy sat on her balcony sipping from a glass of wine and watching the sunset. The meeting with Tuft had left her unsettled, and yet, in an odd way — comforted. He, at least, was considering she could be a target and not the perpetrator.

When she called Paul, he'd been furious she had gone to the sheriff without him.

"I said they would suspect you set the whole thing up," he chided.

She was glad he couldn't see her expression.

"Paul, he said he believed me and thought it was more like someone wanted me gone."

"Of course, he's going to say that," Paul said. "But his first reaction was to accuse you of a cover-up. He put it out there to see how you would respond."

"Maybe you're right. But I don't think so."

"Well, I think the stakes are rising. That bullet was a message, and it complicates things. The sheriff does not like complicated."

CHAPTER TWENTY-THREE

"I don't know why he told you to contact me, I'm not his friend." Ian Winter's voice sounded like gravel, as if he'd just woken.

It was a slow morning, the showroom was quiet, and Remy had taken the opportunity to try again to contact Martin's friend — or not.

"Mr. Winter, I'm calling for Martin's mother, who just moved here and is now trying to administer his estate," she said. "He gave her your name. You're aware he died?"

There was a rustle, silence and then, "Yeah, I knew. What do you need from me?"

"I'm interested in giving his mother peace of mind," she responded. "They hadn't been in touch for the last couple of years. Could you maybe meet with her, talk about Martin's last days and your friendship?"

"Look, like I said, I don't know why he offered my name. We hadn't talked in

238

months," he responded. "Not since he blew off my advice and decided to go to the dark side with his new friends."

Remy frowned.

"I'm sorry; I don't know what you're referring to. What happened to Martin?"

"Lady, I've got to get back to work. I don't want to talk to his mother, so I can't help you."

"Mr. Winter, if you would let me have an hour of your time, so I can tell his mother something. She's very upset. I didn't know Martin at all, so whatever you tell me will help give her closure."

She heard him take a deep breath.

"I'm on a plane to Dallas on Sunday out of Oakland," he said. "Meet me at the Harbor Club in Alameda at six. You'll have an hour. Come by yourself, I don't want to meet his mother."

"Thank you, I'll be there."

Now what was that about? Audra would be so disappointed not to meet with Winter, but she didn't want the woman to be hurt by Winter's unsympathetic attitude.

Remy had scheduled appointment showings to free up her day in order to visit Seems Like Olde Times. The renovation must have concluded, the phone message now announced new store hours. Located in San Francisco, according to the industry directory, it specialized in fine antique furniture. She was unfamiliar with the showroom, Camden's had never dealt with them while she was there, and there was a general reference to the showroom in the LaneWilson files. The unfamiliarity could work in her favor. She would pretend to represent a buyer. She closed LaneWilson a little early.

Seems Like Olde Times was a converted three-story Victorian squeezed in defiance between two mid-rise buildings on the fringe of San Francisco's Design District off Townsend Street. White with marine blue shutters and an overabundance of geraniums flowing from window boxes, if it weren't for a small placard on one of the porch pillars, a person could easily walk past.

The door opened with a faint tinkle of a bell, and she found herself in a narrow foyer flooded with a rainbow of light from the stained-glass dome above. She fell in love with the store as soon as she walked in. Remy wondered why she had never heard of the showroom before. She felt transported to another time and world and couldn't help staring at the dome's workmanship of forget-me-nots tumbling from pots around a flowing fountain hosting goldfinches and robins.

"Good afternoon, may I help you?"

Remy took a step back into reality. She looked into the eyes of a handsome older woman dressed in a moss green pantsuit and pale blue blouse, her face alight with curiosity.

Remy smiled. "Yes," she said. "My name is Remy Bishop. I'm an assistant appraiser with LaneWilson located just outside the East Bay. I'd like to speak with the owner about refectory tables."

"I'm the owner, Lara Nielsen. Perhaps we can talk in my office," she offered, pointing down the hallway. The two women shook hands. "How is Grayden?"

"He's doing well. We had a big jewelry sale last week and he's recuperating."

"It's been awhile since we've seen each other. I don't make it to the usual social functions like I used to." Nielsen's eyes narrowed. "What do you want to know about our refectory tables?"

Nielsen led her to a small room cluttered with catalogs and display cases. An Edwardian reproduction desk was positioned on the diagonal almost at the center of the room, and two overstuffed chintz-covered chairs faced front. She gestured for Remy to sit.

"I'm trying to track down a table I saw for . . . sale." The practiced words sounded true. "It was a late Regency period mahogany table seating twenty. I have a client who is very interested in purchasing. The owner passed away, and I'm hoping the item will show up as part of an estate sale. You have the reputation for being an expert collector in the field. I was hoping perhaps you have, or have seen such a table. And I'm also looking for a Fernier clock."

"Tables, yes, but clocks?" Nielsen shook her head. "Object d'art and fine artworks we leave to others. I find it better to specialize. Now that Regency table, as I'm sure you're aware, is rare and valuable. I know of nine in existence in the United States." Nielsen sat on the edge of her desk, arms crossed. "What is your client willing to pay?"

Remy had done some research and had chosen to describe a table she knew would be difficult to locate. She didn't want her true search to set off any alarms and the Crandall table to vanish into the market ether. She made a mental note it wasn't the Crandall table any more than it was the Kieffer table.

Remy couldn't stop a small look of surprise at Nielsen's matter of fact response. *Was it as easy as that?*

As if reading her thoughts, Lara Nielsen added, "Ms. Bishop, I think you misunderstand me." She moved to sit in the chair behind her desk. "I didn't mean to imply I had such a table here."

"Then what —"

"I meant it will cost your client quite a bit of money," Nielsen remarked. "Come, I'd like you to see our showroom." She came from around the desk and gestured toward the door.

The showroom in effect was a large, somewhat bland decorated converted ballroom. Narrow windows on one side of the room indicated they were at the rear of the house. At the switch of the light, intermittent small chandeliers lit a room full of a dozen refectory tables ranging from the Charles II to the Victorian era. Remy was mesmerized by the beauty of the gleaming wood. She walked toward an oak table that could seat at least twenty persons. Its heavy cabriole legs had elaborate carvings of stags and roses.

Her eyes caught another breath-taking table nearby.

"It's beautiful isn't it?" Nielsen said. "The table belonged to a foreign government official that fell on disgraced times. It had been in his family for generations."

Remy noted that from Lara Nielsen's vague description of a "foreign" official, the provenance would likely have a cloud.

"It's magnificent," she responded.

The mahogany table was large and gleaming with oil. The fine-turned Gillows' reeded legs ended in brass castors singular in design.

It was the table from the Crandall house.

Remy tried to keep a blank face. Her heart pounded in her ears as she ran her shaking fingers along its long edge. She bent to check for the mark.

"The mark is there." Nielsen came to stand next to her. "This is a very nice piece. Very rare. I've had it for some time, and I may be able to convince the owner to be flexible on the price. I'm debating on keeping it for myself."

Remy hid her amazement as the lies rolled off the woman's tongue without pause. Despite the cover story, there was no doubt this was the table she had seen in the Crandall dining room. She walked around it one more time.

"This is a beauty," Remy said, standing back to look at it. "We may have a client who might be interested. You said the price had some flexibility?" She lifted the manila price tag hanging from a thin cord of twine. It was high enough to allow for a lot of latitude in putting in a lower bid.

"Well, as I said, I'll have to consult the owner if the bid is less than the asking price." Her eager voice now took on an edge. "What did you have in mind?"

"Do you mind if I take pictures with my phone?" Remy said, reaching inside her purse. "I want my client to see how beautiful it is."

"Of course."

She snapped a number of photos.

"I'm wondering, is the owner local?"

Nielsen frowned, not smiling now. "Why?"

"It's just this looks like a table I saw in a home in the East Bay," Remy replied, as she stared into the eyes of Lara Nielsen. "The owner said it was a family heirloom."

Nielsen didn't flinch. "Well, you did say you were new to the business. I'm not surprised you haven't developed the skill yet to distinguish fine pieces. I think I mentioned this table has been here for quite a while." She pulled out her phone to glance at the time. "Are you finished? As a policy, I only take showings by appointment, but I extended you professional courtesy. I have a private showing coming up."

"Oh, I'm sorry," Remy said, moving toward the door. "I've taken up too much of your day." She took one last glance at the tables in the room. "I'll check in with my client. I'm sure they will want to make a bid."

Nielsen didn't respond but stood stoical holding open the door.

Sitting in her car, Remy wasn't sure what to do next. Detective Tuft needed to know she'd discovered the Kieffer table, but she wasn't sure if she should contact Paul first. She'd assured him she wouldn't be doing any more detective work. But her discovery was good news, and he may have a strategy approach for the police.

She punched in his number. He picked up immediately, and Remy took him through her findings.

There was a long pause before he spoke. "Where are you now?"

"In my car, down the street from Nielsen's showroom." She looked in her rear viewmirror. "Do you want to meet me at the sheriff's office?"

"What? No, you can't go to the sheriff." His voice rose. "Remy, if the sheriff hears you may have supposedly 'discovered' the Crandall table, they'll think you knew just where to look. You've got to admit, it didn't take you long to find it. And, I hate to say it, they may not want to take the word of . . . your word it was the Crandall table."

"You mean the table *from* the Crandall house," she pushed back. "You think my word is *that* tainted?"

"No, but —"

"Nielsen is a crook. She could be receiving stolen goods. Maybe she was working with Kieffer. I don't have a good feeling about her, and I could tell when I left, I wasn't going to be her favorite person either."

"Okay, okay, you're right." He paused. "But before you go around accusing people, let me do a little checking with the status of the Kieffer investigation, and see if there is any mention of this Lara Nielsen. I'll get back to you later today, but you hold off contacting Tuft until tomorrow. I want to go with you. I don't want them to arrest you."

She had her doubts, but agreed to wait.

CHAPTER TWENTY-FOUR

It was Melanie's mother who arranged the funeral, which was more of a memorial. Paul warned Remy it might be difficult staying out of sight because, due to the weather, the service was to be inside a small chapel at the rear of the mortuary. Other than two representatives from the funeral home who sat alongside the aunt, the room was empty. There were two rows of ten chairs split down the middle, so it appeared attendance was expected to be sparse.

Twenty minutes before start time, Remy was positioned in a small office off the entry. With the door half-opened, she could see the front parking lot as well as the anteroom leading to the chapel. A slamming car door sent her attention to the draped window. Detective Gaines, along with another plain clothes man, strode up the steps. Remy backed herself tight into a corner.

"Let's take seats near the door," Gaines said.

The fading response from his companion sounded in the affirmative.

Remy peeked from the doorway, and then ducked back into the room as the front door once more opened and two men and a woman entered. Dressed in a simple navy-blue dress, the middle-aged woman stood in front of a mirror positioned off to the side of the door. She moistened her lips and ran a finger over her eyebrows.

"Will you come on?" one of the men said. "Let's get this over with."

The woman shot him a scathing look but said nothing as she straightened her dress. The other man, on second glance, looked to be a teenager — he was silent, as well.

Remy caught them all on her camera phone.

More car doors.

A small group of men and women gathered at the entrance. Remy recognized fellow workers from the lab. They entered without speaking, and took their seats.

The door opened again, and she stood to the side. It was Paul. She wanted to get his attention, but thought it better to remain hidden. Paul went straight for the viewing room and took a seat behind the aunt.

As if signaled that everyone who was going to be there was there, the funeral director entered the room through a sliding door. Remy sat down in her safe room and strained to hear his words. She was torn. She felt a slight pang at the loss of her friend, but at the same time she realized their friendship had been built on unnecessary lies. She'd never known the real Melanie.

Outside movement caught her eye. She stood by the side of the window. A dark car had pulled up, but no one got out. A man was just sitting there staring at the building.

What was he doing?

The car door opened, he still didn't emerge, but continued to sit. Then he got out and stood next to the car. Remy gasped. Before she could process what she had just seen, the man got back into the car and drove away.

It was Jay Ross.

Remy had to rummage through her purse to find Ross' phone number. She punched it in and reached his voicemail.

"Jay, just called to see if you were interested in getting together for dinner. Give me a call or text."

He responded with a text:

"Can't talk right now. Dinner sounds great.

What about Saturday at six?"

She texted back: *"Fine. I'll meet you at Gracie's."*

CHAPTER TWENTY-FIVE

Gracie's was a popular restaurant in Fremont. Now known for its tapas creations, fifteen years ago it had started out as a traditional Mexican restaurant and struggled until new management arrived and "rebranded" the menu. Now, it received five-star reviews. Soft notes of the Spanish guitar played in the background. After a full day of errands, any other time Remy would be lulled into relaxed contemplation, but not tonight.

"I was surprised to get your call," Jay said after the server had taken their order. "Although I notice you chose tapas and not a full dining experience."

Remy laughed with him.

· "All right, I admit I didn't know if we were ready for a formal dinner commitment," she said.

He raised his eyebrows. "Hmmm, you have criteria for dinner companions?"

252

She chuckled. "I have criteria for everything. But no, not for dinner companionship. However, I do for friendship."

"I do, too."

They exchanged looks.

She turned her eyes away and took a sip of water from her glass. "Jay, I don't know any other way to ask this, so I'm just going to say it."

"Yeah, please do."

"Did you know Melanie Chase?"

His face took on the countenance of stone. "Why would you ask that?"

"I'll make it easy for you," Remy said. "I saw you at her memorial."

He just stared at her for a moment. His eyes nailed hers with calculation.

"I'm not going to deny I knew her. We were friends and I liked her. I didn't go in because in the parking lot I realized that I hate funerals," he said, twisting the stem of his wine glass.

"How did you two meet?"

He shrugged. "We knew some of the same people, and connected at a holiday party a couple of years ago."

Remy appeared to mull his words over. "I liked her too. So, by 'connected' do you mean you dated?"

"Yeah, we did for a short while, but at the

end we agreed to part as friends. That's why I went to the memorial."

It was her turn to peer into his eyes. "You know when you came to dinner at my parents, I later thought to myself why a successful real estate agent would find Mendleson's 'second home buyer' market substantial enough to spend any real time here." She leaned in. "Were you trying to reconnect with Melanie?"

"No, I knew she was in the area, we'd talked," he said smiling. "But real estate is like farming, you have to keep finding new fields to plant. Nothing is too small."

Remy didn't try to hide her look of skepticism.

"Do you have any idea who might have killed her?" she asked.

Stiffening, he seemed caught off guard.

"The newspapers seem to be implying it could be you," he said. "But, since I don't think you did, I thought it safe to accept your dinner invitation. And, no, before you ask, I have no idea why anyone would want her dead."

His last words were measured and carried a chill.

Remy looked around at the almost full tables. "Well, it's a good thing we just ordered tapas."

CHAPTER TWENTY-SIX

After her evening with Jay Ross, Remy's instincts told her that the pieces of a much larger intrigue were starting to take form.

But what intrigue?

The Harbor Club in Alameda had a stunning view of the San Francisco skyline. It seemed so close she should be able to touch it. Remy had arrived before the agreed time, but Ian Winter had arrived earlier. He'd texted her as she was getting out of her car. He was waiting in the top floor viewing bar.

He was tall, sandy-haired with a muscular body. His trimmed beard and moustache were a darker brunette. The total package made a handsome impression. He looked to be in his thirties, with the energy vibe of a man in a hurry. She walked up to him and introduced herself. He shook her hand, and then looked down at his watch.

"Okay, let's get this over with," he said. "All I can tell you about Martin Dunlap runs the span of about five years."

He stopped to wave at a passing server, and they both ordered iced tea.

He continued, "Like I said, Martin and I knew each other for about five years. He and I met at the Golden State Gym in Emeryville. I'm still a member, but he left a short while after we met. I found out he couldn't afford the fees. It didn't matter, he'd already turned to the dark side and was starting to make his connections."

Remy had a question, but Winter didn't seem like a man who tolerated interruptions.

"You said you never met Martin?" he asked.

Remy shook her head.

"Martin was a ladies' man. He could pull them in with one appealing wink. Young ones, old ones, married, single — he was the man." Winter frowned and looked out the window. "He wasn't a bad dude; he just never found his way. You know what I mean? He never figured out what he wanted to do in life." He turned back to look at Remy. "So, he relied on the one thing he knew he did well."

The server brought their drinks, and there was a momentary break in Winter's story.

"You were saying about what he did well,"

Remy prodded.

"Yeah, he knew how to use them. I mean he knew how to use women," Winter said. "Martin would say it wasn't using if they didn't mind." He looked at her, as if to read her reaction. "And to tell you the truth, he was right. I met one or two, and one admitted to me she knew what he was about, but she didn't care because he was the only man who ever treated her like a lady and made her feel young again." He took a swallow of his beverage. "Jeez."

Remy wanted to agree, but she didn't want him to stop talking.

"Anyway," he continued, "he was doing okay in his own way, until he met this older woman. I think he fell for her, at least, he said he did. And before you ask me, I never met her, and I don't know her name. He referred to her as Ginger."

"*Referred* to her as Ginger?"

"Yeah, I don't think it was her real name. He called all his women Ginger. He said she would give him gifts, never money, but nice stuff, art, antiques, and they'd go out, once even on vacation. He was with her a long time. I should tell you, a long time for him anyway was almost a year."

"Where did Ginger live?"

"I don't know, somewhere in the city, I think."

"You said you two were friends until he turned to the dark side. What did you mean?"

Winter glanced at his phone for the time and took another swallow of drink. "He started selling the stuff she gifted him. That was bad enough. In the beginning, I turned him on to a dealer I knew in Berkeley, but she found out what he was doing, and things started to go downhill."

He stopped speaking and just stared at his glass. Remy waited until he started speaking again, this time much slower.

"He started stealing things out of Ginger's house." He looked Remy in the eyes. "I'd appreciate it if you didn't tell his mother."

She shook her head. He ordered a glass of wine for them both.

"It was small things at first. He justified it because she wouldn't miss them, and whenever he admired something, she'd offer it to him anyway. Too bad he didn't think to tell her. He got so bad he would take photos to show the stuff around, trying to find a buyer." Winter grimaced. "He was unbelievable. At that point, I stopped hanging out with him. I'd had enough. He didn't seem to care. To be fair, I could tell he was a little remorseful, but unfortunately not enough to stop. He would have kept going until he emptied the woman's house of anything valuable."

"What stopped him?"

Ian Winter hesitated before answering, "He was murdered."

CHAPTER TWENTY-SEVEN

"I thought you knew," Winter said.

Remy leaned back in her seat. It had never occurred to her to ask Audra Dunlap *how* her son had died. She had assumed it was from natural causes.

"No, I didn't know. His mother never said," Remy responded. "And I never asked. Do you know the circumstances?"

"Like I said, by that time I had lost touch with him. I did hear through a mutual friend he had been mugged or burglarized — something, I don't know — somewhere in San Francisco. That's the last I heard about him."

She put dollars on the table before gathering her purse and coat. "I know you've got a flight. Thank you for seeing me."

"You okay?" he asked, putting cash down. "Was I able to help you?"

"Yeah, you helped a lot. I won't tell his mother everything you told me, but it will be enough to give her a little peace. But now, I have some questions of my own."

Remy had arranged to meet with Audra in her son's house, which was now her current residence. She wasn't eager to tell Audra her son was a thief and the center of what must be a lucrative and apparently lethal stolen goods operation.

They were having lunch in the kitchen alcove overlooking clustered trees in a grassy yard.

"I have to find a new place to live," Audra said, putting down her napkin. "A friend of a friend has a large home in Berkeley, near Ashby Street with a very nice cottage in the back. I like it, it's just enough for me. I'll be able to afford it once I sell Martin's house. This house is too large."

Remy nodded, half listening. "Audra, we need to talk. I . . . I don't know how to start, but I'm going to jump in."

"Yes?"

"How did Martin die?"

The woman turned away to peer out the window. "If you're asking me that question, then you already know."

"Why didn't you tell me?"

She looked down at her hands and started to wring them. "I told you we were estranged. I guess . . . I guess I didn't want you to think ill of him. They never found out who did it. I didn't want you to. . . . I wanted you to help me find the clock because it was the last thing we shared, he and I. He told me it reminded him of family and tradition and. . . ." Her voice faded.

"Audra, I spoke with Martin's friend, Ian Winter," Remy leaned over and put her hand over those of the woman in front of her. "He said he and Martin went their separate ways before he died. He told me Martin was . . . well, he was selling artifacts from a female friend's home with, or sometimes maybe without, her knowledge."

Audra gasped and put her hand to her mouth.

"I wasn't going to tell you at first, but . . . but I didn't want you to go to the police without knowing," Remy continued. "It's possible those items in the photos weren't . . . didn't belong to Martin." She squeezed the woman's hand. "Tell me what you know; I can't help you if I don't know the whole story."

Audra looked so forlorn, Remy could almost feel, as well as see her grief.

"I didn't know for sure," Audra said, looking away. "I didn't know anything for sure. The police contacted me to tell me Martin had been . . . killed. I came to California right away. I told you the truth; he and I hadn't spoken in months. We didn't have any family left, so I identified the body and had him cremated. It was when I was going through his things that I found little notes from women, and . . . and pictures. I could tell they were older women, some much older."

Remy frowned. "Did the police search his house for any evidence leading to the person who killed him?"

"Yes, they'd been there," she said. "When I talked to the detective in charge, he said the case was still unsolved. A neighbor called the police about seeing an open front door from a possible burglary. They couldn't tell if anything had been taken. They found fingerprints, but Martin was killed in his car, parked in a public garage in the city. He was shot. They didn't get any prints from the . . . the scene." She took a deep swallow.

Remy was surprised to hear there wasn't trace evidence found, though maybe they didn't tell the mother. They fell into silence for a few moments. Audra got up to refresh their glasses.

"Audra, can I hold on to the photos? I may have some news about the clock, but I want to check something out first."

"But you said he stole —"

"Not the clock," she said. "The Fernier clock has been in your family. You know what it looks like. There's a chance I know where it is. I need to think about how to give you a chance to identify it."

"From the way you talk, I'd assumed he put it up for sale," her voice began to waver.

"If it's the one I think it is, then, yes, he was trying to sell it."

"You must have guessed by now I was a terrible mother," Audra said, fingering her napkin. "I was the reason Martin and I didn't have a relationship. His father wasn't around after he saw having a family required more than what was pictured in a television ad. And I wasn't much better. Martin never had a chance."

"Having parents around doesn't always make a difference."

Audra stared at her. "Do you have family?"

"Yes."

"Are you close?"

Remy remembered she had to call her mother. "Yes."

"I'm not shocked he went the way he did, but I am so sorry . . . so sorry." She broke into sobs.

Remy got up and took the woman into her arms, until her shoulders went still, and her tears subsided. Audra pulled away and reached for tissue. She wiped at her nose and eyes.

"If you know where the clock is, I want to buy it back."

"I understand, but I haven't seen it. I was told a showroom in the city may have it up for sale. And I'm not positive it's your clock."

Audra seemed to collect herself. "I'll come with you to verify. Let me know when." She looked at Remy, taking another dab at her eyes. "I'll be getting quite a bit of money from this house. I want that clock. It will remind me of Martin and how easy it is to take time for granted, when we forget time is running out."

CHAPTER TWENTY-EIGHT

"Remy you're back. I didn't see you this much when you worked here." Victor Camden chuckled, putting down the newspaper he'd been reading from behind the reception desk.

She wanted to return his smile, but couldn't.

"I think I mentioned I had a client who might be interested in a few of your items," she said. "Well, it turns out I was right."

"You may want to wait until my next sale this Friday. The prices may be more to your client likes." He gestured over the room. "What has caught your eye?"

She looked around. "The Urbino vase and the Tiffany lamp, but I don't see either of them now."

She thought she saw his eyes narrow, but a moment later, he grinned. "Good looking out. But those were reproductions; I sold them the same day you were here last time."

He didn't look at her but went back behind the desk. "You were my best student. If I fooled you, my customer should be pleased with his purchase."

"They weren't reproductions, Victor."

Remy placed two of the Dunlap photos on his desk.

Camden leaned over and lifted them up. He tossed the photos down. "I don't know where these were taken but it wasn't my shop. And yes, I've had both items, but like I said they were very good reproductions."

"They were in your store. I saw them when I worked here."

His face flushed. "What are you trying to say?"

"I'd swear they were the real deal."

"And you would be wrong." He dug into a stack of papers in front of him. "Look, here's the sales receipt. Claudine hasn't had a chance to file it yet." He held out a yellow form receipt. "If I sold originals at those prices, I'd be out of business in a heartbeat."

Remy held the paper and could see there were three items that were sold to an unintelligible scribbled name. In addition to the two items she'd questioned, a pair of Meissen porcelain peasants had been sold, all for less than ten-thousand dollars. She held her gasp and kept her eyes lowered.

The same peasants had been in one of Audra's photos.

"Who bought them?" she asked regaining her composure. "I'm afraid I've raised my client's hopes with their description. Maybe your buyer might be interested in a quick resale."

"I don't think so, but I'll ask," he said in a flat voice. "Didn't you say your client wanted originals? Besides, I treat sales as confidential, you know that."

Not always.

"Well, I guess I was wrong," Remy said, raising her eyes to meet the ones boring into hers.

Camden turned away and sat down, speaking over his shoulder as he reached for a pad of paper and a pen.

"I can't guarantee anything, but I come across Tiffany lamps every day. As you can tell, some are excellent reproductions. I can —"

"Don't bother, Victor." Remy stood. "I could have sworn the Tiffany lamp in that case was authentic. I even noticed how the light hit the confetti glass. The glass changed color in the light, one sign of an original Tiffany."

"Remy, calm down. Along with being one of my best students, you were also one of the most dogged." Camden put away his pad and folded his hands across the desk. "I'm sorry you can't accept what I'm telling you. At any rate, I no longer have the reproductions you seek. Is there anything else?"

She took a moment to control the outburst that perched on the edge of her tongue.

"No, I'm sorry for being a pest." She paused, then, "Are you going to the San Francisco trade show this weekend? I might see you there."

He appeared surprised at the change in subject, and his shoulders visibly relaxed. "Yes, we're doing a booth and a small workshop on cleaning." He looked at his watch. "In fact, I'm supposed to meet with the coordinators in an hour."

"Then I'll let you get on with your day."

"Sorry about the lamp."

"Me, too."

"Remy Bishop, what are you doing here? I thought you forgot about me."

Claudine Eberly had worked as office manager and receptionist for Camden House almost from the very beginning. She took Remy under her tutelage, a circumstance, she assured her she did not take on often.

Claudine never said how old she was, but Remy estimated her age to be in the 50s. Her jet-black hair was dyed and contrasted dramatically with her pale skin, and the fine wrinkles that crept around her mouth and eyes. Her frequent trips to the dermatologist for Botox injections were evidenced by the slick shine of the skin on her forehead and chin. Her expressions appeared frozen in place, and her eye lids were becoming slits. She was losing the battle of holding on to youthful looks.

She hugged the woman. "Claudine, it is so good to see you."

Remy had made sure Victor's car was out of the lot before returning to Camden House.

"Victor told me you came by the other day. I'm surprised you came back again, but pleased," she said, holding her at arm's length to look. "How's working for Grayden Lane? Is he still a pompous ass?"

They hugged.

Remy laughed. "Still the same old Claudine. I admit I miss you guys, but no regrets. LaneWilson is a good house. It was time for me to find my place in the world."

"Want some tea?" Claudine asked. "Or, are you in a hurry? I've got to get these flyers out but that will take no time." She patted a stack of garish yellow papers.

Remy stared at the sheets, trying to catch a memory but let it slip. She was here for a purpose. She pulled out her phone for the time.

"We just finished a sale. I can stay for a short while, but a brief visit with one of my favorite people sounded like a great way to make the day."

"Good."

The woman turned to a small serving table behind an ornate Chinese screen.

"If you came back to see Victor again, you just missed him. He's at the Art and Antiques Show for the rest of the afternoon," Claudine brought out two steaming cups. "We've got a new intern. Not a bad kid if you ignore his acne and lisp. Victor is showing him the ropes."

"Ah, I remember those days," Remy chuckled. "Grayden's at the show too, which is why I can't stay long. Sorry to miss Victor. I thought of something I wanted to ask him." She wrinkled her forehead. "Say, there is one thing while I'm here. I could use your recollection."

The woman straightened in her chair. "What's that?"

"I was going to ask Victor, but you're as knowledgeable as he is," Remy said, looking in her purse and pulling out two photos. "Have you seen this clock?"

"Maybe." Claudine peered at it and nodded. "We get so many clocks these days. I think clocks have fallen out of favor in this world of instant digital time on the device of your choice. This is a Fernier soniere clock. We had one similar not too long ago. If this one still keeps time, it should bring a good price." She looked at Remy. "Why?"

She handed her the second photo of the clock bottom. "Look at the stamp. Was this the clock you had?"

"Yes, it looks like it. You're giving me a picture of a picture, but if the authentication holds up, I'd say it was the same."

"Who sold it to you?"

Claudine tossed the picture onto the desk and crossed her arms over her chest. "No more answers, what's going on?"

"Sorry, I didn't mean to sound like an interrogator. An elderly friend is trying to track down family heirlooms that were sold at an estate sale years ago to see if she can buy them back." She had practiced her story and hoped it would allay Claudine's fears and curiosity. "I told her it was a long shot, but I would do a little asking around."

"Oh, poor thing," she said. "Still, I'm not sure I can help you. You know how Victor feels about the identity of his sellers."

"Claudine, forget the seller, what about the buyer? Can you take a peek at your records and let me know if the clock is still in private hands or did another house purchase it?"

The woman was clearly exasperated. But she walked to the rear of the store where a bank of file cabinets lined a wall. "We'll be converting to digital files soon, but Victor wants to keep hardcopy for a while longer. I used to be able to recite from memory our buyers and sellers after a sale, but now, not so much. We hire out for personnel to assist with transactions and to them it's just a paycheck. Ah, here it is," she said, lifting out a form. "Lara Nielsen from Seems Like Olde Times. Her showroom is in the downtown district. She bought several items in a lot, and the clock was one of them."

CHAPTER TWENTY-NINE

The interior lights could be seen through the windows of Seems Like Olde Times' showroom. The preview reception had been underway for just an hour. But the street was full of parked cars as valets scrambled to give tickets to owners in exchange for their keys. Remy had suggested to Audra they rent a driver for the least amount of hassle possible. They were dropped off about a half-block from the showroom.

Grayden hadn't asked any questions when Remy inquired if he could get her an invitation for two to the Seems Like Olde Times Wednesday function.

"I'm sure I can. Lara wants as many dealers as she can to buy her stock. She travels to Europe in a few weeks to purchase new pieces, and I know she needs the space." He peered at her over his glasses. "I think it's a good idea for you to attend. Her parties are a little too showy for me. If you go,

274

I don't have to give my regrets."

"I guess I thought a place that was taking in stolen goods would look a little less glamorous," Audra whispered, keeping pace with Remy's stride.

Remy pulled her vintage 1920s shawl close and bent down to Audra's ear. "Remember, we're not here to make a scene or make any accusations. I'll follow-up with the police later. If the clock is here, we want to buy it and leave. I'm not even sure the clock will be featured, but if you see it find me, and if I spot it, I'll do the same."

"Why does it feel like we're the ones doing something illegal?" Audra whispered, walking up the steps.

"Well, we're not." Remy grinned at the man greeting guests at the door, and spoke over her shoulder to Audra and said, "We're the good guys." She handed him their invitation.

The hallways and rooms were near to capacity. Champagne and tiny finger foods were held aloft on silver trays by tuxedo-garbed servers. Remy need not have worried about Audra finding the clock on her own; the woman hadn't left her side.

"Let's check out the rooms at the rear for artifacts," Remy said. "I've seen the ones up front, and they all hold large furniture."

They moved toward a huddle of persons just outside a door leading to a room with a huge crystal chandelier. Remy stood on her toes to see the cases along the walls of the room.

Lara Nielsen spoke from behind her.

"Ms. Bishop, at first I was surprised to see you here." Nielsen said, holding a glass of champagne and wearing a cold but wide smile. "But then I realized Grayden had passed on his invitation."

Remy swirled around at the woman's voice.

"Lara, I'd like you to meet Audra Dunlap, she's the client I told you about," she said, nudging the woman forward. "I understand you have included a small collection of artifacts in tonight's sale."

Nielsen stiffened but the now fixed smile never left her face. She shook Audra's hand, in response to Audra's mumbled greeting. Remy noticed the owner's furtive look behind her in the direction of a small room near the staircase.

"Ah, yes the clock you were interested in. I think I told you I only carry large furniture pieces, but from time to time I do sell items for other dealers, who for whatever reason choose not to have their own sale."

"So, you might have the clock after all?"

Remy pushed.

Lara Nielsen took a sip from her glass. "Just so we're clear. I did not have any such clock in my showroom when you came by, but as I said, I have allowed others to bring in items to assist in their sales. It's common practice," she said. "I have no idea what is available. My assistant works out all the details."

"Well, we'll continue to walk around." Remy said.

Nielsen's look of fury could not be contained. Her face flushed red, causing face-lift scars near her scalp line to appear. Without speaking further, she sidestepped them to greet an older couple coming through the door.

"I don't think you should expect a Christmas card," Audra said under her breath. "That lady has issues."

Remy put her glass down on a passing tray.

"Come on, Audra, we've got to find the clock before she removes it."

"You think it's here?"

"Oh, I'd bet on it," Remy said, moving through the throng toward the staircase into what must have once been the butler's pantry. "She doesn't want us to see it. But I noticed she glanced toward this room —"

"There it is!" Audra cried out.

In a narrow passage way, which was once a butler's pantry, the small clock was displayed on a marble counter centered between two Tiffany egg reproductions. Remy let Audra pass ahead of her, and at the same time caught the eye of Nielsen who was moving hurriedly away from the opposite side. A server came from nowhere, slithered in front of Remy and blocked Audra's progress.

"Champagne?"

"No, thank you," Remy snapped, advancing to go through him if she had to.

Audra shook her head in refusal and slipped past to reach the small alcove. She lifted up the clock and turned it over.

"I thought . . ." she said.

"Audra, are you saying this isn't your clock?" Remy asked.

Turning the clock around, the woman looked puzzled. "No, this isn't my clock, nor is it the clock I saw a moment ago from the doorway." She put it back down. "I don't understand."

Remy stretched to see the back of Lara Nielsen making her way toward the main showroom.

"But it wasn't the clock?" Chief Warren said, writing a quick note on his pad.

They were meeting in the LaneWilson showroom.

Remy took a breath. "The clock was switched, Audra Dunlap identified it as we were coming up to it, but by the time we got there, Lara Nielsen had swapped it with another similar but different clock."

He tossed his pen on the table. "Remy, you said Mrs. Dunlap is an older woman, could she have seen what she wanted to see? From what you told me, she has a lot of emotion tied up with this clock."

"No, even I could tell the first clock had gold settings and the replaced clock had brass."

"But she never saw her clock? She never verified it as her own?"

Her shoulders sank. "No."

He leaned forward. "Then you must see the sheriff's problem. First, she's not in their jurisdiction and second, there's no basis for interrogating Ms. Nielsen, let alone justification for a warrant."

Remy bit down on her bottom lip. "Suppose I told you I saw a certain valuable table stolen from a house in East Mendleson in Lara Nielsen's showroom."

He frowned. "What are you saying?"

"I mean the table I saw in the Crandall house was in her showroom."

Warren ran his hand through his hair. "Are you trying to tell me Lara Nielsen — prominent San Francisco leader and philanthropist, is guilty of receiving and selling stolen goods?"

She winced. "I'm not sure about all that. I know the table I saw in the Seems Like Olde Times showroom a couple of days ago was in the Crandall house a couple of weeks ago."

"Did you see the table last night?"

She frowned. "No, it was very crowded. I didn't have enough time. We were focused on the clock."

He looked past her.

"Tell you what, I'll check out Nielsen and Olde Times," he said. "I'll see if she's come up on any law enforcement databases. There's someone I know who's a consultant with SFPD who might be able to shed some light. Maybe he'll be willing to help you. I'll let you know."

CHAPTER THIRTY

Remy reached across the kitchen table for the copied case notes Andy had retrieved. When she got to the Lennox file, her hand shook. The victim's body was discovered on a wet day in an open field, with a bloody knife alongside her body. The scene was processed by police, who were able to identify her from identification and directed to her condo. Neighbors in her complex were more than willing to recount how, days before, a male visitor was seen running down the hallway and stairs. Their descriptions, while generic enough to fit a current boyfriend, were too varied and the DA relied on forensics from the murder weapon to seal the conviction.

Remy rubbed her eyes.

Her Lennox notes were detailed and echoed the format and syntax of her other past cases. She stared at the signature on the bottom line. It was hers. The computer printout showing her entries bore her passcode. She picked up the photos of the evidence bags. Each forensic technician had a badge with a barcode that was scanned at the time of initial assignment of evidence from the property officer and each instance of evidence access and transfer. She recognized the knife by its bloody handle. Her eyes went to the barcode, attesting to the date, time and her name. Her notes reflected the same.

Andy had taken the photo of the second evidence bag holding the knife tip. She squinted to see the smear of blood. She would swear she had never seen this evidence before. But, suppose it had been a rush time when an agency dropped off a large amount of evidence all at once from multiple cases? It was possible, unlikely, but possible, she could have overlooked it. She went back over her notes, line by line. There was nothing referencing a knife tip, and in the chain of custody section was her barcode.

She sighed and poured herself a cup of tea. She had signed off on an evidence log that had allowed the killer to stay free.

The mistake appeared to be hers.

CHAPTER THIRTY-ONE

"Audra, remember when you showed me Martin's bedroom, and the cabinet near his balcony?" Remy held the woman's hands. They were sitting in the Dunlap kitchen. Remy had asked to come by on Monday before she went to work.

Audra frowned. "Sure, I remember. Why?"

"I need to see that cabinet. If I'm right, I should be able to get Lara Nielsen's fingerprints."

"Lara Nielsen! Remy, why would Lara Nielsen's prints be here?"

She sighed. "Because, I think Nielsen was having an affair with your son. I discovered the items in those photos you showed me, in a San Francisco dealer's showroom. Those items were handled, or bought, or stolen by Lara Nielsen."

"Martin and Lara Nielsen," Audra murmured.

"I learned that Martin had an affair with

a . . . a much older woman. My gut tells me it was Nielsen. There is a chance he brought her here and either showed her or she wandered around and discovered his . . . collection. You're sure Martin would never relinquish the clock willingly, so let's say she had an opportunity to take the clock and maybe a few other things. She could sell them through her 'special' sales receptions."

"You can take still get fingerprints?"

"Well, yes. I've never done it in the field, but everyone's fingers are coated with perspiration, and the oiliness of our fingers create latent, or invisible prints on everything we touch, leaving behind a little piece of us as we go about our everyday life. That's the stuff powders pick up."

"Do you have fingerprint powder with you?"

Remy took a large plastic bag from her purse. "I brought along a few other things that will help me to lift any prints." She gestured toward the stairs. "I'd like to see that cabinet. There's the chance Lara Nielsen left her prints on the wood frame or the glass. If we can show she was here, then maybe the police would be willing to get a warrant to search her showroom."

Audra led the way.

Peering at the glass panel adjacent to the cabinet knob, Remy spotted a possible print. There were also several along the dark wood. She took out her phone and took pictures. It was a good idea to take pictures of the print before she tried to lift it just in case her attempts to lift the print altered or destroyed it. The furniture piece did not appear to be dusty, so after putting on latex gloves, she opened a jar of latent print powder and, using a small fiberglass print brush with care, she spread the powder over several prints. After gently blowing on the powder, she took out her lifting tape dispenser, pulled off two-inch squares and covered each suspected print. Then, making sure there were no air pockets she lifted them off and marked each on the space at the bottom for labeling.

"Do you always carry a fingerprint kit with you?" Audra asked, peering over her shoulder.

Remy chuckled. "No, but I do keep one in my trunk and at home." She placed each lift into a filing box. "It's a habit from a former life." She frowned and labeled the container.

"You used to be a cop?"

"No."

Her abrupt tone had the desired effect of

stifling any further questions on the topic and Audra moved to sit on the side of the bed.

"What are you going to do now?" Audra asked.

"I'm going to take this to a sheriff's detective who can help us." She lifted up the box. "He can run the prints to see if there is a match in the system." Remy opened up an inked pad. "I'd like to take your prints, so we can exclude them from any I got today."

In less than five minutes, Remy took Audra's prints, and they were back in the kitchen.

"I guess I never imagined the police would get involved," Audra mused. "I think I was so sure LaneWilson had cheated my son that . . . it didn't occur to me my son might be the cheat." Her eyes glistened with brimming tears. She gripped Remy's forearm. "You never knew Martin. The things that are coming out now make him out to be a bad person, but I tell you he had a good heart, and he would not have sold that clock."

Remy patted her hand. "Then let's see if we can get it back."

She was going to be late again. Traffic on the Nimitz Freeway was bumper-to-bumper and based on the road alert board; it would be twenty minutes before she could break free. Remy wanted to get to the office, because she was meeting Noah Larson for lunch to hand over the prints. At this rate, she'd be lucky to get to work for lunch.

She left a message for Larson to change her appointment to late afternoon.

At last, she passed a two-car accident off to the right side of the road. The participants were still pointing and waving their hands in front of a bored-looking police officer. Traffic picked up and she, along with a number of cars, took the next exit.

She noticed the dark navy Volvo sedan when she maneuvered onto the two-lane roadway leading into Mendleson. Narrow with a deep channel on either side, it was a short cut used by locals when the freeway was slower. The vehicle was several car lengths back and she couldn't see the driver. They were alone on the road. Then, when she could hear a muffled roar of an engine, getting louder and louder that she realized the car was bearing down on her at a speed that foretold an impending crash.

Remy forced herself to relax her body, and at the last moment moved into the vacant oncoming traffic lane. The move saved her life. When the impact occurred, she was side-swiped. The car half spun, ending at an angle teetering precariously over the downward slope of a gulley. The Volvo slowed, turned around and then sped away.

Someone had tried to kill her.

Afraid to make any sudden moves for fear the car would tilt further, with care she reached for her phone and punched 9-1-1.

CHAPTER THIRTY-TWO

"How long before you hear back about the Dunlap prints?" Remy asked, sitting at the small table in a diner down the street from the sheriff's office.

"Whoa, let's hold off a minute. I understand you were almost killed yesterday. Are you okay?"

Grateful that Grayden was out of town at a trade show, she'd gotten Roberta to reset her meeting with Larson for the next day. Chief Warren had introduced her to Detective Noah Larson and suggested he would be her best chance to get the information she needed, as well as pass on any information she discovered. Larson, a twenty-year law enforcement veteran with the sheriff, was working as a consultant to Patterson County. Tall and not a pound overweight, he had a light brush of gray at the temples of his blond hair. His doe brown eyes seemed to see through her. The chief said she could trust him.

"Yes, it looks like it was deliberate," she said. "Chief Warren is investigating. He may need help from the sheriff, but —"

"Ms. Bishop, you seem very calm. Why do you think someone would want to kill you?"

Remy didn't want to tell him how she couldn't stop shaking with fear and alarm as she waited for the police. How she could hear her own heart beat as it pounded in her chest, and how she broke into a steady flow of tears when she got home waiting for her doctor's prescribed sedative to kick-in.

"I'm always calm. Besides, I walked away without a scratch," she said. "But I do think someone is trying to silence me, or keep me from finding out who killed Edmund Kieffer or Melanie Chase. I must be getting close."

"I don't know you, Ms. Bishop. I'm listening to you because I owe the chief. I don't like working with civilians who think detective work is conducted like it is on television."

Remy fought not to react to his words. She pushed the small box containing the fingerprints forward.

"Detective, I assure you, I don't wish to waste your time nor am I a detective wanna-be. I do, however, want to clear my name and be removed from everyone's suspect list."

"As long as we have an understanding that you'll stay in your lane." Noah Larson looked at his watch. "I'll ask the lab supervisor to put a rush on it, so maybe late this afternoon, at the latest tomorrow morning."

"I've always been on the receiving-end of running the tests," Remy said. "What happens next?"

"Once we get the results, I'll take things, or not, from there." He cleared his throat. "Okay, listen to me. I'm working with you as a favor to the chief. He's been a mentor to me and has helped me more than a couple of times. I work cold homicide cases, not theft and robbery. It's not law enforcement procedure to involve civilians in a possible investigation, but since you're the one that asked for the investigation, and you're coming in with your own evidence — although I'm not sure it will stand up in court — I'll be a little flexible." He held his hand up when Remy grinned relief. "But I still have to verify anything you give or tell me, I'm not going to take your word for it."

"I do understand," she said. "Detective, I'm going to be upfront with you. You don't recognize my name, but I was the forensic tech that blew the Lennox case." She waited for the look of recognition cross his face. When it did, she continued, "I figured if you work cold cases, then Lennox was on your list. I didn't want you to think . . . I mean when you found out it was me . . . I wanted to be the one to let you know."

He folded his hands. "You're too late, the chief told me."

"Oh." Remy straightened in her seat. "I should have realized he would." She looked down at her hands. "I was set up, but that's a discussion for another day. It's not why I'm here, now."

"Fine, let's focus on why you're here now. The chief asked me to check out Lara Nielsen to see if she'd been on our radar. Well, it turns out our general crimes division has her on our persons of interest list. She hasn't committed any crime we know of, but her name keeps cropping up on the periphery of other criminal cases. They're watching her."

"So," she said. "If her prints are on Martin Dunlap's cabinet, then we know two things. She had access to the clock and there's a good chance she was Martin's front for stolen goods."

"More important, we'll have probable cause and maybe enough to get a search warrant."

"What makes you so sure Nielsen's prints are on file?"

"Because when we first met, she told me she oversees the annual fundraiser for a children's foundation," Remy replied. "And, I happen to know anyone associated with children in a public setting must go through live-scan and be fingerprinted."

"You're correct, Ms. Bishop, I'm impressed," he said, curiosity evident on his face. "Let's hope those prints tell us something."

"I know they will."

Remy couldn't help looking in her rear-view mirror as she turned onto the roadway that had almost ended her life. But this afternoon there was mild traffic and she gradually relaxed.

In the LaneWilson showroom she forced herself to concentrate on work by answering mail and returning calls. After a couple of hours, she got a text that the results had been emailed to Detective Larson with a blind copy to her. With that, she put out the "Will Be Right Back" sign and left to meet with Larson.

"Congratulations," he said. "Nielsen's prints were all over the cabinet. We've already got a warrant request in front of a judge. We should be able to go in tonight."

"Can I —"

"No," he said with firmness. "I know what you're going to ask. You cannot be there, this is a police action."

"I was thinking I could be waiting in my car down the street. I'd be out of harm's way," Remy offered. "You might need me to identify the antique piece."

"No."

Remy frowned. "Look, there's another reason I'd like to be there."

"Yeah, what's the other reason?"

"It's a long story. I don't think the chief shared this one with you." She moistened her lips and over the next minutes recounted a short version of the Kieffer murder. "I'm pretty sure, but not positive; a table I saw in the Crandall House was in Nielsen's showroom."

Larson wrinkled his brow and tapped a pen against his writing pad.

"You know, the Kieffer murder isn't solved," he said. "I was wondering how you stumbled onto Seems Like Olde Times. You've been playing detective, haven't you?"

"No, I —"

"How did you track the table to Nielsen's store?" he asked, not waiting for an answer. "You know there's a good chance she's hauled all her stolen stuff out of there, particularly if she thinks you've recognized a few things."

"I know the clock might be gone, but not that table."

"How can you be so sure?"

"For one, it's huge," she said. "Second, it is priceless. The care it would take to move it without harm would take many hours. Tell your guys to look everywhere. Those old houses have a lot of small side rooms. Look on the floors and see if there are signs on the carpet near the wall or even tracks of furniture legs being dragged."

She handed him photos of the Dunlap clock and of the mahogany table she'd captured during her first visit before Nielsen made her leave.

Larson leaned forward and accepted the material. "All right, Ms. Bishop, I assure you we know how to do our job. I'll let you know if we find anything."

"I haven't heard from you in a few days," Paul said. "What's been going on?"

Remy was in the showroom finishing up a sale, and when he called, she thought it might be the detective. She debated on telling Paul about her visit to Noah Larson.

"I've been helping a customer locate an

295

heirloom. The police are going to raid a showroom in San Francisco based on a tip I supplied them. I want to show them I'm a good guy, and I thought it best to show Grayden I'm an asset by staying close to LaneWilson."

"Good idea," Paul agreed. "Have you heard from Tuft?"

"No, nothing." She was glad to speak the truth. "They must be working on some angle that doesn't involve me, and for that I always be grateful. Did you learn anything about the people who attended Melanie's funeral?"

He blew out his cheeks. "Nah, nothing unusual."

Remy wondered how hard he looked.

"Paul, I need to get back to work." She hesitated, and then said, "You know, I appreciate having your support and advice regarding this terrible Kieffer mess, but I can't go on taking money from my parents to pay you. I —"

"Wait, you're not firing me, are you? I haven't even billed your father yet." Paul's voice wavered. "This is not the time to let me go. I've seen this situation many, many times before. The sheriff hasn't approached you, because they think they have everything they need, and they're tightening their case before you're arrested."

"But, I —"

"Remy, will you please listen to me?" The exasperation in his voice was evident. "Don't be foolish. I know the legal system, and I know how the DA thinks and works. You are the only person of interest they've got. You're their 'smoke' to a raging fire. First, Kieffer then this Chase woman — you need me to block for you."

He stopped speaking and waited a long moment for her response.

"Okay," she said with reluctance. "But you have to bill me from now on, which means I'll need your special deferred payment plan."

"You got it," he chuckled. "Now, what have you been up to?

She wasn't ready to incur his ire over her progress in her pursuit of the Kieffer table. "Like I said, I'm helping a client locate a family heirloom and I'm pretty sure it involves a prominent San Francisco arts dealer at a showroom called Seems Like Olde Times."

Her cellphone rang. Remy squinted at the time and the name of the caller. It was close to ten o'clock. She must have fallen asleep watching a rerun.

"Detective, did you find anything?"

"No, we didn't," Larson growled. "No clock, no table and nothing else on our stolen goods list. We had three men go out there tonight for a complete waste of time."

Remy shoulders sank.

"I'm so sorry. But I still know it's her."

"Right," he said. "I'll give my captain your reassurance. Goodnight, Ms. Bishop."

CHAPTER THIRTY-THREE

Remy clicked off her phone. With her promised call to her mother out of the way, she could concentrate on her job. Larson's unspoken rebuke still burned in her ears. She knew Nielsen was a criminal, and probably celebrating she had once more dodged the police.

She tackled answering customer inquiries and arranging for shipping of purchased items. Grayden was in his office with his sister, and she could hear their low murmur. He had a last-minute lunch in the city and would have to leave soon. With him away, she'd have her afternoon free to contact dealers. Nielsen may have sold or placed the clock with another showroom.

Grayden's door opened, and the two appeared.

"Like I've been saying," Grayden said. "I don't see any reason to change how we've done things in the past. But you appear to be fixated, so I'm willing to give it a try."

"Thank you." Joan gave him a quick kiss on the cheek. "That's all your partners ask."

He stood next to Remy's desk and flipped through the small stack of mail. "I'm on my way to lunch. I won't be back. I'll be working out of the San Francisco office."

"Not a problem," Remy said.

Joan glanced at her phone for the time. "Remy, how about you and I get an early lunch? It would be a chance for us to get to know each other better. I've got some time to kill before my meeting with a potential client."

Remy swallowed her groan. She had planned to make search calls to a couple of showrooms in the city.

"I —"

"No offense, Remy," Grayden said, and he turned to his sister shaking his head. "But Joan, we hired her to keep the show-room opened during the lunch hour. There may be clients who take off from work to catch us open."

She waved him off. "We had a successful sale; a little longer lunch closing won't deter the possible hordes of walk-in traffic." She gestured toward Remy. "What do you say?"

Remy glanced up to see Grayden's resigned expression, and she didn't think it wise to reject an offer from a business partner. "Grayden, I'll hurry back. I've got some things I've got to take care of today, but a short break for lunch won't hamper that. I'll put the sign on the door."

The Crystal Bay Café was a tiny establishment just outside Mendleson, serving the basics for breakfast, lunch and dinner. It didn't have an extensive menu, but what it did serve was delicious. After Remy left home to start her adult life, she'd been surprised to read the reviews in several touristy magazines touting the Crystal Bay as one of the Bay Area's best hidden secrets. Which unfortunately had created a rush of foodies on the weekends, locals had learned to patronize during the week.

Being Thursday, the café had few customers. Remy and Joan took no time placing their order with the server.

"Let's order a glass of wine," Joan said. "I need something stronger than iced tea after meeting with my brother.

"Sounds good to me."

The server, who was part owner, also helped with the cooking, and soon returned with two glasses and a small carafe of wine.

"So," said Joan. "How do you like working for LaneWilson? Is it what you expected?"

Remy poured a half-filled glass for Joan and herself.

Joan was dressed very town and country in charcoal gray slacks, a crisp white linen blouse and a subtle plaid blazer. Her thick dark hair was pulled back and held in place with expensive sun glasses perched on top of her head.

"I like it a lot," Remy said. "As far as being what I expected, I guess you can say it meets my expectations."

"Hmm," Joan said, taking a sip of wine. "I know you must be curious about all the closed-door sessions we've been having."

Remy started to shake her head, but Joan raised her hand in protest.

"Please, I'm not going to report you to the police."

Remy's face blanched.

"Oh, I'm sorry, Remy," Joan said. "I was kidding. I didn't mean by . . . I mean it was a turn of phrase; I wasn't referring to your situation. Look, I'm an excellent read of people. In no way do I think you're a criminal. If I did, you would have been gone week one."

Remy took a sip of her wine. "I'm okay. I guess I'm a little punchy from having people dying around me." She took another sip. "Yes, I am curious. What's going on with the LaneWilson partners?"

"Grayden is going to sell LaneWilson."

Remy's eyes widened. She hadn't expected that. "Why? When?"

The server brought their orders, and Joan leaned back in her chair before speaking.

"First, forgive me. I should have mentioned your job is secure. Evan Wilson and I want Grayden to sell the Mendleson showroom to us. He will continue to operate the San Francisco and Novato showrooms. If all goes well, our transaction should close within sixty days." She paused to take a bite from her salad then continued, "You know I just realized you don't know anything about me, or Evan."

"No, I don't, and I've never met Evan Wilson," Remy replied, comfortable in not mentioning her search through the files. "I guess I assumed I'd get to know you both over time. I'm not shocked Grayden wants to sell, but it is something to consider."

"Well, we hope you consider staying," Joan said. "You're a quick study. We're going to be changing some things, but Mendleson is doing well as it is. And as much as I like fine art goods, I'm not a salesperson. Evan is another matter." She looked at her phone for the time. "I don't want to make you late getting back. My older brother will point out I have no idea what it takes to run a business, but he'd be wrong."

They talked for the next minutes in a free-flowing fashion getting to know each other.

"Joan, I know you don't know me, but I am trying to help a friend who is convinced she saw a family heirloom for sale in the showroom of a local dealer." Remy hesitated. "They deny it. Do you know of any dealers with questionable reputations? I met my friend since I've worked for LaneWilson. She's an older woman, a nice older woman, who needs help. I tried going to the police, but they say they don't have enough to move forward."

Joan twisted the stem of her glass without looking up. "I take it she says the heirloom was stolen?"

"And, without going into a lot of detail, I believe her. I've seen it."

"Would I know the dealer?"

Remy looked the woman in the eye. "I think it's a good possibility," she said.

Joan returned the look. "I assume you're hesitating to give me the name because either you don't want to risk besmirching the character of a dealer who could be a friend of mine, or maybe you think I could be involved and would give an alarm?"

Remy made an apologetic face.

"On the other hand, you must have some feeling I can be trusted because you wouldn't have raised your friend's situation with me at all, unless you needed help," Joan prodded. "So, in the interest of time, I think you're going to have to make a leap of faith."

"I suppose you're right." Remy moistened her lips and straightened her shoulders. "I don't know for certain it's the dealer. It could be the showroom. I have no proof of anything."

"Disclaimer noted."

"My friend is missing a Fernier clock," she said. "We saw it on display in the Seems Like Olde Times showroom night before last."

Joan looked down at her hands and played with her napkin. "Lara Nielsen has a solid reputation, but I've never liked her," she said. "Fortunately, I've had a minimum of transactions with her. I too had a friend who had a bad experience with her showroom, but I didn't believe his complaint for a number of reasons. None of which had to do with antiques. But maybe I did him a disservice. There were insider rumors she needed big money to pay off bigger debts. She had an expensive boy toy, and he left her for another."

"I don't think I'm wrong about the clock." Remy did not want to speculate about the name of the "boy toy."

"No, I can see that," Joan said frowning. "But a Fernier? Lara doesn't carry artifacts, she specializes in furniture."

"I know. So, you can imagine my surprise when I glanced at a display of clocks, vases and Tiffany eggs in one of her side rooms." Remy sighed. "Look, I realize I'm walking on a thin wire. I don't want to discredit the name of LaneWilson, but —"

"I'm in."

"What? What are you talking about?"

"I'm in," said Joan. "I haven't had an adventure in some years."

Remy raised her eyebrows. "Er, thank you, but I wouldn't presume to ask for your help," she said. "I would be happy with your opinion. I'm working off a gut feeling. But I'm new and disposable so this could all go south very fast. If you get involved, LaneWilson's reputation might be damaged."

It was clear Joan had stopped listening.

"Joan?"

"Grayden and I are eight years apart. We share our mother, but different fathers. Unlike most people in society, he likes to come off being a lot older. He streaks his hair with gray to make himself look more distinguished, and those glasses are fake."

"Really?"

"Really. Anyway, it was my idea to open LaneWilson ten years ago. Grayden thought it was a brilliant idea. I will say this about him, he's got a great business mind and combined with my eye for antiques, I knew we couldn't fail — and we didn't."

Remy wasn't sure where this was going. "So, what happened?"

"My divorce," she said, wiping her mouth with the napkin. "Suffice to say, the showroom ownership escaped being a line item in a settlement battle. Thanks to Grayden's good business sense, my ex couldn't lay a hand on our operations. It was pretty messy. And it meant Grayden had to be present a lot more than he wanted, and I had to be absent a lot more."

That explained all the calls for Joan.

"I can imagine your situation," Remy said. "And now?"

Joan grinned. "My divorce was final a week ago. I'm free," she said, looking once more at the time. "I'm sorry, Remy, but I need to keep an appointment with my lawyer for a different reason." She stood. "I'd like to continue our conversation, maybe at dinner when we both don't have to rush to another place." She paused. "Let me think about how I can help you. Lara is far from stupid, any approach by a LaneWilson associate will raise her suspicions. So, we've got to be careful, and quick."

"I agree," Remy said, gathering her purse. "But I have a couple of ideas myself."

CHAPTER THIRTY-FOUR

"I didn't expect to hear from you so soon," Joan said.

"I'd hoped I wouldn't need your help," said Remy.

They were sitting in the LaneWilson break room the next day. It was after closing, and both women had their feet up on adjacent chairs. Grayden was still working out of the San Francisco showroom and for once it had been a quiet day.

"You acknowledge the dealer as Lara Nielsen?" Joan said. "I told you I was in."

"Yes, you did," she said. "I had hoped the police would discover her cache of stolen goods, but by the time they got there, she'd already gotten rid of everything. Anyway, they didn't find anything, and I look like a fool."

Joan frowned. "So, are you just looking for this clock? Or, are you trying to nail Lara?"

"At first, I wanted both." Remy shrugged. "But now, if I can't retrieve the clock, I want her caught."

"Have you got a plan?"

"A rough one." Remy sat up in the chair. "Do you know where she lives?"

"Yes, but she keeps it private to most people. She has a beautiful home in Pacific Heights. What do you have in mind?" Joan said. "I don't think I'd be a good burglar."

Remy chuckled at the thought of the sophisticated Joan wearing her Jimmy Choos, as she climbed in through a window.

"No, of course not. But now the police have raided her showroom, I am for sure on her banned list."

She got a bottle of water from the refrigerator and offered one to Joan, who shook her head.

"Agreed. I would not want to get on her wrong side. She used to have an assistant, who committed an unforgivable sin in Lara's mind. Lara destroyed him. She spread rumors about his reputation, and then filed a lawsuit against him. She had the attorneys, and she won. He had no job prospects, no money, and in this town, he lost most of his friends. In the end, I heard he had a breakdown."

Remy sniffed. "What did he do to her?"

"He rejected her."

Remy raised her eyebrows. "Well, at least we know who we're dealing with."

"Remy, I understand why you might want to help a friend find her clock. But this seems more than that. What's going on?"

"You're right, and if I have the nerve to ask you to help, then you deserve to know everything."

Remy was tempted to take out the clipping and share her quest for redemption, but she wasn't ready to be that open. Instead, she spoke of her first week with Lane Wilson, her meetings with Edmund Kieffer and the call for help from Audra Dunlap.

"My lawyer thinks until the police find the real killer, I'm number one on their list," she said. "And then my friend was killed, and she may have been seeing Kieffer."

"Hmm, so you're connected to them both," Joan murmured. "Are you sure the refectory table you saw in Mendleson is the same one you saw in Olde Times?"

Remy nodded. "Refectory tables are not common, and I'm not a novice. I know a Gillows table when I see one. They're very rare."

"True enough," said Joan. "I have never seen one except in a museum. So, if I am to understand you, we are trying to locate a Fernier clock and a Gillows table, hoping Lara has not already sold, or got them out of her possession. Is that correct?"

Remy took a swallow of water.

"I'm not sure about the clock, but I have to think she still has the table."

"Unless it was stolen to meet a specific buyer's demand," Joan pointed out.

Remy winced. "I know. Why else would she risk holding such an item? It's my biggest fear."

"The last time I was in her house, it was for a reception for a French artist showing his work at San Francisco's Museum of Modern Art. She had quite a few pieces from her showroom there." Joan leaned back. "I may have an idea. She sent my ex an invitation to another reception she's hosting next week. She doesn't know of our breakup. I think I should go, what do you think?"

Remy jumped up. "Joan, take Detective Noah Larson with you," she said excited. "He's working on cold cases, and he seems to believe me. He was the one who got the police to raid Seems Like Olde Times. I have photos of the clock, and I can describe the table and its mark. If those pieces are around at all, they'd be in her home, or . . .

or they're just gone." She couldn't avoid the dejection in her voice.

"I suppose I could work with the police." Joan looked doubtful. "I did say I was ready for an adventure."

As Remy suspected, it took much longer to convince Noah Larson to participate. He was even less inclined to accompany Joan to Lara Nielsen's soiree. Remy found herself in his office once more pleading for his faith in her plan.

"Ms. Bishop, do you have any idea how much it costs, first to get a warrant and then to gather the human resources needed to search the premises of Lara Nielsen's establishment? And then to find nothing."

Sitting in his office, across the desk, Remy felt she was in front of the school principal.

"I know, Detective, and I'm sorry things didn't pan out," she pleaded. "But the same reason I asked you to search Nielsen's showroom, is the same reason why you have got to search her house."

"No, it's not justified." He turned his mouth down. "And we don't work with civilians who think they are detectives," he said, pointing at her with his pen. "If we didn't already have suspicions about Nielsen, I wouldn't be spending my time talking to you. But you don't seem to know when to quit."

"Detective Larson, if Lara Nielsen sees me, she'll know something's up. You didn't go out on the warrant," she said. "I'll be outside waiting in the car. Joan's a pro. She knows what she's doing."

"I told you, I don't like working with civilians," he said.

"But she can recognize the clock *and* the table."

He shook his head.

Remy let out an exasperated breath and went over what Joan had told her about Nielsen.

"This is crazy." Larson took a breath, ran his hand over his head and stood. "Okay, this is the deal. I'll do this on my own time — off duty," he said, pacing. "But if we don't get anything on Lara Nielsen after that night, I don't want you back in my face about this clock, or a table or for any other reason. Do we have a deal?"

"Deal."

He rubbed the back of his neck. "All right, but we do it my way," he said. "I want to meet this Joan the day before we go in, and to coordinate our visit."

"Tomorrow evening at LaneWilson," Remy rushed.

■ ■ ■ ■

Joan Lane Durbin and Detective Noah Larson eyed each other, and turned in unison to Remy for introductions.

"Joan, describe to the detective what you know of Nielsen and her special receptions," she said.

"Lara takes great pride in them. I've got an invitation, and you will be my 'plus one,' " Joan said. "They're catered affairs covered by the *Chronicle* and *San Jose Mercury News.* And there will be valets, so we don't have to worry about finding parking."

Larson shook his head. "No valets for us. We might have to leave in a hurry."

Remy protested, "But parking —"

"Ms. Bishop, if we do this, we do it my way," he said. "Ms. Durbin and —"

"Please, call me Joan. It will be very odd if you don't."

"Joan," he emphasized. "Joan and I will arrive soon after the start —"

"No," said Joan. "We should come about an hour later, when the crowd will be thickest, and we can move around without attracting notice."

Larson shook his head. "How will we

recognize the artifact if the rooms are full of people blocking the view of the items?"

"First of all, *"we"* won't be attempting to recognize the items. I will," she said. "I'll need you to act as my shield as I move around. Just follow me."

Larson looked uncomfortable in taking a back seat, but Remy knew he saw the correctness of her approach.

"What if Nielsen catches on?" Remy asked.

Joan straightened. "I don't see how she could, but at any rate she's not going to create a scene. If I were her, I'd realize my days as a free person were numbered, and I'd be looking for the nearest exit."

"That's where I come in," Larson said. "If you think we've been made, let me know at once. Depending on the circumstances, I'll take it from there."

CHAPTER THIRTY-FIVE

The dense fog made the house lights look as if they were covered in gauze. One block down and across the street, Remy could see the valets scrambling to park cars as they pulled up to the gated path. Larson had given her a swift nod as he and Joan walked past. Joan hadn't noticed her.

So here she sat. It was cold, but she had layered up with a sweater and heavy coat. They'd been in the house about a half-hour. She knew that because it was twenty-five minutes after her car heater stopped blowing warm air. People were still arriving, but intermittent now. The bulk of the invitees were inside. Muffled music wafted through the trees. Remy slid down in her seat.

She perked up soon after. A silent black and white drove up the driveway and then two others followed. The valets backed up to the fence to get out of their way as two uniforms went to the side yard, two remained on the sidewalk and two went to the door.

The pounding of her heart sounded in her ears.

This was it. Joan had made the identification.

Remy brought her window down. The music had stopped. Minutes later, people departed in a rush down the steps. The two valets appeared unnerved, and kept dropping keys as they scrambled to bring up cars. There were loud conversations as attendees walked down the street and into their self-parked vehicles. Then, about five minutes later, in the midst of the crowd, a handcuffed Lara Nielsen was led down the steps by one of the officers, followed by Larson and Joan.

Lara looked up. Remy thought it was to locate her, but the fog provided an indefinite cover, and Nielsen was hustled into the back seat of a police car.

Larson and Joan headed toward Remy. She got out and leaned against the door.

"You were right!" said Joan, giving Remy a squeeze hug. "They caught her. I can't believe how stupid some people can be. If I were receiving stolen property, do you think I would keep it in my home? No way. I didn't want to mention this, Remy, because

I knew how much you were counting on it. But I thought this was a real long shot. Boy was I wrong."

"What happened?" Remy asked, looking to Larson's smug face.

He looked up and down the street. "Why don't we go to a coffee shop and talk?" he said. "There's a pretty good one not far from here."

The Tipsy Teacup was a combination bar, coffee shop, and tea house, and for that reason the crowd was a bit eclectic. It was packed, but Larson knew the owner who brought out a small round table from a back room, and set it off to the side of the counter. He pulled chairs from other tables, and the three sat down. A server took their orders, and then left.

"So, what happened?" Remy repeated.

"I'll tell you what happened," Joan interjected, gesturing to Larson she could take it from here. "There was a real nice crowd. I'm going to have to suggest to Grayden we do something like this. It doesn't have to cost a lot either, and people —"

"Joan," said Remy. "Please."

"Right," she said. "Well, there are so many places you can put a refectory table that seats twenty, and I spotted it in the dining room. I think she was going to keep it for herself. I would. It's an exquisite piece. Anyway, I waited until I saw her leave the room, and I checked underneath for the numbered mark, and there it was."

"She didn't recognize you?" asked Remy.

"No, and she had a lot of security," Joan said. "We were checked at the door for a driver's license and the invitation. It was a little strange. But, when I saw what exclusive items she had inside, I would have been careful, too."

Remy looked at Larson, but he sat without comment allowing Joan to tell the story. "So, what happened next?"

"I started walking around looking for the clock. I knew the table wasn't going anywhere. We walked throughout the house, and I'd almost given up finding it, when I saw from across the room, one of the guests pick it up and examine it. But I wasn't certain so, as soon as she put it down, I went to see. I could tell it was a Fernier, but to make sure, I looked for the family maple leaf marking you indicated, and there it was."

Remy leaned back on the chair. "Wow."

"Wow, is right," Joan said. "Up to this point we were on a roll, but what I didn't notice, and Noah did, was Lara had spotted me sleuthing around and was becoming suspicious." With a shaking hand, Joan took a long sip from her glass of pinot noir and gestured to Larson. "Noah, can you take it from here? I think my adrenaline is abating."

Remy noticed Joan's use of Larson's first name. It sounded almost odd he should have one.

He cleared his throat. "After Joan provided the signal that the table was the one in question, I sent a pre-arranged code to the robbery division that we had spotted one of the items, and they should approach, as planned, on a 10-29." He stopped when he saw the puzzled looks on their faces. "Sorry, it's the department's code to check for stolen goods. They have a full list of items that haven't been recovered from numerous high-end thefts over the months. Anyway, I saw Nielsen's glare when Joan turned the clock upside down, and my gut told me she suspected something was up, and we needed to move fast."

He took a drink of his coffee and continued. "I confirmed with Joan that she'd identified the clock and told her to stay put. With that, I followed Nielsen who was headed upstairs. She saw me, and when I identified myself as a sheriff's detective, she tried to bolt herself inside a bedroom. I kicked the door in, and caught her trying to leave by way of a balcony. I stopped her, cuffed her, read her rights, and turned her over to my fellow officers."

For the first time since she'd known him, a broad smile crossed his face.

"It was a good bust," he said.

CHAPTER THIRTY-SIX

Remy called Audra first thing in the morning and told her they had found the Dunlap clock and the Kieffer table.

"Audra, your search is over," she said, after recounting the night's events. "However, it may be some time before the clock can be returned to you since it's evidence for the prosecution."

"But, at least, I'll have it back," the woman exclaimed. "Remy, thank you so much, but I wonder . . . I wonder if it's really mine. I mean, maybe no one stole it. Martin had changed. He wasn't the son I once knew. I've been thinking, maybe he did sell it. All these older women . . . he . . . I mean, maybe he had to sell it to Nielsen to get money."

"I've thought about that, too," she said. "But if Nielsen had a legitimate claim she would have said so. It would have been the quickest way to get rid of me. No, Nielsen felt used by your son, and I think she took the clock as compensation, or revenge."

Audra was silent for a moment. "The house goes on the market this week," she said. "I can't thank you enough, Remy. I wish I could do something to show you how thankful I am, but know you'll always have a friend in me. I hope your troubles work themselves out."

Me, too.

CHAPTER THIRTY-SEVEN

Remy tapped in Paul's number. She'd promised him she would let him know if she was going to speak with the sheriff. He was getting more agitated the longer the investigation dragged on, but he should be pleased with the Nielsen arrest. She had weighed the option of telling him about her findings at the Crandall house, but she could hear his protestations and it wasn't worth it. She would reserve the story for the sheriff.

"What do you mean you're off the hook?" Paul questioned.

Remy chuckled. "I don't think you understood me," she said. "They have the Crandall table. It means I was telling the truth. I did not kill Edmund Kieffer. My story holds up."

"That's not what it means at all. One conclusion does not lead to the other. You're still a suspect because of your motive to kill

Melanie Chase. I think it's a weak one, but you're not in the clear until they say you are," he said with gruffness. "Look, we need to meet before you see the sheriff. They can wait."

"I don't understand," Remy said annoyed. "What do you see that I don't?"

"I can't talk now. Can we meet after you get off work?"

"I'll be home after six."

Remy wasn't going to let Paul's warning bring her down, but it did.

A call to Detective Larson underscored there would be no problem meeting the next day. They were still logging all the stolen items discovered in Lara Nielsen's home.

"It was a ring," Larson said. "Most of the stuff came from southern California burglaries. They could fence goods easier up north without as much detection. We don't have final proof, but without a doubt Kieffer was in the middle of it. So far, Nielsen refuses to give up her partners. Still I have a feeling once it sinks in she's going away for a long time, she won't be so loyal."

"That's good to hear," Remy said, then cleared her throat. "Detective Larson, since you found the Kieffer table, doesn't it mean I'm no longer a suspect? I mean my story checks out."

"Yes and no. If we could capture the ring, then we would have all the parties, but . . . but as it is, there are still some unanswered questions," he said. "As far as I'm concerned, I think you're in the clear, but Tuft . . . well, Tuft is not quite ready to release you from the suspect list, yet."

"Yet," Remy repeated.

Maybe Paul was right.

"You're early," Remy said dropping grocery sacks onto the kitchen counter.

Paul entered behind her, shutting the door. "I hope you don't mind," he said. "My last appointment finished earlier than planned, and I didn't want to sit in the car for forty-five minutes."

He took a seat in the overstuffed chair facing the sofa.

"No, it's fine. But you enter at your own risk. Don't look at the dust. I'm going to put my things down," Remy called out heading for her bedroom. "There's a beer in the refrigerator."

Remy returned and flopped down on the sofa. "You didn't want the beer?" she asked, looking at Paul's empty hands.

"Maybe next time, I have to get some work done this evening."

"I'm ready to talk. Let's get this conversation over with. Why don't you want me to be upfront with the sheriff's office?"

"I know you think because of your background you're up to date with law enforcement procedure and practice, but until they capture the real murderer you will stay a person of interest."

"I get that feeling."

Paul leaned over. "Why?"

She told him about her conversation with Larson.

"See, that's what I mean."

Remy frowned. "What are you talking about? Why would I lead the police to Nielsen if we were conspirators?" she said. "Anyway, I'm sure that's what they're discussing now. I'm not going to sit around. I'm working on a couple of strong leads."

"Oh, that's just great. But, I'm not sorry you heard how they think of you and your status. Tuft needs an arrest." He stood. "I think I'll have that beer. Work can wait a few minutes." He went to the refrigerator.

She spoke over her shoulder. "So, what do I do?"

"First, did Larson give you any idea how they're looking at this?" He took a swallow from a bottle. "Where are they in their investigation?"

"Just what we already knew." She

shrugged. "He confirmed Tuft was still in charge of the Kieffer murder. They combined the Kieffer and Chase investigations under one detective because of Melanie's connection to Kieffer."

"Well, that's one thing we can get an answer to when we go there tomorrow," he said. "You'll just be dealing with Tuft, and he's not a friendly."

"I know."

Paul was quiet with thought.

"How's your state of mind?" he asked.

"Well, of course, I'm a bit worried, because I know what it's like to be wrongly accused and punished." She paused. "But I'm more irritated than anything else."

"I think you should play on their sympathy. Tell them you can't sleep or eat," he said. "Tell them you're feeling depressed and the pressure is becoming too much."

Remy frowned. "I don't feel that way at all," she said. "Besides, I don't think either would care how I felt about things one way or the other."

"Would you listen to me for once?" His voice rose. "This isn't my first rodeo; this is why you need me as your attorney. If you show your human side, they may think you're an improbable murderer. If you seem too self-reliant or indifferent, that will fit their profile."

She peered at him, and then deliberately spoke in a low tone to offset his. "Paul, I'm not sure I can do what you ask. You want me to dumb it down." She raised her hand when he moved to speak and then continued, "I keep remembering there is a real killer out there, and I will do what I have to do to get across my sincerity."

"That's all I ask."

For once, after a busy day at the showroom, Remy was able to close the store and meet Paul at the sheriff's office without any additional angst. With his warning words in her ear, she realized her visits were becoming an all too regular occurrence when the security officer recognized her with a greeting.

In the interview room, Tuft clicked his pen on and off while they waited for Larson to return from a phone call. Remy's gut told her his silence was deliberate; he was waiting for them to speak first, to be uncomfortable with the quiet. She met his stare with calm.

"So, Detective, how are things with the investigation?" Paul said, drumming his fingers.

"We're making progress."

"There are all kinds of progress." Paul gave a self-conscious chuckle. "Have you gotten any more information on Edmund Kieffer? Did he know Nielsen?"

"I think those answers would best wait until Detective Larson returns," Tuft responded. "Your client is here to sign a statement. I'm included because her account may contain information that could be useful to another case where she's a person of interest."

Remy frowned and bit her tongue. She refused to take Tuft's bait by speaking.

Paul cleared his throat. "Person of interest does that —"

The door opened, and Larson swept in, dumping a folder on the table. "Sorry, that call took a lot longer than I anticipated," he said. "Where are we?"

"We," Tuft emphasized. "*We* thought it best to wait for you. Is that Ms. Bishop's statement?" He pointed to the folder.

"Yes," he said, taking a sheet of paper out of the folder. "Read it, and if you . . . and your lawyer say it's complete you can sign it now."

Remy reached across the table. Paul edged closer to read over her shoulder. It was complete. She glanced up to Larson.

"I'm ready to sign."

"My client may sign," Paul added.

Remy saw the look exchange between Larson and Tuft.

"Good," Larson said, passing a pen. "Sign and I'll give you a copy before you leave."

"Before we go, I've got to say this." She set her shoulders. "Detectives, I've done everything I can to cooperate in the Kieffer murder as well as Melanie's murder. I've answered all your questions, gone over the site with you, shared what I know, and . . . and even helped you solve another crime."

She looked at Paul, who gestured go-ahead, and then stared at the detectives sitting across from her.

"What do you want from me?" she said. "I don't want to be a person of interest. It's . . . it's making me crazy."

Tuft expression held blatant condescension. "We're sorry to cause you distress, Ms. Bishop but we have a job to do, and right now you're still suspect in the Chase murder."

Larson jumped in.

"Ms. Bishop, we appreciate the leads you provided to arrest Lara Nielsen. We uncovered a stolen goods ring that has plagued us for years. In fact, there's another reason why I'm here today."

Remy was curious. "Yes?"

"Lara Nielsen was arraigned yesterday," Larson said. "She's being held, for now, without bail pending a hearing, but she's made an interesting allegation. She left us with a link between Kieffer and Chase. Kieffer told Lara Nielsen your friend Melanie had a gambling problem. He met her at the casino where she worked, dated her off and on. Nielsen thinks Chase referred him to your showroom. Maybe it was his child she was carrying. The lab is going to run tests."

Both Remy and Paul exchanged wary looks.

Tuft leaned forward. "We know you are anxious to be eliminated as a suspect in one, maybe two, murders," he said. "But, one thing doesn't clear with me: why you? Why did Kieffer insist on having you do his appraisal? Do you have you an answer for that one?"

Remy froze.

"Hold it a minute, Detective," Paul jumped in. "I'm going to recommend my client not answer any more questions, since you just stated she's a prime suspect in two murders." He hit the table with his fist. "We came down here in an open and above-board way to continue to help any way we could. She is going crazy with worry and depression, but she told you everything she knows. She may appear composed, but you don't see her like I do."

"Paul —" Remy put her hand on his sleeve.

He shook it off. "No, I'm tired of seeing you beat down by these guys and still try to answer their endless questions. And —"

"Mr. Scott, it is up to your client if she wants to talk to us," Tuft said evenly. "But I'm not going to leave any questions unanswered in a murder case."

"Excuse me, I'm the one on the line," Remy raised her voice to catch their attention, and then turned to Larson. "Let me answer your question Detective. I don't know why Kieffer sought me. I've given this a lot of thought, and because I agree it does seem like he chose me. Maybe Melanie did refer him. When I —"

"Don't say another word." Paul stood. "We're leaving. Remy and I need to talk before she says something unintentional and damaging. She's not been herself since all this happened."

Remy frowned. "Paul, I'm —"

"No," he said. "Nothing more, we're out of here."

The detectives once again exchanged looks.

"You know how to get in touch with us," Larson said.

Paul gripped her elbow and led her out the door. She glanced back to the detectives who huddled in conversation.

She pulled her arm back. "Was that necessary?"

Paul gestured for her silence until they were outside. He unlocked the car door.

"You don't get it, do you?" he said angry, pulling into traffic.

Remy's lips formed a thin line. "Oh, I get it," she said, checking her phone. "I don't think I'm the best client for you, Paul. I think I should go forward on my own." She stared straight out the windshield.

He smiled. "Hey, don't get upset. I may have overreacted trying to protect you. Besides, you already tried to fire me once. Look, why don't I take you home and you get some rest. This whole thing would put anyone on edge. We'll talk strategy tomorrow."

"I don't think so. Just send me your final bill."

They said nothing for the next five minutes as he drove.

"Remy, I —"

"Paul, I don't want us to end on a bad note," Remy said. "I appreciate all your advice and all you've done. But I think it's best for me if I go with my own instincts."

"That so?" he muttered. "All right, I have to admit I liked having your case to work on, and I do understand." He pulled up in front of her condo. "Tell you what; let's share a glass of wine to toast the resolution of your case. I have no worries you will come out victorious. I have a bottle of Argentinian Malbec at home, waiting for a good reason to toast, and I can't think of a better one."

"Paul, that's sweet, but I was thinking of returning to the department, or meeting with the chief, maybe I'll tell Tuft some of my own theories."

He tapped his head on the steering wheel.

"Humor me on this one. Wait until tomorrow morning when you've had a chance to sleep on it," he said. "It's late in the day; I bet they've already gone home."

"It seems you're always putting me off a day," she said. "I'm sorry, Paul, but I don't want you to represent me anymore."

"I wished you would've trusted me on this." He said with exasperation.

She patted his shoulder. "It's me, not you," she said, trying to get him to smile. "Now, tell me the truth. Why it was so important to you that I remain a client,"

Remy asked.

He frowned.

"I don't need . . . it's not . . . I mean I don't. . . ." Paul's words stumbled and stopped. "All right, I'll be honest with you since you've fired me for the last time," he said, looking straight ahead out the windshield. "You're what my firm calls a 'high profile' case. To keep it simple, if I can win your murder case at trial, I'll make partner."

"Oh." She slammed back on the seat. "You too, Paul, another user? I must have a sign on my forehead."

Paul took off his glasses and wiped the lens on a tissue.

"I know, I'm fired for real this time. You're right, you don't need me. I wouldn't say this to all my clients, but you've already punched holes in their case. It would have been a no-brainer to clear you." He looked over at her. "So, I guess this is goodbye, Remy Bishop."

"Goodbye, Paul. And don't bother sending a bill."

CHAPTER THIRTY-EIGHT

Call it dogged determination, or plain stupidity. Remy had to revisit the Crandall house. She wanted to take her time and see the house through the eyes of a forensic specialist. She pushed aside thoughts that she could be the next victim. She was not reckless, and she took care to keep checking her rearview mirror.

Her visit before had raised more questions in her mind. And, since Nielsen's arrest she had a feeling that she was close to being completely exonerated. If she could clear up the Kieffer murder, then any connection to Melanie Chase would also be suspect. Of course, if caught, she'd have no defense to her presence at a recent crime scene — supposedly looking for evidence. She knew better. The clipping in her wallet was a constant reminder.

There was a big difference between a misdemeanor and a felony. One was jail, and the other was prison.

The morning was once again cloaked in fog. She parked to the side of the house in front of the four-car garage. Over to her right was a shed and just outside the door, leaned a rake. It was possible it was used to disguise tracks. Crime scene tape criss-crossed the door. She slipped on her latex gloves. The remains of police presence were evident, with fingerprint powder on the latch and door edge. She peered in the side window. There, plywood floors were covered with dust and dirt. But it was empty; nothing had been stored there for some time. Kieffer had said they had a caretaker; it was another lie.

She walked to the back of the shed. There was a generous roadway leading off into the trees and then an open field. The start of the roadway was covered by brush and leaves, not enough to be completely hidden, but tucked away from casual sight. The police would not have missed it.

The exit route for removing the goods inside the house.

Remy took pictures with her phone, and then walked to the rear of the house which was stark and unimpressive. The exterior was stucco and, while there was a small patio and porch leading off to a winding path and the remnants of an English garden, it was clear the former residents spent little time outdoors. She bent and picked up a handful of gravel and placed it in one of the several quart-sized plastic bags she'd shoved into her purse that morning. The rear entrance was a Dutch door. She took a picture of the scuff marks and what appeared to be dark blue streaks of color spread on the lower half of the door. She'd have to think about what it meant.

The wide steps were made of redwood, leading up to a small porch. At the foot of the steps her gaze caught the glint of grey metal through the leaves of a small shrub nestled against the foundation. It was a water meter, and fastened to the meter was a lock box.

She smiled.

The padlock-shaped box was the type that real estate agents attach somewhere to a house that is on the market. The digital device held the house keys to allow communal access for real estate agents to show the house. Stored in the box, the key, and therefore the house would remain secure. The agent would punch in an identification code take out the key during the showing, and then return it at the end, snapping the box shut. The digital record would also give the listing agent the number and name of the agents who came to show the house, making it a resource for follow-up.

In this case, whoever had the listing on the Crandall house had left the keys in the box to accommodate buyers' agents. Now, after bending down, and brushing aside the branches, Remy could see the box hung open and the key was gone.

To keep peace, and to ensure her family didn't take it upon themselves to "help" her, she had taken advantage of the time to visit for dinner.

"Dad, can you identify the company a lock box belongs to?" Remy asked.

"Sure, just check the listing on the house address," Mitch Bishop said. "The box might be registered with the Multiple Listing Service, too. You could get more complete information from them. Why?"

Remy tried to sound as nonchalant as she could.

"Out of curiosity, I noticed a lock box at a house the other day. It was open with no key, maybe it was left behind?"

"I doubt it. Those boxes are expensive. An agent would claim it as soon as the listing expired or was cancelled." Mitch said. "Where was this house?"

"I was doing a bunch of errands; I think it was in the city. Anyway, it's not important."

"You're not eating," Belinda Bishop said, pushing a bowl of potatoes toward her daughter.

Remy picked up her fork and stabbed at the meatloaf on her plate. "Mom, I assure you I'm just not hungry. The dinner is delicious."

"Remy," her mother said. "You're making me nervous. What have you got on your mind?"

Her father looked up. "Is the attorney still working out? He hasn't sent me a bill yet."

"It will be his first and last bill," her mother interjected. "She's innocent. The police don't think she did those murders anymore. Right, Remy?"

"They haven't told her that," her father said. "Until they do, she's got to play it safe and assume the tide could change at any time and —"

"Hey, I'm over here. I can hear you," Remy said. "I liked Paul. But —"

"Liked?" her father questioned. "What happened to him?"

"Dad, I told him I didn't need his services anymore." She didn't see the need to go into Paul's career ladder plan. "He agreed. We parted amicable."

Belinda got up and put her arm around her daughter's shoulders. Although, she was a couple of inches shorter and Remy always wondered how her mother always managed to make her feel as if she was looking down on her. "This thing you have on your mind, is it about your friend, Melanie? Why did you fall out?"

Remy sighed and shook her head. "Now that she's gone it seems trivial. She borrowed money I didn't have to give, and she didn't pay me back when she said she would."

"Oh," her mother said, leaving unsaid her: " 'I told you so.' "

"Remy," her father said. "We want to be here for you. You're not a child, but . . . but you have to understand seeing your name in the paper like that, well, no parent wants to have their child in trouble."

Of course, she understood.

"Dad, Mom, I'm so sorry you have to defend me among your friends. I never thought I would be considered a suspect in not one, but two murders," she said.

She didn't miss the look that passed between her parents. But her father changed the subject and the next hour went fast, and Remy found herself surprised that she was able to put her situation aside and enjoy her parents' company. Her mother served her comfort desert of peach cobbler, and her father kept her laughing with anecdotes of showing open houses.

She was returning the last plate to the kitchen sink when she felt her mother's look of concern.

"What? What's the matter, Mom?"

"You don't fool me, Remy Loh Bishop," she said, her finger pointing at her daughter. "I can't believe I'm sounding like my own mother, something I said I would never do, but I can't stop myself."

Remy put her towel down and leaned against the sink. "What are you trying to say?"

"I know there's something wrong, very wrong. And I know you're trying to protect us from worry, but it makes us worry more." She put her hand on Remy's shoulder. "But if you are in danger or bad trouble, I'll —"

"Mom, please." Remy begged. "There is no danger, there is no bad trouble. But I do need to make a stop before I go home, so don't call me every fifteen minutes to see if I arrived safe. I have a bit of research to do."

"Fine. You call me." Her mother sniffed in affront and stepped back. "Go, but visit with your father for a few minutes before you leave. He worries the most about you." She had a stern look. "Call more often. If we don't hear from you — well, you don't want to know what we will do if left to our own imaginations and devices."

Remy laughed, and her mother laughed with her.

Then like a light switch, her mother's face turned serious. "I'm not kidding."

She plugged in the address from the business card Kieffer had handed her into the GPS. Thirty minutes later she entered The Best of Wine Bar, which was located about five miles from Stanford University, in a popular upscale commercial district. Happy hour was almost over, and the patrons had drifted into couples or huddled in companionable clusters along the huge horseshoe shaped bar. Remy smiled at an approaching young female.

"Here's our pour list," the hostess said, opening up a navy blue and silver menu and putting it in front of her. "You still have a few minutes of happy hour."

Remy gazed through the many pages. Her eyes widened at the prices.

"Do you have any specials?"

"We have a modest Barbera that's pretty good. Would you like a taste to see if you like it?" the server offered.

"Sure, that would be fine."

Moments later she took a large sip from a generous sample. She nodded at the server.

"This is pretty good. I'll have a glass."

"It's one of our customers' favorites." She started to move away.

"Wait." Remy stopped her. "What's your name?"

"Nadia."

"Nadia, I'm looking for a friend who used to come here," Remy said, then shook her head when she saw Nadia's knowing expression. "No, not *that* kind of friend. I should have said I'm looking to locate someone for a friend."

The server paused and gestured for her to go on.

Remy pulled a newspaper picture out of her purse. "Did this guy come in here?"

Nadia looked down at the picture and frowned. "Look, we respect our customers' privacy. Who are you? Are you law enforcement?"

"No, I'm not a cop, but a friend of mine is in trouble, and this guy might be able to help."

"I don't know how to tell you this, but he's dead."

Remy sagged onto the stool; she'd been

hoping news of Kieffer's murder had not travelled this far.

"Yeah, I know." Remy ran her hand through her hair. "I wanted to find where he used to hang out so I could locate any of his friends."

"I thought you said *you* were helping his friend."

Remy looked her in the eyes. "She's dead, too."

"Oh."

A voice called out to her from the cash register.

"Sorry, I've got to get back to work." Nadia turned to leave and then turned back. "He used to come here with one of the owners. Check the pictures on the wall leading to the restrooms."

Remy hurried her thanks, and gulped down the glass of wine. Leaving extra money under her glass, she stood and headed for the narrow hallway to the left of the bar. Along its walls was a gallery of pictures. Famous faces with bold signatures, and some not so famous standing with what must be the owners. Remy squinted, trying to identify Edmund Kieffer, while side-stepping the occasional visitor to the bathroom. At one picture, she closed her eyes and shook her head.

It was him.

Kieffer was standing in a group with smiling men and women holding a toast almost in the same spot at the table where she'd just sat. But what caused her to catch her breath was the figure that leaned into the shot holding what looked like a bottle of champagne.

CHAPTER THIRTY-NINE

Moving the menu aside, she slipped the folded newspaper clipping into her tote bag. She glanced at her phone, and when she looked up her companion was approaching the table.

"Ms. Bishop, I'm still not sure why you're so secretive and why we had to meet outside of the department," Noah Larson said, slipping into the chair. "I want to add my congratulations to all the others you've gotten. I'm sorry if we seemed a bit stiff and bureaucratic the other day. Your attorney tends to put us on guard. Tuft hasn't stopped smiling and the DA is happy to take all the credit. There are a couple of loose ends. We're still trying to work out who tipped Nielsen off the first time about the search of her showroom."

Remy grinned with vindication.

"Thank you, for saying this," she said. "I think I might be able to help you with one of those loose ends.

He nodded for her to speak.

"Detective did your people ever take note of the lock box on the water meter at the rear of the Crandall house? It could be a loose end."

"Lock box, what are you talking about?" he said exasperated. He squinted. "Miss Bishop, you first told us that you had only seen the front of the house, are you now changing your story?"

She raised her hands in front of her in protest. "Not at all, Detective, I'm trying to clear my name."

"Then, may I ask how you know about a real estate lock box secured to a meter at the back of a crime scene house?"

"Well, I admit to going to the Crandall house just to see it from a forensic point of view. Besides, the rear yard wasn't cordoned off with crime scene tape. My father's in real estate so I know how a lock box works.

"In addition to the access code, an agent has to put in an identification code or phone number. That box would have the information on the person who put it there and accessed it last," she said.

His silence confirmed he was considering the implication of her words.

"It may be that you have stumbled on new

evidence," he acknowledged. "Anything else?"

Remy looked past him, and then said, "I gave my attorney a piece of information to pass on to you, but he didn't think much of it and neglected to." She moistened her lips. "When I met Edmund Kieffer, he scribbled his name on another's business card. Last night, I followed up with the business card and discovered a photograph of Kieffer and a group of people who looked pretty chummy." She paused.

Larson looked at her in disbelief. "Go on."

"I recognized one face, a real estate agent named Jay Ross."

Larson insisted that they continue their discussion at the sheriff's department. He held back to take out his phone and give orders sending deputies out to The Best of Wine Bar. Remy noticed he chose to meet in a small conference room and not one for interviews.

"The ring was well organized," Larson said. "Nielsen already gave up Victor Camden and Martin Dunlap. You're right. Dunlap would ID the items worth stealing and Camden would set up the new buyers. Kieffer's job was to find a location to house the goods and arrange for deliveries."

"Victor?" Remy shook her head with sadness. "Camden's Showroom taught me everything I know."

"You know that flyer you found on your first trip to the Crandall House?" Larson asked. "If you had opened it up you would have seen that it belonged to Victor Camden. We found it in one of the vases we confiscated."

Remy slowly nodded her head, remembering seeing the bright flyers on Cordelia's desk and trying to remember where she'd seen them before.

"Jay Ross was the guy in the picture with Edmund Kieffer. I think they might have worked together with warehousing the stolen antiques," she said. "He was also at Melanie's funeral."

Larson could not hold back his surprise. Over the next minutes he took notes as Remy went through her updates.

"I have to tell you, Ms. Bishop, I'm of two minds. I am very impressed with your findings, but I'm also irritated because you can't seem to stop playing amateur detective. You are one remarkable lady."

Remy beamed, and then her smile disappeared.

"Now, Detective, I need your help," She said. "I think I might have a lead that could result in the capture of Sandra Lennox's killer."

Larson glanced around the office, his lips forming a thin line. He made a sympathetic face.

"Now I know why you don't like meeting in the department. You're still labeled as the tech who lost the case by tampering with evidence."

"I know what law enforcement thinks of me," she admitted. "And don't forget, I'm on record as being professionally incompetent. Yes, I have a motive; I want to clear my name."

"And you know I close cold cases."

Remy shook her head. "I did not contaminate the Lennox evidence." She clasped her hands in front of her. "I loved my job too much to not take it serious. I was set up by someone who worked there, too, someone who had access to the Lennox file and to me. Someone who killed Sandra Lennox or was convinced to cover for her killer. It took me a while to think through the reason, but I figured it out at last."

Larson said nothing for a moment but peered at her with a steady gaze. Finally, he tilted his head in acknowledgment.

"Go ahead, you've got my attention."

"You see, when I got the evidence sample

there was the knife — undamaged. Other evidence, clothing, hairs, whatever, went to other techs. We do that when it's an expedited analysis. The knife was intact as the officer, who bagged it at the scene, said it was. I did not drop the knife and cause the tip to break off. What sense does that make? Do you know how hard I'd have to drop that knife, and from what distance? It's long odds at best, and totally unlikely."

Larson straightened. "The supervising detective said you put the now contaminated tip in a separate bag, did the blood analysis and signed off. It appeared as if you hoped the officer would never have to verify the forensic evidence. And —"

"Sorry to interrupt, but I'm not crazy, and that's just nuts. Don't you think we know how important our analysis is to get a murder conviction? The suspected murder weapon would be the first thing they would ask an officer on the scene to identify."

He rocked back and forth in his chair. "Okay, okay, keep going. Tell me what you think happened. You said you tested and signed off on an intact knife. Then what?"

"Someone *did* tamper with the evidence." She moistened her lips. "Someone took my badge to use my barcode, that's how I'm identified in the database and the chain of custody. That someone gained access to the evidence storage, broke the tip, whether by accident or deliberate. They wrote up another evidence bag and completed a chain of custody entry, used my badge, forged my signature and returned everything to the Lennox file in storage."

"Wow, talk about unlikely, how probable is that?"

"Not very, but if you know our system, and you've got a lot at stake . . . you'd only have to wait for the right time."

"What you're saying is one of your fellow workers would have had to have the access needed to do that much damage." Larson looked deep in thought. "If you're right, there was a conspiracy to kill Sandra Lennox."

"Or, the conspiracy was in the cover up."

"All right, who do you think the someone is who tampered with the evidence?"

"I think it was my false best friend, Melanie Chase."

"Melanie Chase." Noah Larson frowned. "She was interviewed along with everyone else in your section. She defended you."

"Well, if anyone knew I was innocent, it would be her," Remy retorted. "She either killed Sandra Lennox or knew who did. I think more likely the later. I think she knew the real killer and had extorted money in exchange for contaminating the evidence and framing me. She tried to get money from him for her abortion, maybe he wouldn't pay up, or she didn't want him to know about the baby. At any rate, she didn't get what she needed and was forced to borrow money from me."

"She tracked down the Lennox killer and kept quiet about it?" He raised his eyebrows. He went back to rocking. "I don't buy it. I've worked on this case for seven months; the killer's identity is not obvious. She'd have to have access to law enforcement databases, too."

"Okay, I admit there's a timing issue I haven't worked out. But somehow Melanie found out the identity of the killer," she conceded. "It was Melanie who sent Kieffer to me. I think she must have sent him my way to give me business in my new job." She paused. "I guess she didn't hate me. But she didn't know he had enemies who wanted him dead, sooner rather than later."

With that Larson made more notes. Finishing, he said, "Look, I need to follow up on the Chase connection to Lennox. If Kieffer knew Lennox *and* Chase, then we've got a new ball game. How can I reach you?"

"Wait. I need your help." Remy took out a

file with several pages. "I've thought about the Lennox case a lot." She pointed to a sheet of paper. "First, if I could get back into the lab and check my case files and the tests run on that second bag of evidence — the knife tip. It's a long-shot, but I bet my prints aren't on it. They used my signature on the custody form to condemn me. The district attorney wanted me punished as an example, and I didn't blame him. But I was overwhelmed, and I didn't think to make sure there were prints."

"Okay, I heard you out. But I can tell you now, that's not going to happen," he said with finality. "Haven't you been affected enough? No DA is going to give you access to a forensic lab with a tampering charge handing over your head."

"It's not just about me." Remy looked up to the ceiling. "I'm trying to close a cold case and maybe find a killer."

"I'm sorry, but it's a non-starter," he said. "We'll continue our informal partnership as long as I can, but don't be surprised if I can't always reciprocate." He tapped his pad. "However, I will check to see if Melanie Chase's prints are on the evidence bags."

"I don't think you'll find her prints. If she were framing me, she would have used gloves, but it gives my argument some plausibility. There should be at least some prints on them. It shouldn't be clean of all prints. I wouldn't have taken my prints off my own sample and still filled out a form."

Larson wrote on his pad.

"You may have helped us here, Ms. Bishop. We'll wrap up the Kieffer and Chase murders first. It may be a while, but I promise you that the Lennox cold case will be my next priority." He made a notation. "I'm almost afraid to ask again, but anything else?"

She sighed. "No, Detective I'm done."

CHAPTER FORTY

Andy slid the folder across the cafe table. He'd agreed to meet Remy for lunch midway distance between their jobs.

He took a deep breath. "From what I could find out, Sandra Lennox's file was assigned to you with a chain of custody form attached. See, here, it's your barcode. You accepted the transfer." He pulled a sheet out of a folder.

"I did so many of these samples a day, to be honest I didn't, and I still don't remember the Lennox file." Remy took a sip of iced tea and opened the folder. "When I conducted the serology tests, I checked blood samples on just one evidence item — a single, unbroken, knife." She looked at the paper. "Andy, I swear there was no second bag, there was no knife tip. That's a rookie mistake."

He held up his hand. "Hey, I believe you." He leaned in and lowered his voice. "But I don't know how you can prove a negative."

Remy rubbed her forehead, "You saw both bags?"

"No, I don't have the access. But I saw copies of both custody forms." He looked away from her crestfallen face.

"Don't feel bad," she said. "I saw those copies, too. That's what they used to throw in my face in order to get rid of me." She took another sip, and shook her head. "I don't get it. I admit that's my signature, such as it is, my scribble."

"I wouldn't keep harping on this case. You've got a new job and you're going to be successful," Andy said in a lowered voice.

"What?"

"You're taking this too hard. You should move on."

She took a deep breath and shook her head. "I need to get back in to see the actual evidence bags."

"Are you crazy?" Andy shook his head. "I told you, you weren't thinking with a clear head. You're talking about a felony."

Remy's jaw tightened in frustration.

"I don't know what else to do. Nobody else knows how *I* do things. I know what I'm looking for." She poked at her own chest. "I need to test the bags and forms, maybe. . . ." She paused to think.

"What?"

"Unless I could see my. . . ." Her face turned blank. "I won't tell you what I'm planning. Deniability is your best bet."

Andy frowned. "My best bet for what?"

"For the lie detector test you'll be given if this doesn't go my way."

"You want to find your paperwork on the Lennox murder, don't you?"

"Andy, trust me on this. You can't afford to lose your job."

He gave her a small smile. "You're going to break into the lab, aren't you?" He nodded in the affirmative to his own question. "You're going to break in and examine the evidence bags." He shook his head. "I can tell you're not going to give up. What the hell, all right I'll get you in," he said. "You can't say I didn't try to discourage you."

Remy gave him a quick hug. "Andy, you are the best. I will never forget this."

He sighed. "We'll do it Sunday."

Remy hadn't been in the lab for over a year. It hadn't changed. Typical of a weekend, the parking lot was empty and the surrounding neighborhood, quiet. Andy entered the building's current access code and then slid in his own ID tag. It wasn't unusual for employees to come in on a weekend to catch up on work. His presence wouldn't be questioned.

Entering the long hallway that divided the firearm testing labs from the forensic section, she realized how much she missed the smell. Subtle chemical odors mixed with unnamed scents. She took a deep breath and closed her eyes.

"Is it bringing back memories?"

She nodded. She was home.

Although, this time "home" was full of potential danger. With Andy's nod of approval, she pulled a pair of latex gloves out of her pocket and slipped them on, followed by disposable shoe covers out of her other pocket. She couldn't take a chance of being found out. If she went down, she'd jeopardize Andy's career. He'd insisted on helping her, but she wasn't going to mess his life up like hers.

Pretty much nothing had changed since her employment. They entered through the property manager's office and made their way past the cubicles to the evidence file room. Andy punched in another code.

With a small beep the door opened.

Remy's heart thumped in her chest. Following Andy, from habit she knew the file room, and she soundlessly closed the door behind them. He flipped on the lights.

"You're here now, I hope you're happy."

Remy ran her fingers along the tabbed folders on the ceiling-high row of shelves.

"I'm not sure if happy is the word I'd use," she said, searching the boxes of files, making her way to the farthest corner before turning up the next aisle.

She'd been through these files many times. She looked up to see Andy standing by the door, watching her.

"I wish you had let this go," he said.

"I'm here now. I'm going as fast as I can."

She rose from her crouched position, and went to him.

"Andy, thank you so much for helping me." Remy gave him a peck on the cheek.

He had slipped on similar gloves and a lab coat. He stood. "I can't let you bring me down."

"I won't." Remy wrinkled her forehead. "I told you I'll take the blame."

"Too late, things have gone too far." He ran his fingers through his hair. "I didn't want to go along with her."

She frowned and stepped back. Like the lights in the room, the light came on in her head.

He noticed.

"She found out, Remy, she knew about Sandra." Andy ran his gloved hand over his head. "Melanie was working on the fibers from the case. She could see in the scene photos that Sandra and I had the same tattoo. She confronted me. She bled me dry. I didn't have any more money. My parents . . . she knew I would do anything . . . *anything* to. . . . I didn't want to go to jail."

It took Remy just seconds to make sense of Andy's scattered explanation.

"It was you. You killed Sandra Lennox," Remy said in disbelief.

Andy's lowered his head and rubbed the nape of his neck.

"It just happened, I didn't plan it," he insisted. "We'd been going out for months. She said she loved me. Then, all of a sudden, she wanted to see other people. Translate: not me. I loved her." He looked away. "It was an accident."

Remy doubted a jury would go along with multiple stab wounds as an accident.

"And how did I get dragged into all this?"

"Melanie had your database code. She knew where you kept it. She arranged the evidence, and then entered your code."

She shook her head.

"You and Melanie conspired to ruin my life to save your own criminal butts."

Andy seemed to stand taller. "We didn't think you'd get fired. Melanie thought they might suspend you, but not let you go."

She could feel the adrenaline pumping through her system. Her mind worked fast. Her phone was in her back pocket, and she edged backwards toward the shelf to cover her movement.

"But they did fire me, Andy," she said. "And you two — my two so-called friends, let it happen. Melanie must have thought she wouldn't be able to own up to it and get money from you."

"You should have let it go. It was just a job, Remy." Andy shook his head. "You have a family that could support you, Melanie and I didn't. But, no, you had to keep at it. It was all about you." His voice took on an edge. "When you went to appraiser school, I hoped you'd move on. Melanie kept saying you would. She even sent you her old boyfriend to give you a big contract to distract you. But, no, you had to keep at it."

He took a step toward her, and she stiffened.

"Melanie wanted money. Was . . . was it your baby?"

His eyes grew large. "A baby? No, it wasn't my baby. From me, she just wanted cash." He rubbed his forehead with the back of his hand and then stared through her. "Toward the end, she said she needed more money, but she knew I didn't have any more. Didn't make a difference, she wanted additional money from each of my pay-checks to keep quiet about Lennox."

Remy said nothing as her thoughts swirled with consequences.

"It got out of hand, Remy. Things got away from me, I couldn't stop. . . ."

Remy felt a chill. "Andy, why did you come here with me? You know they can trace you here. You used your access number to get in. Why did . . ." her words drifted.

She knew.

He gave a slow grin. "That's right, I came to work on the weekend." He took a deep breath. "You know, it came to me that in a way you were using me, too. You didn't care I could lose my job, or that my parents would be harmed. You just wanted to prove your innocence."

He lifted his shirt and brought out a .32 caliber revolver from the waist of his pants and pointed it at her. Remy backed further into the shelves.

Everyone had a gun but her.

"I'm so sorry." His voice shook, but his hand was steady.

"Andy, what are you thinking? What are you going to do?" Remy hurried. "I'd never use you. If I get caught, I'll say I stole your number. I would never leave you hanging."

"Interesting use of words," he said.

He gripped her arm and motioned for her to go out into the larger room. Then he grabbed her wrist to stop her from going further than the first desk.

"Oh, I should tell you that this little trip of yours was a waste of time. It isn't there anymore, you know," he said.

"What are you talking about?"

"I destroyed the evidence bag. I didn't think I had left anything to chance, until you told me what I had overlooked. You were right; there weren't any prints on the second bag. Not yours, not mine and not Melanie's. I wore gloves. I forgot someone's prints should be on the bag. An evidence bag without any fingerprints, was evidence in itself," he mused. "Anyway, thanks for the heads up."

"What happens now?"

"Now? I'm going to kill you. What's one more?" He laughed when he heard her gasp. "Yeah, I killed Melanie. You almost caught me at her place that day. I can't tell you the satisfaction I felt when I read the newspaper about her demise."

"You modified your voice and told the guard to let me in." Remy took a deep breath. "Andy, I know you, killing . . . killing — it's not you. Give yourself up," she said, taking a step toward him.

"That's not going to happen. Evidently, you don't know me well, since I've killed twice. You'd also know I'd never make it in jail. Besides, I have to take care of my parents," he said. "Once I get rid of you, I'll wait until the heat calms down, and then I'll get out of California."

"I'll tell you what's not going to happen, you getting away with this," she protested. "You left a clue, Andy. I didn't realize what kept nagging me, but if I could figure it out, the police will too."

"What clue?"

Good question.

"Melanie figured it out, didn't she? That gave her power to torment you. She believed in insurance; she kept the proof in a safe place."

Andy frowned. "Proof?" His eyes flitted back and forth. "Proof, what are you talking about? She's dead, and soon so are you."

"Maybe, but one of the detectives will figure it out." Remy closed her eyes. "Melanie knew my routine, but I also knew hers."

There was a distant thump and a slamming sound.

Andy jerked around. He motioned her with his gun toward the entrance doors.

"You go out there first."

"Give yourself up," she said. "You know how this is going to end. I called 9-1-1."

He laughed. "So did I," he said. "I wanted to report that our file room had been burglarized. I wanted to wound the intruder, but you ran. I didn't see who it was, and I killed you by accident." He shook his head. "What a shame."

She took a deep swallow. She'd lied. She hadn't been able to make the emergency call.

He raised his arm taking aim at her chest. "Go on, go out the door. I'm right behind you."

"I don't think so. For your story to hold up, you have to shoot me in the back."

"No, by the time they figure out how to get access to the building, it will be over. You panicked." He shrugged. "It's up to you. We don't have a lot of time. I'm going to have to use my backup plan, I trapped you, it was dark, you tried to get the gun, and . . . well, it was all over so sudden."

Someone banged on the door and called out, "Andrew Carter are you in there?"

Andy shrugged and pulled the trigger.

CHAPTER FORTY-ONE

She was being dragged. Why was Andy yelling? The gun, he had a gun. Now pain. Her chest? So much pain. Where was she?

"Remy Loh," her mother whispered in her ear. "Please wake up, I'm not worried, but your father is at his wits end. The doctors say you're still in there somewhere, but you can't find the door out." She squeezed her daughter's hand. "Here's my hand, follow my voice." She brushed the tears from her own eyes.

"Bee," her father said. "Why don't you go home? I'll stay with Remy until you get back. You haven't had any sleep since yesterday. You won't do her any good, if you end up in the next room."

Her mother voice revealed her fear. "What if she has brain damage? What if she doesn't make it?" She blew her nose. "What I don't understand is why would she go back to that place? She knew she'd get in trouble. She wasn't crazy, she was angry."

"Andrew Carter said she was despondent, and the police said she did seem upset when she met with them." His own voice was ready to break. "Mr. Carter, did she say anything else to you?"

"No," he said with a lowered voice. "Er . . . ah, when I saw her yesterday, she said she was tired. She was kind of weepy and maybe drank a little too much. I made her promise she wouldn't drive. I thought she was going to . . . to go to bed. If I had known she was going to try to break into the lab . . . well, I. . . . I'm so sorry about the shooting, it was a terrible mistake."

Andy's voice. Andy's here.

"Of course," Mitch Bishop said.

Bee Bishop patted her Remy's hand. "You know, I think I will go home," she said. "I do need the rest. But Mitch you'll call me if anything changes?"

"I'll call you if anything changes, I promise. I can rest here."

Andy's voice held certainty. "Look, why don't you both go home? I'll call you if her condition changes," he said. "You live minutes away. I'm on leave and don't have to be at work. I've got my laptop, and I can read a book."

Her father gave a slight cough. "I think

371

we'll take you up on your offer," he said. "We appreciate this. I just need an hour or two. Will that work for you?"

"Without a doubt."

Andy waited for the door to click shut. He hurried to Remy's side.

Eyes closed; she lay still with an oxygen tube in a plastic cover over her face. In order for the blood splatter and GSR evidence to support his story she had to run for the door. He wasn't able to take aim the way he wanted, and the doctor said he'd missed her heart by less than two inches.

"I can't seem to get rid of you," he said in a low voice. "You should have bled out, but no, here you are still with us." He flicked a curl from her forehead. "How did you ever manage that? Anyone else would have been long dead."

Bastard, I'll see you rot.

The pump of air into her lungs was her response.

He bent over the bed. "If I could be sure there's brain damage, I wouldn't have to worry," he muttered, as he straightened her covers, and then patted the back of her hand. He paused. "Maybe, just a few seconds off the oxygen and . . ."

He's going to kill me.

The door opened, and a nurse entered.

"Sorry, we're not to leave Ms. Bishop alone without a nurse. I didn't know she still had visitors, but you're going to have to go. I need to take her vitals and get her ready for the doctor's visit." She moved about the room, waiting to see if he was following her directives.

"I better be going," Andy said, uttering a curse under his breath as he left the room.

Noah Larson approached the Bishops who sat huddled holding hands in the waiting room.

"Have you seen Carter?" he asked. "I have some questions for him. I want to know why he carried a gun into a forensic lab." He looked at the couple in front of him exhausted and worried about their daughter. He sat across from them. "Mr. and Mrs. Bishop, your daughter was sure there was evidence she could find that would clear her name. It's too bad it turned out this way."

"Remy is very pragmatic. She wouldn't risk everything if she didn't know for sure she would be cleared," Mitch said. "It's been eating at her ever since she was let go. And no, Mr. Carter was with her until the nurse came in. He left a little while ago."

"We need your daughter to tell her side of

the story," Larson said. "I'm —"

The doctor entered. Head down, he was holding a chart and flipping its pages.

"Mr. and Mrs. Bishop? Good news, I've just finished examining your daughter." He looked questioningly at Larson.

"Look," said Larson. "I'll leave you to discuss her condition with the doctor. I'm going to take a peek at Ms. Bishop, and then I have a few questions for Mr. Carter. I'll need his statement. Meanwhile, we'll get a deputy here to sit outside her door."

Larson noted that the view from the bay window in Remy's room wasn't half bad. Someone had designed the parking lot with interspersed little pocket parks. The greenery broke up the expanse of concrete.

"De . . . Detective."

Larson spun around to Remy's muffled and raspy voice spoken through an oxygen mask. He rushed to her side.

"Am I glad to hear you." He choked on his words and cleared his throat. "Who did this?"

He bent down to hear the sound from her lips.

She cracked, "Andy . . . killer."

Larson nodded, and pulled back with narrowed eyes that searched hers. "I understand. I'll go get the doctor and your parents." He mustered a smile and said, "Stay put."

Her eyes closed, but she gave a small nod.

He dashed into the hallway and grabbed the arm of a passing nurse. "Stay with her, and no matter what happens don't leave her alone until the doctor comes."

Moments later, Remy's parents ran into her room followed on their heels by her doctor. They made way for him, and he carefully removed the oxygen mask.

Noah Larson, standing by the door, tapped her father on the shoulder.

"I've got an arrest to make."

EPILOGUE

"I have to give it to you Ms. Bishop," Detective Tuft said. "With your help we were able to clear up a cold case and two homicides. Andrew Carter tried, but wasn't able to slip away fast enough; we caught up to him in Nevada. It took us three days after his attempt to kill you, and he spent last night as a guest of the Patterson County Jail. Another thing, we also located your friend, Jay Ross. Nielsen told us they hired him to get rid of you."

He was no friend of mine.

"Good," Remy responded, amazed at how someone could break bread so easily with a person they were ready to kill. But then there was Andy. "To think all these months, he knew I was going through hell because of what he did, and he had no remorse at all for killing Melanie or Sandra Lennox."

"As an added bonus we were able to shut down a major theft ring," Tuft continued.

"As you speculated with Larson, it turns out Edmund Kieffer was using the Crandall house as his halfway-storage locker. He needed an innocent, such as you Ms. Bishop, to legitimize appraisals on the proper forms with respectable letterhead. You can be sure; the ring already knew the values. Turns out your former boss, Victor Camden, killed Kieffer. He says they fought because Kieffer was stealing items, such as that fancy mirror for himself, and it was self-defense. I wouldn't want to be his defense lawyer." He glanced at his phone. "And, it took some doing but I was able to convince the county officials not to prosecute you."

"Prosecute her!" her mother said, gripping Remy's hand on top of the hospital blanket. "What for?"

"Calm down, Mom. Regardless of how things turned out, I broke into a secured government facility," Remy said. Her voice was strained, and still not at full strength. "Thank you, Detective."

He gave a dismissive gesture. "Well, I've got to get back to the department, and there are others waiting outside to see you. They only allow you to have two visitors at a time."

Her mother did not turn around but said

over her shoulder, "Sorry to see you go."

"Mom," Remy said with reproach.

The door didn't close before Noah Larson entered with Audra Dunlap holding onto his arm.

"I won't stay," she said, coming to stand on the opposite side of Remy's bed. "I had to see you for myself. I caused so much trouble for you, and I'm so sorry." Tears glistened in her eyes.

Remy reached for her hand. "I'm already on the road to recovery. I'll be out of here in a week or so, and we can share a cup of tea."

"No, I'll be gone far from here by then. Martin's house sold in two days." She reached into her purse and pulled out a card in an envelope. "I just wanted to give you this get-well card." She squeezed Remy's hand. "Thank you again, and goodbye." She motioned to Noah Larson and then smiled at Belinda Bishop. "You've got a very special daughter."

She left.

"So, Audra Dunlap will eventually get her clock back," Larson said.

"Speaking of clocks," Belinda said, "I've got to check the time of your sister's flight. I'll be back." She walked out the door.

Remy moaned.

"Are you in pain?"

"I'm anticipating a huge headache," Remy said, half-kidding. "Tell me, Detective, what happens to Andy, now?"

"He's already got some attorney laying the ground work for temporary insanity, but it will be a little hard to show he was temporarily insane three times," Larson said. "Don't worry, he'll do some major time."

"I can't wait to testify against him." She sighed. "He destroyed the evidence that could have cleared me, and then tried to destroy me."

"I hear you got your old job back."

A big smile crossed her face. "Yes, I got a letter this morning from the director indicating I had been vindicated, and that they were happy to have me return."

"Good for you. I better get going, too." He straightened. "I think your current employer is waiting to see you."

As if on cue, Joan poked her head in the room.

"Hi, Remy. Noah, are we still on for this evening?" Joan said to the detective on his way out.

"Ah, yeah, I'll call you when I'm on the road." He lowered his voice, and then, "Take care of yourself, Ms. Bishop."

"Remy, I think you can call me Remy, now."

Larson smiled and closed the door.

Joan pulled a chair close to the side of the bed. "I told your mother I would stay until she returned."

"Joan, are you and Detective Larson seeing each other?" Remy asked, with a more than a little interest.

"Maybe, we'll see." Joan picked at an invisible piece of lint on her sweater. "Grayden sends his regards. We didn't know about your involvement in the Lennox murder. Now, I can understand how frantic you were to clear your name."

"I was obsessed," she said. "I realize now, in a way, not only am I an appraiser of fine art and artifacts, I'd slipped into appraising my own life. The value I gave 'me' depended on convincing others, as well as myself that I didn't deserve shunning." Remy thought for a moment. "I don't want, nor do I need my old position back."

"Well, good then. Grayden wants you to know he will hold your job open as long as we need to, until you're ready. It appears your notoriety is bringing in new business from the peninsula." She made a sympathetic face. "When you're up to it a friend of mine wants to meet you. He read in the

380

paper about how you tracked down the Dunlap clock and his family has a similar issue."

"Hmm, interesting," Remy said. "Joan, can you reach me my purse?" She pointed to a small dresser near the top of her bed.

"Sure." Joan handed her the handbag.

Remy reached inside and pulled out her wallet. With the clipping in her hands, she read it one last time, and then tore it in half, then in quarters, and then crumbled it into a ball. She motioned for Joan to pass the trash can, and tossed it inside.

It's done.

Joan looked on with curiosity but before she could ask, the door opened, and Belinda Bishop stepped in. "Thank you, for sitting with Remy. I know you and that handsome detective have dinner plans."

Remy exchanged knowing smiles with Joan, and they said their goodbyes.

Her mother went about straightening her bed and cart. "Mom, go home."

"What's this?" Belinda said, ignoring her daughter and holding Audra's card. "How considerate, we should put it on your table to cheer you up. I'll bring the cards from home. There's at least a dozen." She handed the card to her daughter.

Remy opened the envelope. A check fluttered out.

She gasped.

It was for six figures.

ABOUT THE AUTHOR

R. Franklin James grew up in the San Francisco Bay Area and graduated from the University of California at Berkeley. As a UC Berkeley grad, she cultivated a different type of writing — legislation and public policy. After a career of public advocacy and serving as Deputy Mayor for the City of Los Angeles, she went back to her first love — writing. In 2013, her debut novel, *The Fallen Angels Book Club,* was published by Camel Press. Her second book in the Hollis Morgan Mystery Series, *Sticks & Stones,* was released in 2014, and her third book, *The Return of the Fallen Angels Book Club,* was released in 2015, followed by *The Trade List* in 2016 and in 2017, *The Bell Tolls.* R. Franklin James lives in Northern California with her husband. For more information, go to www.rfranklinjames.com.

The employees of Thorndike Press hope you have enjoyed this Large Print book. All our Thorndike, Wheeler, and Kennebec Large Print titles are designed for easy reading, and all our books are made to last. Other Thorndike Press Large Print books are available at your library, through selected bookstores, or directly from us.

For information about titles, please call:
(800) 223-1244

or visit our website at:
gale.com/thorndike

To share your comments, please write:
Publisher
Thorndike Press
10 Water St., Suite 310
Waterville, ME 04901